CLASSIC ADVENTURES

This book belongs to

Name . . . .

Date . . . .

The Silver Skates
or Hans Brinker

The Silver Skates
or Hans Brinker

By
Mary Mapes Dodge

The Classic Adventures Series

First published by Blackie and Son Ltd
This facsimile edition
© Fabbri Publishing Ltd 1992
Printed and bound in Spain by Printer
Industria Gráfica, Barcelona

ISBN 1-85587-334-6

CONTENTS

THE SILVER SKATES

OR

HANS BRINKER

CHAPTER I

HANS AND GRETEL

ON a bright December morning long ago, two thinly-clad children were kneeling upon the bank of a frozen canal in Holland.

The sun had not yet appeared, but the grey sky was parted near the horizon, and its edges shone crimson with the coming day. Most of the good Hollanders were enjoying a placid morning nap; even Mynheer von Stoppelnoze, that worthy old Dutchman, was still slumbering "in beautiful repose."

Now and then some peasant woman, poising a well-filled basket upon her head, came skimming over the glassy surface of the canal; or a lusty boy, skating to his day's work in the town, cast a good-natured grimace toward the shivering pair as he flew along.

Meanwhile, with many a vigorous puff and pull, the brother and sister, for such they were, seemed to be fastening something upon their feet—not skates, certainly, but clumsy pieces of wood, narrowed and smoothed at their lower edge, and pierced with holes, through which were threaded strings of raw hide.

These queer-looking affairs had been made by the boy Hans. His mother was a poor peasant woman, too poor to even think of such a thing as buying skates for her little ones. Rough as these were, they had afforded the children many a happy hour

7

upon the ice; and now, as with cold, red fingers our young Hollanders tugged at the strings—their solemn faces bending closely over their knees—no vision of impossible iron runners came to dull the satisfaction glowing within.

In a moment the boy arose and, with a pompous swing of the arms, and a careless "Come on, Gretel," glided easily across the canal.

"Ah, Hans," called his sister plaintively, "this foot is not well yet. The strings hurt me on last market-day; and now I cannot bear them tied in the same place."

"Tie them higher up, then," answered Hans, as without looking at her he performed a wonderful cat's-cradle step on the ice.

"How can I? The string is too short."

Giving vent to a good-natured Dutch whistle, the English of which was that girls were troublesome creatures, he steered towards her.

"You are foolish to wear such shoes, Gretel, when you have a stout leather pair. Your klompen [1] would be better than these."

"Why, Hans! Do you forget? The father threw my beautiful new shoes in the fire. Before I knew what he had done they were all curled up in the midst of the burning peat. I can skate with these, but not with my wooden ones. Be careful now——"

Hans had taken a string from his pocket. Humming a tune as he knelt beside her, he proceeded to fasten Gretel's skate with all the force of his strong young arm.

"Oh! oh!" she cried in real pain.

With an impatient jerk Hans unwound the string. He would have cast it upon the ground in true big-brother style, had he not just then spied a tear trickling down his sister's cheek.

"I'll fix it—never fear," he said, with sudden tenderness; "but we must be quick; the mother will need us soon."

Then he glanced inquiringly about him, first at the ground,

[1] Wooden shoes.

next at some bare willow branches above his head, and finally at the sky, now gorgeous with streaks of blue, crimson, and gold.

Finding nothing in any of these localities to meet his need, his eye suddenly brightened as, with the air of a fellow who knew what he was about, he took off his cap, and removing the tattered lining, adjusted it in a smooth pad over the top of Gretel's worn-out shoe.

"Now," he cried triumphantly, at the same time arranging the strings as briskly as his benumbed fingers would allow, "can you bear some pulling?"

Gretel drew up her lips as if to say "hurt away," but made no further response.

In another moment they were laughing together, as hand-in-hand they flew along the canal, never thinking whether the ice would bear or not, for in Holland ice is generally an all-winter affair. It settles itself upon the water in a determined kind of way, and so far from growing thin and uncertain every time the sun is a little severe upon it, it gathers its forces day by day, and flashes defiance at every beam.

Presently, squeak! squeak! sounded something beneath Hans' feet. Next his strokes grew shorter, ending ofttimes with a jerk, and finally he lay sprawling upon the ice, kicking against the air with many a fantastic flourish.

"Ha! ha!" laughed Gretel, "that was a fine tumble!" But a tender heart was beating under her coarse blue jacket, and, even as she laughed, she came, with a graceful sweep, close to her prostrate brother.

"Are you hurt, Hans? Oh, you are laughing! Catch me now"—and she darted away, shivering no longer, but with cheeks all aglow, and eyes sparkling with fun.

Hans sprang to his feet and started in brisk pursuit, but it was no easy thing to catch Gretel. Before she had travelled very far, her skates too began to squeak.

Believing that discretion was the better part of valour, she turned suddenly, and skated into her pursuer's arms.

"Ha! ha! I've caught you!" cried Hans.

"Ha! ha! I caught *you*," she retorted, struggling to free herself.

Just then a clear, quick voice was heard calling, "Hans! Gretel!"

"It's the mother," said Hans, looking grave in an instant.

By this time the canal was gilded with sunlight. The pure morning air was very delightful, and skaters were gradually increasing in numbers. It was hard to obey the summons. But Gretel and Hans were good children; without a thought of yielding to the temptation to linger, they pulled off their skates, leaving half the knots still tied. Hans, with his great square shoulders, and bushy yellow hair, towered high above his blue-eyed little sister, as they trudged homeward. He was fifteen years old and Gretel was only twelve. He was a solid, hearty-looking boy, with honest eyes, and a brow that seemed to bear a sign, "goodness within," just as the little Dutch zomerhuis [1] wears a motto over its portal. Gretel was lithe and quick; her eyes had a dancing light in them, and while you looked at her cheek, the colour paled and deepened just as it does upon a bed of pink and white blossoms when the wind is blowing.

As soon as the children turned from the canal they could see their parents' cottage. Their mother's tall form, arrayed in jacket and petticoat and close-fitting cap, stood like a picture in the crooked frame of the doorway. Had the cottage been a mile away, it would still have seemed near. In that flat country every object stands out plainly in the distance; the chickens show as distinctly as the windmills. Indeed, were it not for the dykes and the high banks of the canals, one could stand almost anywhere in middle Holland without seeing a mound or a ridge between the eye and the "jumping-off place."

None had better cause to know the nature of these same dykes than Dame Brinker and the panting youngsters now running at her call, But before stating *why*, let me ask you to take a rocking-chair trip with me to that far country, where you may see, perhaps for the first time, some curious things that Hans and Gretel saw every day.

[1] Summer-house.

CHAPTER II

HOLLAND

HOLLAND is one of the queerest countries under the sun. It should be called Odd-land or Contrary-land, for in nearly everything it is different from other parts of the world. In the first place, a large portion of the country is lower than the level of the sea. Great dykes or bulwarks have been erected at a heavy cost of money and labour, to keep the ocean where it belongs. On certain parts of the coast it sometimes leans with all its weight against the land, and it is as much as the poor country can do to stand the pressure. Sometimes the dykes give way, or spring a leak, and the most disastrous results ensue. They are high and wide, and the tops of some of them are covered with buildings and trees. They have even fine public roads upon them, from which horses may look down upon wayside cottages. Often the keels of floating ships are higher than the roofs of the dwellings. The stork clattering to her young on the house-peak may feel that her nest is lifted far out of danger, but the croaking frog in neighbouring bulrushes is nearer the stars than she. Water-bugs dart backward and forward above the heads of the chimney swallows; and willow trees seem drooping with shame, because they cannot reach as high as the reeds near by.

Ditches, canals, ponds, rivers, and lakes are everywhere to be seen. High, but not dry, they shine in the sunlight, catching nearly all the bustle and the business, quite scorning the tame fields stretching damply beside them. One is tempted to ask, "Which is Holland—the shores, or the water?" The very verdure that should be confined to the land has made a mistake and settled upon the fish-ponds. In fact, the entire country is a kind of saturated sponge, or, as the English poet, Butler, called it,

> A land that rides at anchor, and is moor'd
> In which they do not live, but go aboard.

Persons are born, live, and die, and even have their gardens on canal-boats. Farm-houses, with roofs like great slouched hats pulled over their eyes, stand on wooden legs with a tucked-up sort of air, as if to say "we intend to keep dry if we can." Even the horses wear a wide stool on each hoof to lift them out of the mire. In short, the landscape everywhere suggests a paradise for ducks. It is a glorious country in summer for bare-footed girls and boys. Such wadings! such mimic ship sailings! such rowing, fishing, and swimming! Only think of a chain of puddles where one can launch chip boats all day long, and never make a return trip! But enough. A full recital would set all my readers rushing in a body toward the Zuider Zee.

Dutch cities seem at first sight to be a bewildering jungle of houses, bridges, churches, and ships, sprouting into masts, steeples, and trees. In some cities vessels are hitched, like horses, to their owners' door-posts, and receive their freight from the upper windows. Mothers scream to Lodewyk and Kassy not to swing on the garden gate for fear they may be drowned! Water-roads are more frequent there than common roads and railways; water-fences, in the form of lazy green ditches, enclose pleasure-ground, polder, and garden.

Sometimes fine green hedges are seen; but wooden fences such as we have in America are rarely met with in Holland. As for stone fences, a Dutchman would lift his hands with astonishment at the very idea. There is no stone there, excepting those great masses of rocks that have been brought from other lands to strengthen and protect the coast. All the small stones or pebbles, if there ever were any, seem to be imprisoned in pavements or quite melted away. Boys with strong, quick arms may grow from pinafores to full beards without ever finding one to start the water-rings or set the rabbits flying. The water-roads are nothing less than canals intersecting the country in every direction. These are of all sizes, from the great North Holland Ship Canal, which is the wonder of the world, to those which a boy can leap. Water-omnibuses, called *trekschuiten,*[1] constantly ply up and down these roads for the conveyance of passengers; and water-drays, called *pakschuyten,*[1] are used for carrying fuel and merchandise. Instead of green country-lanes, green canals stretch from field to barn and from barn to garden; and the farms or *polders,* as they are termed, are merely great lakes pumped dry. Some of the busiest streets are water, while many of the country-roads are paved with brick. The city boats, with their rounded sterns, gilded prows, and gaily-painted sides, are unlike any others under the sun; and a Dutch waggon, with its funny little crooked pole, is a perfect mystery of mysteries.

"One thing is clear," cries Master Brightside, "the inhabitants need never be thirsty." But no, Odd-land is true to itself still. Notwithstanding the sea pushing to get in, and the lakes struggling to get out, and the overflowing canals, rivers, and ditches, in many districts there is no water fit to swallow; our poor Hollanders must go dry, or drink wine and beer, or send far into the inland to Utrecht, and other favoured localities, for that precious fluid older than Adam yet young as the morning dew. Sometimes, indeed, the inhabitants can swallow a shower, when they are provided with any means of catching it; but generally they are like the albatross-haunted sailors in Coleridge's famous poem of *The Ancient Mariner*—they see

> Water, water everywhere,
> Nor any drop to drink!

Great flapping windmills all over the country make it look as if flocks of huge sea-birds were just settling upon it. Everywhere one sees the funniest trees, bobbed into fantastical shapes, with their trunks painted a dazzling white, yellow, or red. Horses are often yoked three abreast. Men, women and children go

---

[1] Canal-boats. Some of the first named are over thirty feet long. They look like green houses lodged on barges, and are drawn by horses walking along the bank of the canal. The trekschuiten are divided into two compartments, first and second class, and when not too crowded the passengers make themselves quite at home in them; the men smoke, the women knit or sew, while children play upon the small outer deck. Many of the canal-boats have white, yellow, or chocolate-coloured sails. This last colour is caused by a preparation of tan which is put on to preserve them.

clattering about in wooden shoes with loose heels ; peasant girls
who cannot get beaux for love, hire them for money to escort
them to the Kermis ; [1] and husbands and wives lovingly *harness*
themselves side by side on the bank of the canal and drag their
pakschuyts to market.

Another peculiar feature of Holland is the *dune* or sand-
hill. These are numerous along certain portions of the coast.
Before they were sown with coarse reed-grass and other plants
to hold them down, they used to send great storms of sand over
the inland. So, to add to the oddities, farmers sometimes dig
down under the surface to find their soil, and on windy days
dry showers (of sand) often fall upon fields that have grown wet
under a week of sunshine.

On the other hand, many of the oddities of Holland serve
only to prove the thrift and perseverance of the people. There
is not a richer, or more carefully-tilled garden-spot in the whole
world than this leaky, springy little country. There is not a
braver, more heroic race than its quiet, passive-looking inhabitants. Few nations have equalled it in important discoveries
and inventions ; none has excelled it in commerce, navigation,
learning and science,—or set as noble examples in the promotion
of education and public charities ; and none in proportion to its
extent has expended more money and labour upon public works.

Holland has its shining annals of noble and illustrious men
and women ; its grand, historic records of patience, resistance,
and victory ; its religious freedom, its enlightened enterprise, its
art, its music, and its literature. It has truly been called, " the
battle-field of Europe,"—as truly may we consider it the Asylum
of the world, for the oppressed of every nation have there found
shelter and encouragement.

There are said to be at least ninety-nine hundred large
windmills in Holland, with sails ranging from eighty to one
hundred and twenty feet long. They are employed in sawing
timber, beating hemp, grinding, and many other kinds of work ;
but their principal use is for pumping water from the lowlands
into the canals, and for guarding against the inland freshets that

[1] Fair.

so often deluge the country. Their yearly cost is said to be nearly ten millions of dollars. The large ones are of great power. Their huge, circular tower, rising sometimes from the midst of factory buildings, is surmounted with a smaller one tapering into a cap-like roof. This upper tower is encircled at its base with a balcony, high above which juts the axis, turned by its four prodigious, ladder-backed sails.

Many of the windmills are primitive affairs, seeming sadly in need of modern ingenuity; but some of the new ones are admirable. They are so constructed that, by some ingenious contrivance, they present their fans, or wings, to the wind in precisely the right direction to work with the requisite power. In other words, the miller may take a nap and feel quite sure that his mill will study the wind, and make the most of it, until he wakens. Should there be but a slight current of air, every sail will spread itself to catch the faintest breath; but if a heavy "blow" should come, they will shrink at its touch, like great mimosa leaves, and only give it half a chance to move them.

One of the old prisons of Amsterdam, called the Rasphouse, because the thieves and vagrants who were confined there were employed in rasping log-wood, had a cell for the punishment of lazy prisoners. In one corner of this cell was a pump, and in another, an opening through which a steady stream of water was admitted. The prisoner could take his choice, either to stand still and be drowned, or to work for dear life at the pump and keep the flood down until his jailer chose to relieve him. Now it seems to me that, throughout Holland, Nature has introduced this little diversion on a grand scale. The Dutch have always been forced to pump for their very existence, and probably must continue to do so to the end of time.

Every year millions of dollars are spent in repairing dykes, and regulating water-levels. If these important duties were neglected the country would be uninhabitable. Already dreadful consequences, as I have said, have followed the bursting of these dykes. Hundreds of villages and towns have from time to time been buried beneath the rush of waters, and nearly a million of persons have been destroyed. One of the most fearful in-undations ever known occurred in the autumn of the year 1570 Twenty-eight terrible floods had before that time overwhelmed portions of Holland, but this was the most terrible of all. The unhappy country had long been suffering under Spanish tyranny; now, it seemed, the crowning point was given to its troubles. When we read Motley's *History of the Rise of the Dutch Republic*, we learn to revere the brave people who have endured, suffered, and dared so much.

Mr. Motley in his thrilling account of the great inundation tells us how a long-continued and violent gale had been sweep-ing the Atlantic waters into the North Sea, piling them against the coasts of the Dutch provinces; how the dykes, tasked beyond their strength, burst in all directions; how even the Hand-bos, a bulwark formed of oaken piles, braced with iron, moored with heavy anchors and secured by gravel and granite, was snapped to pieces like packthread; how fishing-boats and bulky vessels, floated up into the country, became entangled among the trees, or beat in the roofs and walls of dwellings, and how at last all Friesland was converted into an angry sea. "Multitudes of men, women, children, of horses, oxen, sheep, and every domestic animal, were struggling in the waves in every direction. Every boat and every article which could serve as a boat, were eagerly seized upon. Every house was inundated, even the graveyards gave up their dead. The living infant in his cradle, and the long buried corpse in his coffin, floated side by side. The ancient flood seemed about to be renewed. Every-where, upon the tops of trees, upon the steeples of churches, human beings were clustered, praying to God for mercy, and to their fellowmen for assistance. As the storm at last was subsid-ing, boats began to ply in every direction, saving those who were struggling in the water, picking fugitives from roofs and tree tops, and collecting the bodies of those already drowned." No less than one hundred thousand human beings had perished in a few hours. Thousands upon thousands of dumb creatures lay dead upon the waters; and the damage done to property of every description was beyond calculation.

Robles, the Spanish Governor, was foremost in noble efforts to save life and lessen the horrors of the catastrophe. He had formerly been hated by the Dutch because of his Spanish or Portuguese blood, but by his goodness and activity in their hour of disaster, he won all hearts to gratitude. He soon introduced an improved method of constructing the dykes, and passed a law that they should in future be kept up by the owners of the soil. There were fewer heavy floods from this time, though within less than three hundred years six fearful inundations swept over the land.

In the spring there is always great danger of inland freshets, especially in times of thaw, because the rivers, choked with blocks of ice, overflow before they can discharge their rapidly-rising waters into the ocean. Added to this, the sea chafing and pressing against the dykes, it is no wonder that Holland is often in a state of alarm. The greatest care is taken to prevent accidents. Engineers and workmen are stationed all along in threatened places, and a close watch is kept up night and day. When a general signal of danger is given, the inhabitants all rush to the rescue, eager to combine against their common foe. As everywhere else straw is supposed to be of all things the most helpless in the water, of course in Holland it must be rendered the mainstay against a rushing tide. Huge straw mats are pressed against the embankments, fortified with clay and heavy stone, and, once adjusted, the ocean dashes against them in vain.

Raff Brinker, the father of Gretel and Hans, had for years been employed upon the dykes. It was at the time of a threatened inundation, when in the midst of a terrible storm, in darkness and sleet, the men were labouring at a weak spot near the Veermyk sluice, that he fell from the scaffolding, and was taken home insensible. From that hour he never worked again; though he lived on, mind and memory were gone.

Gretel could not remember him otherwise than as the strange, silent man, whose eyes followed her vacantly whichever way she turned; but Hans had recollections of a hearty, cheerful-voiced father, who was never tried of bearing him upon his

shoulder, and whose careless song still seemed echoing near when
he lay awake at night and listened.

CHAPTER III

DAME BRINKER earned a scanty support for her family by
raising vegetables, spinning, and knitting. Once she had
worked on board the barges plying up and down the canal, and
had occasionally been harnessed with other women to the towing-
rope of a pakschuyt plying between Broek and Amsterdam. But
when Hans had grown strong and large, he had insisted upon
doing all such drudgery in her place. Besides, her husband had
become so very helpless of late, that he required her constant
care. Although not having as much intelligence as a little child,
he was yet strong of arm and very hearty, and Dame Brinker
had sometimes great trouble in controlling him.

"Ah! children, he was so good and steady," she would sometimes say, "and as wise as a lawyer. Even the burgomaster
would stop to ask him a question ; and now, alack ! he don't
know his wife and little ones. You remember the father, Hans,
when he was himself—a great brave man—Don't you ?"

"Yes, indeed, mother ; he knew everything, and could do
anything under the sun—and how he would sing ! why, you
used to laugh, and say it was enough to set the windmills
dancing."

"So I did. Bless me, how the boy remembers ! Gretel,
child, take that knitting-needle from your father, quick ; he'll
get it in his eyes maybe ; and put the shoe on him. His poor
feet are like ice half the time, but I can't keep 'em covered all I
can do." And then half wailing, half humming, Dame Brinker
would sit down, and fill the low cottage with the whirr of her
spinning-wheel.

Nearly all the out-door work, as well as the household labour, was performed by Hans and Gretel. At certain seasons of the year the children went out day after day to gather peat, which they would stow away in square, brick-like pieces, for fuel. At other times, when home-work permitted, Hans rode the towing horses on the canals, earning a few stivers[1] a day; and Gretel tended geese for the neighbouring farmers.

Hans was clever at carving in wood, and both he and Gretel were good gardeners. Gretel could sing and sew, and run on great, high, home-made stilts, better than any girl for miles around. She could learn a ballad in five minutes, and find, in its season, any weed or flower you could name; but she dreaded books, and often the very sight of the figuring-board in the old school-house would set her eyes swimming. Hans, on the contrary, was slow and steady. The harder the task, whether in study or daily labour, the better he liked it. Boys who sneered at him out of school, on account of his patched clothes and scant leather breeches, were forced to yield him the post of honour in nearly every class. It was not long before he was the only youngster in the school who had not stood at least *once* in the corner of horrors, where hung a dreaded whip, and over it this motto:

Leer! leer! jou luigaart, of dit endje touw zal je le ren![2]

It was only in winter that Gretel and Hans could be spared to attend school; and for the past month they had been kept at home because their mother needed their services. Raff Brinker required constant attention, and there was black bread to be made, and the house to be kept clean, and stockings and other things to be knitted and sold in the market-place.

While they were busily assisting their mother on this cold December morning, a merry troop of girls and boys came skimming down the canal. There were fine skaters among them, and as the bright medley of costumes flitted by, it looked from a distance as though the ice had suddenly thawed, and some gay tulip-bed were floating along on the current.

There was the rich burgomaster's daughter, Hilda van Gleck,

---

[1] A stiver is worth about a halfpenny.
[2] (Learn! learn! you idler, or this rope's end shall teach you!)

with her costly furs and loose-fitting velvet jacket; and, near by, a pretty peasant girl, Annie Bouman, jauntily attired in a coarse scarlet jacket and a blue skirt, just short enough to display the gray homespun hose to advantage. Then there was the proud Rychie Korbes, whose father, Mynheer van Korbes, was one of the leading men of Amsterdam; and, flocking closely around her, Carl Schummel, Peter and Ludwig [1] van Holp, Jacob Poot, and a very small boy rejoicing in the tremendous name of Voostenwalbert Schimmelpenninck. There were nearly twenty other boys and girls in the party, and one and all seemed full of excitement and frolic.

Up and down the canal, within the space of a half mile they skated, exerting their racing powers to the utmost. Often the swiftest among them was seen to dodge from under the very nose of some pompous lawgiver or doctor, who, with folded arms, was skating leisurely toward the town; or a chain of girls would suddenly break at the approach of a fat old burgomaster, who, with gold-headed cane poised in air, was puffing his way to Amsterdam. Equipped in skates wonderful to behold, from their superb strappings, and dazzling runners curving over the instep and topped with gilt balls, he would open his fat eyes a little if one of the maidens chanced to drop him a courtesy, but would not dare to bow in return for fear of losing his balance.

Not only pleasure-seekers, and stately men of note were upon the canal. There were workpeople, with weary eyes, hastening to their shops and factories; market-women with loads upon their heads; pedlars bending with their packs; bargemen with shaggy hair and bleared faces, jostling roughly on their way; kind-eyed clergymen, speeding perhaps to the bedsides of the dying; and after a while, groups of children, with satchels slung over their shoulders, whizzing past, towards the distant school. One and all wore skates, excepting, indeed, a muffled-up farmer, whose queer cart bumped along on the margin of the canal.

Before long our merry boys and girls were almost lost in the confusion of bright colours, the ceaseless motion, and the gleam-

[1] Ludwig, Gretel, and Carl were named after German friends. The Dutch form would be Lodewyk, Grietje, and Karel.

ing of skates flashing back the sunlight. We might have known no more of them had not the whole party suddenly come to a standstill, and, grouping themselves out of the way of the passers-by, all talked at once to a pretty little maiden, whom they had drawn from the tide of people flowing toward the town.

"Oh, Katrinka!" they cried, in a breath, "have you heard of it? The race—we want you to join!"

"What race?" asked Katrinka, laughing. "Don't all talk at once, please; I can't understand."

Every one panted and looked at Rychie Korbes, who was their acknowledged spokeswoman.

"Why," said Rychie, "we are to have a grand skating match on the twentieth, on Mevrouw [1] van Gleck's birthday. It's all Hilda's work. They are going to give a splendid prize to the best skater."

"Yes," chimed in a half-a-dozen voices, "a beautiful pair of silver skates—perfectly magnificent! with, oh! such straps and silver bells and buckles!"

"*Who* said they had bells?" put in the small voice of the boy with the big name.

"*I* say so, Master Voost," replied Rychie.

"So they have,"——"No I'm sure they haven't,"——"*Oh*, how can you say so?"——"It's an arrow"——"And Mynheer van Korbes told *my* mother they had bells"——came from sundry of the excited group; but Mynheer Voostenwalbert Schimmelpenninck essayed to settle the matter with a decisive—

"Well, you don't any of you know a single thing about it; they haven't a sign of a bell on them, they——"

"Oh! oh!" and the chorus of conflicting opinion broke forth again.

"The girls' pair are to have bells," interposed Hilda, quietly, "but there is to be another pair for the boys, with an arrow engraved upon the sides."

"*There!* I told you so!" cried nearly all the youngsters in a breath.

Katrinka looked at them with bewildered eyes.

[1] Mrs. or Madame (pronounced MEFFROW).

"Who is to try?" she asked.

"All of us," answered Rychie. "It will be such fun! And you must, too, Katrinka. But it's school-time now, we will talk it all over at noon. Oh! you will join of course."

Katrinka, without replying, made a graceful pirouette, and laughing out a coquettish—"Don't you hear the last bell? Catch me!"—darted off towards the school-house, standing half-a-mile away, on the canal.

All started, pell-mell, at this challenge, but they tried in vain to catch the bright-eyed, laughing creature, who, with golden hair streaming in the sunlight, cast back many a sparkling glance of triumph as she floated onward.

CHAPTER IV

HANS AND GRETEL FIND A FRIEND

AT noon our young friends poured forth from the school-house intent upon having an hour's practising upon the canal.

They had skated but a few moments when Carl Schummel said mockingly to Hilda:

"There's a pretty pair just coming upon the ice! The little rag-pickers! Their skates must have been a present from the king direct."

"They are patient creatures," said Hilda, gently. "It must have been hard to learn to skate upon such queer affairs. They are very poor peasants, you see. The boy has probably made the skates himself."

Carl was somewhat abased.

"Patient they may be, but as for skating, they start off pretty well only to finish with a jerk."

Hilda laughed pleasantly and left him. After joining a small detachment of the racers, and sailing past every one of them, she halted beside Gretel, who, with eager eyes, had been watching the sport.

"What is your name, little girl?"

"Gretel, my lady," answered the child, somewhat awed by Hilda's rank, though they were nearly of the same age, "and my brother is called Hans."

"Hans is a stout fellow," said Hilda, cheerily, "and seems to have a warm stove somewhere within him, but *you* look cold. You should wear more clothing, little one."

Gretel, who had nothing else to wear, tried to laugh as she answered:

"I am not so very little. I am past twelve years old."

"Oh, I beg your pardon. You see I am nearly fourteen, and so large of my age that other girls seem small to me, but that is nothing. Perhaps you will shoot up far above me yet; not unless you dress more warmly, though—shivering girls never grow."

Hans flushed as he saw tears rising in Gretel's eyes.

"My sister has not complained of the cold; but this is bitter weather they say"—and he looked sadly upon Gretel.

"It is nothing," said Gretel. "I am often warm—too warm when I am skating. You are good, jufvrouw,[1] to think of it."

"No, no," answered Hilda, quite angry at herself. "I am careless, cruel; but I meant no harm. I wanted to ask you—I mean—if—" and here Hilda, coming to the point of her errand, faltered before the poorly-clad children she wished to serve.

"What is it, young lady?" exclaimed Hans eagerly. "If there is any service I can do? any—— "

"Oh! no, no," laughed Hilda, shaking off her embarrassment, "I only wished to speak to you about the grand race. Why do you not join it? You both can skate well, and the ranks are free. Any one may enter for the prize."

Gretel looked wistfully at Hans, who, tugging at his cap, answered respectfully.

"Ah, jufvrouw, even if we could enter, we could skate only a few strokes with the rest. Our skates are only made of wood, you see" (holding up the sole of his foot), "and they soon become damp, and then they stick and trip us."

---

[1] Miss—Young lady (pronounced YUFFROW). In studied or polite address it would be jongvrowe (pronounced YOUNGFROW).

Gretel's eyes twinkled with fun as she thought of Hans' mishap in the morning, but she blushed as she faltered out timidly :

"Oh no, we can't join ; but may we be there, my lady, on the great day to look on ? "

"Certainly," answered Hilda, looking kindly into the two earnest faces, and wishing from her heart that she had not spent so much of her monthly allowance for lace and finery. She had but eight kwartjes[1] left, and they would buy but one pair of skates at the most.

Looking down with a sigh at the two pair of feet so very different in size, she asked :

"Which of you is the better skater ? "

"Gretel," replied Hans, promptly.

"Hans," answered Gretel, in the same breath.

Hilda smiled.

"I cannot buy you each a pair of skates, or even one good pair ; but here are eight kwartjes. Decide between you which stands the best chance of winning the race, and buy the skates accordingly. I wish I had enough to buy better ones—good-bye ! " and, with a nod and a smile, Hilda, after handing the money to the electrified Hans, glided swiftly away to rejoin her companions.

"Jufvrouw ! jufvrouw von Gleck ! " called Hans in a loud tone, stumbling after her as well as he could, for one of his skate-strings was untied.

Hilda turned, and, with one hand raised to shield her eyes from the sun, seemed to him to be floating through the air, nearer and nearer.

"We cannot take this money," panted Hans ; "though we know your goodness in giving it."

"Why not, indeed ? " asked Hilda, flushing.

"Because," replied Hans, bowing like a clown, but looking with the eye of a prince at the queenly girl, "we have not earned it."

[1] A kwartje is a small silver coin worth one quarter of a guilder, or three-pence.

Hilda was quick-witted. She had noticed a pretty wooden chain upon Gretel's neck—

"Carve me a chain, Hans, like the one your sister wears."

"That I will, lady, with all my heart; we have white-wood in the house, fine as ivory; you shall have one to-morrow," and Hans hastily tried to return the money.

"No, no," said Hilda, decidedly. "That sum will be but a poor price for the chain," and off she darted, outstripping the fleetest among the skaters.

Hans sent a long, bewildered gaze after her; it was useless he felt to make any further resistance.

"It is right," he muttered, half to himself, half to his faithful shadow, Gretel; "I must work hard every minute, and sit up half the night if the mother will let me burn a candle; but the chain shall be finished. We may keep the money, Gretel."

"What a good little lady!" cried Gretel, clapping her hands with delight. "Oh! Hans, was it for nothing the stork settled on our roof last summer? Do you remember how the mother said it would bring us luck, and how she cried when Janzoon Kolp shot him? And she said it would bring him trouble. But the luck has come to us at last! Now, Hans, if mother sends us to town to-morrow you can buy the skates in the market-place."

Hans shook his head. "The young lady would have given us the money to buy the skates; but if I *earn* it, Gretel, it shall be spent for wool. You must have a warm jacket."

"Oh!" cried Gretel, in real dismay, "not buy the skates! Why, I am not often cold! Mother says the blood runs up and down in poor children's veins humming 'I must keep 'em warm! I must keep 'em warm.'"

"Oh, Hans," she continued, with something like a sob, "don't say you won't buy the skates; it makes me feel just like crying—besides, I want to be cold—I mean I'm really quite warm—so now!"

Hans looked up hurriedly. He had a true Dutch horror of tears, or emotion of any kind, and, most of all, he dreaded to see his sister's blue eyes overflowing.

"Now mind," cried Gretel, seeing her advantage, "I'll feel

awful if you give up the skates. *I* don't want them. I'm not such a stingy as that; but I want *you* to have them, and then when I get bigger they'll do for me—oh-h—count the pieces, Hans. Did ever you see so many!"

Hans turned the money thoughtfully in his palm. Never in all his life had he longed so intensely for a pair of skates, for he had known of the race, and had, boy-like, fairly ached for a chance to test his powers with the other children. He felt confident that, with a good pair of steel runners, he could readily distance most of the boys on the canal. Then, too, Gretel's argument was so plausible. On the other hand, he knew that she, with her strong but lithe little frame, needed but a week's practice on good runners, to make her a better skater than Rychie Korbes or even Katrinka Flack. As soon as this last thought flashed upon him his resolve was made. If Gretel would not have the jacket, she should have the skates.

"No, Gretel," he answered at last, "I can wait. Some day I may have money enough saved to buy a fine pair. You shall have these."

Gretel's eyes sparkled; but in another instant she insisted, rather faintly:

"The young lady gave the money to *you*, Hans. I'd be real bad to take it."

Hans shook his head resolutely as he trudged on, causing his sister to half skip and half walk in her effort to keep beside him; by this time they had taken off their wooden "rockers," and were hastening home to tell their mother the good news.

"Oh! *I* know!" cried Gretel, in a sprightly tone, "you can do this. You can get a pair a little too small for you, and too big for me, and we can take turns and use them. Won't that be fine?" and Gretel clapped her hands again.

Poor Hans! This was a strong temptation, but he pushed it away from him, brave-hearted fellow that he was.

"Nonsense, Gretel. You could never get on with a big pair. You stumbled about with these like a blind chicken, before I curved off the ends. No, you must have a pair to fit exactly, and you must practise every chance you can get, until the Twentieth comes. My little Gretel shall win the silver skates."

Gretel could not help laughing with delight at the very idea.

"Hans! Gretel!" called out a familiar voice.

"Coming, mother!" and they hastened toward the cottage, Hans still shaking the pieces of silver in his hand.

On the following day, there was not a prouder nor a happier boy in all Holland than Hans Brinker, as he watches his sister, with many a dexterous sweep, flying in and out among the skaters, who at sundown thronged the canal. A warm jacket had been given her by the kind-hearted Hilda, and the burst-out shoes had been cobbled into decency by Dame Brinker. As the little creature darted backward and forward, flushed with enjoyment, and quite unconscious of the many wondering glances bent upon her, she felt that the shining runners beneath her feet had suddenly turned earth into Fairyland, while "Hans, dear, good Hans!" echoed itself over and over again in her grateful heart.

"By den donder!" exclaimed Peter Van Holp to Carl Schummel, "but that little one in the red jacket and patched petticoat skates well. Gunst! she has toes on her heels, and eyes in the back of her head! See her! It will be a joke if she gets in the race, and beats Katrinka Flack after all."

"Hush! not so loud!" returned Carl, rather sneeringly. "That little lady in rags is the special pet of Hilda van Gleck. Those shining skates are her gift, if I make no mistake."

"So! so!" exclaimed Peter, with a radiant smile, for Hilda was his best friend. "She has been at her good work there, too!" And Mynheer van Holp, after cutting a double 8 on the ice, to say nothing of a huge P, then a jump, and an H, glided onwards until he found himself beside Hilda.

Hand in hand, they skated together, laughing at first, then staidly talking in a low tone.

Peter van Holp soon arrived at a sudden conviction that his little sister needed a wooden chain just like Hilda's.

Two days afterwards, on St Nicholas' Eve, Hans, having

burned three candle-ends, and cut his thumb into the bargain, stood in the market-place at Amsterdam, buying another pair of skates.

CHAPTER V

SHADOWS IN THE HOME

GOOD Dame Brinker! As soon as the scanty dinner had been cleared away that noon, she had arrayed herself in her holiday attire, in the honour of Saint Nicholas. "It will brighten the children," she thought to herself, and she was not mistaken. This festival dress had been worn very seldom during the past ten years; before that time it had done good service, and had flourished at many a dance and Kermis, when she was known, far and wide, as the pretty Meitje Klenck. The children had sometimes been granted rare glimpses of it as it lay in state in the old oaken chest. Faded and threadbare as it was, it was gorgeous in their eyes, with its white linen tucker, now gathered to her plump throat, and vanishing beneath the trim bodice of blue homespun, and its reddish brown skirt bordered with black. The knitted woollen mitts, and the dainty cap showing her hair, which generally was hidden, made her seem almost like a princess to Gretel, while master Hans grew staid and well-behaved as he gazed.

Soon the little maid, while braiding her own golden tresses, fairly danced around her mother in an ecstasy of admiration.

"Oh, mother, mother, mother, how pretty you are! Look, Hans! isn't it just like a picture?"

"Just like a picture," assented Hans, cheerfully,—"*just* like a picture—only I don't like those stocking things on the hands."

"Not like the mitts, brother Hans! why they're very important—see—they cover up all the red. Oh, mother, how white your arm is where the mitt leaves off, whiter than mine, —oh, ever so much whiter. I declare, mother, the bodice is tight for you. You're growing! you're surely growing!"

Dame Brinker laughed.

"This was made long ago, lovey, when I wasn't much thicker about the waist than a churn-dasher. And how do you like the cap?" turning her head from side to side.

"Oh, *ever* so much, mother. It's beautiful! see! The father is looking!"

Was the father looking? Alas, only with a dull stare. His vrouw turned toward him with a start, something like a blush rising to her cheeks, a questioning sparkle in her eye. The bright look died away in an instant.

"No, no," she sighed, "he sees nothing. Come, Hans" (and the smile crept faintly back again), "don't stand gaping at me all day, and the new skates waiting for you at Amsterdam."

"Ah, mother," he answered, "you need many things. Why should I buy skates?"

"Nonsense, child. The money was given to you on purpose, or the work was—it's all the same thing. Go while the sun is high."

"Yes, and hurry back, Hans!" laughed Gretel, "we'll race on the canal to-night, if the mother lets us."

At the very threshold he turned to say—"Your spinning-wheel wants a new treadle, mother."

"You can make it, Hans."

"So I can. That will take no money. But you need feathers, and wool, and meal, and——"

"There, there! That will do. Your silver cannot buy everything. Ah! Hans, if our stolen money would but come back on this bright Saint Nicholas' Eve, how glad we would be! Not a sight have I had of it since the day before the dear father was hurt—as you well know, Hans."

"That I do, mother," he answered sadly, "though you have almost pulled down the cottage in searching."

"Ay; but it was of no use," moaned the dame, "*hiders* make best finders."

Hans started. "Do you think the father could tell aught?" he asked mysteriously.

"Ay, indeed," said Dame Brinker, nodding her head, "I think so, but that is no sign. I never hold the same belief in the matter two days. Mayhap the father paid it off for the great silver watch we have been guarding since that day. But, no—I'll never believe it."

"The watch was not worth a quarter of the money, mother."

"No, indeed; and your father was a shrewd man up to the last moment. He was too steady and thrifty for silly doings."

"Where *did* the watch come from, I wonder," muttered Hans, half to himself.

Dame Brinker shook her head, and looked sadly toward her husband, who sat staring blankly at the floor. Gretel stood near him, knitting.

"That we shall never know, Hans. I have shown it to the father many a time, but he does not know it from a potato. When he came in that dreadful night to supper, he handed the watch to me and told me to take good care of it until he asked for it again. Just as he opened his lips to say more, Broom Klatterboost came flying in with word that the dyke was in danger. Ah! the waters were terrible that holy Pinxter-week! My man, alack, caught up his tools and ran out. That was the last I ever saw of him in his right mind. He was brought in again by midnight, nearly dead, with his poor head all bruised and cut. The fever passed off in time, but never the dulness—*that* grew worse every day. We shall never know."

Hans had heard all this before. More than once he had seen his mother, in hours of sore need, take the watch from its hiding-place, half-resolved to sell it, but she had always conquered the temptation.

"No, Hans," she would say, "we must be nearer starving than this before we turn faithless to the father!"

A memory of some such scene crossed her son's mind now; for, after giving a heavy sigh, and filliping a crumb of wax at Gretel across the table, he said:

"Ay, mother, you have done bravely to keep it—many a one would have tossed it off for gold long ago."

"And more shame for them?" exclaimed the dame, indignantly, "*I* would not do it.   Besides, the gentry are so hard on us poor folks that if they saw such a thing in our hands, even if we told all, they might suspect the father of—— "

Hans flushed angrily.

"They would not *dare* to say such a thing, mother! If they did—I 'd—— "

He clenched his fist, and seemed to think that the rest of his sentence was too terrible to utter in her presence.

Dame Brinker smiled proudly through her tears at this interruption.

"Ah, Hans, thou'rt a true, brave lad. We will never part company with the watch. In his dying hour the dear father might wake and ask for it."

"Might *wake*, mother!" echoed Hans, "wake—and know us?"

"Ay, child," almost whispered his mother, "such things have been."

By this time Hans had nearly forgotten his proposed errand to Amsterdam. His mother had seldom spoken so familiarly with him. He felt himself now to be not only her son, but her friend, her adviser.

"You are right, mother. We must never give up the watch. For the father's sake, we will guard it always. The money, though, may come to light when we least expect it."

"Never!" cried Dame Brinker, taking the last stitch from her needle with a jerk, and laying the unfinished knitting heavily upon her lap. "There is no chance! One thousand guilders! and all gone in a day! One thousand guilders—oh! what ever *did* become of them? If they went in an evil way, the thief would have confessed by this on his dying bed—he would not dare to die with such guilt on his soul!"

"He may not be dead yet," said Hans, soothingly; "any day we may hear of him."

"Ah, child," she said, in a changed tone, "what thief would ever have come *here*? It was always neat and clean, thank God! but not fine; for the father and I saved and saved that we might have something laid by. 'Little and often soon fills the pouch.'"

We found it so in truth; besides, the father had a goodly sum already, for service done in the Heernocht lands, at the time of the great inundation. Every week we had a guilder left over, sometimes more; for the father worked extra hours, and could get high pay for his labour. Every Saturday night we put something by, except the time when you had the fever, Hans, and when Gretel came. At last the pouch grew so full that I mended an old stocking and commenced again. Now that I look back, it seems that the money was up to the heel in a few sunny weeks. There was great pay in those days if a man was quick at engineer work. The stocking went on filling with copper and silver—ay, and gold. You may well open your eyes, Gretel. I used to laugh and tell the father it was not for poverty I wore my old gown;—and the stocking went on filling—so full that sometimes when I woke at night I'd get up, soft and quiet, and go feel it in the moonlight. Then, on my knees, I would thank our Lord that my little ones could in time get good learning, and that the father might rest from labour in his old age. Sometimes, at supper, the father and I would talk about a new chimney and a good winter-room for the cow; but my man, forsooth, had finer plans even than that. 'A big sail,' says he, 'catches the wind—we can do what we will soon,' and then we would sing together as I washed my dishes. Ah, 'a smooth sea makes an easy rudder,'—not a thing vexed me from morning till night. Every week the father would take out the stocking, and drop in the money, and laugh and kiss me as we tied it up together.——Up with you, Hans! there you sit gaping, and the day a-wasting!" added Dame Brinker tartly, blushing to find that she had been speaking too freely to the boy; "it's high time you were on your way."

Hans had seated himself, and was looking earnestly into her face. He arose, and, in almost a whisper, asked—

"Have you ever *tried*, mother?"

She understood him.

"Yes, child, often. But the father only laughs, or he stares at me so strange I am glad to ask no more. When you and Gretel had the fever last winter, and our bread was nearly gone, and I could earn nothing, for fear you would die while my face was turned, oh! I tried then! I smoothed his hair, and whispered to him, soft as a kitten, about the money—where it was—who had it? Alack! he would pick at my sleeve, and whisper gibberish till my blood ran cold. At last, while Gretel lay whiter than snow, and you were raving on the bed, I SCREAMED to him —it seemed as if he *must* hear me—' Raff, where is our money? Do you know aught of the money, Raff?—the money in the pouch and the stocking, in the big chest?'—but I might as well have talked to a stone—I might as——"

The mother's voice sounded so strangely, and her eye was so bright, that Hans, with a new anxiety, laid his hand upon her shoulder.

"Come, mother," he said, "let us try to forget this money. I am big and strong—Gretel, too, is very quick and willing. Soon all will be prosperous with us again. Why, mother, Gretel and I would rather see thee bright and happy than to have all the silver in the world——wouldn't we, Gretel?"

"The mother knows it," said Gretel, sobbing.

CHAPTER VI

SUNBEAMS

DAME BRINKER was startled at her children's emotion; glad, too, for it proved how loving and true they were.

Beautiful ladies, in princely homes, often smile suddenly and sweetly, gladdening the very air around them; but I doubt if their smile be more welcome in God's sight than that which sprang forth to cheer the roughly-clad boy and girl in the humble cottage. Dame Brinker felt that she had been selfish. Blushing and brightening, she hastily wiped her eyes, and looked upon them as only a mother can.

"Hoity! toity! pretty talk we're having, and Saint Nicholas' Eve almost here! What wonder the yarn pricks my fingers! Come, Gretel, take this cent,[1] and while Hans is looking for the skates you can buy a waffle in the market-place."

"Let me stay at home with you, mother," said Gretel, looking up with eyes that sparkled through their tears; "Hans will buy me the cake."

"As you will, child; and Hans—wait a moment. Three turns of the needle will finish this toe, and then you may have as good a pair of hose as ever were knitted (owning the yarn is a grain too sharp) to sell to the hosier on the Heireen Gracht.[2] That will give us three-quarter guilders if you make good trade; and as it's right hungry weather, you may buy four waffles. We'll keep the feast of Saint Nicholas after all."

Gretel clapped her hands. "That will be fine! Annie Bouman told me what grand times they will have in the big houses to-night. But we will be merry too. Hans will have beautiful new skates—and then there'll be the waffles! Oh-h! Don't break them, brother Hans. Wrap them well, and button them under your jacket very carefully."

"Certainly," replied Hans, quite gruff with pleasure and importance.

"Oh! mother!" cried Gretel in high glee, "soon you will be busied with the father, and now you are only knitting. Do tell us all about Saint Nicholas!"

Dame Brinker laughed to see Hans hang up his hat and prepare to listen. "Nonsense, children," she said, "I have told it to you often."

"Tell us again! oh, *do* tell us again!" cried Gretel, throwing herself upon the wonderful wooden bench that her brother had made on the mother's last birthday. Hans, not wishing to appear childish, and yet quite willing to hear the story, stood carelessly swinging his skates against the fireplace.

"Well, children, you shall hear it, but we must never waste the daylight again in this way. Pick up your ball, Gretel, and let your sock grow as I talk. Opening your ears needn't shut your fingers. Saint Nicholas, you must know, is a wonderful saint. He keeps his eye open for the good of sailors, but he

[1] The Dutch cent is worth a farthing.   [2] A street in Amsterdam

cares most of all for boys and girls. Well, once upon a time, when he was living on the earth, a merchant of Asia sent his three sons to a great city, called Athens, to get learning."

"Is Athens in Holland, mother?" asked Gretel.

"I don't know, child. Probably it is."

"Oh, no, mother," said Hans, respectfully. "I had that in my geography lessons long ago. Athens is in Greece."

"Well," resumed the mother, "what matter? Greece may belong to the king, for aught we know. Anyhow, this rich merchant sent his sons to Athens. While they were on their way, they stopped one night at a shabby inn, meaning to take up their journey in the morning. Well, they had very fine clothes—velvet and silk, it may be, such as rich folks' children, all over the world, think nothing of wearing—and their belts, likewise, were full of money. What did the wicked landlord do, but contrive a plan to kill the children, and take their money and all their beautiful clothes himself. So that night, when all the world was asleep, he got up and killed the three young gentlemen."

Gretel clasped her hands and shuddered, but Hans tried to look as if killing and murder were everyday matters to him.

"That was not the worst of it," continued Dame Brinker, knitting slowly, and trying to keep count of her stitches as she talked; "that was not near the worst of it. The dreadful landlord went and cut up the young gentlemen's bodies into little pieces, and threw them into a great tub of brine, intending to sell them for pickled pork!"

"OH!" cried Gretel, horror-stricken, though she had often heard the story before. Hans still continued unmoved, and seemed to think that pickling was the best that could be done under the circumstances.

"Yes, he pickled them, and one might think that would have been the last of the young gentlemen. But no. That night Saint Nicholas had a wonderful vision, and in it he saw the landlord cutting up the merchant's children. There was no need of his hurrying, you know, for he was a saint; but in the morning he went to the inn and charged the landlord with the murder. Then the wicked landlord confessed it from beginning to end, and fell down on his knees, begging forgiveness. He felt so sorry for what he had done, that he asked the saint to bring the young masters to life."

"And did the saint do it?" asked Gretel, delighted, well knowing what the answer would be.

"Of course he did. The pickled pieces flew together in an instant, and out jumped the young gentlemen from the brine-tub. They cast themselves at the feet of Saint Nicholas and he gave them his blessing, and—oh! mercy on us, Hans, it will be dark before you get back if you don't start this minute!"

By this time Dame Brinker was almost out of breath and quite out of commas. She could not remember when she had seen the children idle away an hour of daylight in this manner, and the thought of such luxury quite appalled her. By way of compensation she now flew about the room in extreme haste. Tossing a block of peat upon the fire, blowing invisible dust from the table, and handing the finished hose to Hans, all in an instant—

"Come, Hans," she said, as her boy lingered by the door, "what keeps thee?"

Hans kissed his mother's plump cheek, rosy and fresh yet, in spite of all her troubles. "My mother is the best in the world, and I would be right glad to have a pair of skates, but" —and, as he buttoned his jacket, he looked, in a troubled way, toward a strange figure crouching by the hearth-stone—"if my money would bring a meester [1] from Amsterdam to see the father, something might yet be done."

"A meester would not come, Hans, for twice that money; and it would do no good if he did. Ah! how many guilders I once spent for that; but the dear, good father would not waken. It is God's will. Go, Hans, and buy the skates."

Hans started with a heavy heart, but since the heart was young, and in a boy's bosom, it set him whistling in less than five minutes. His mother had said "thee" to him, and that was quite enough to make even a dark day sunny. Hollanders

[1] Doctor (dokter in Dutch), called meester by the lower class.

do not address each other, in affectionate intercourse, as the
French and Germans do. But Dame Brinker had embroidered
for a Heidelberg family in her girlhood, and she had carried its
"thee" and "thou" into her rude home, to be used in moments
of extreme love and tenderness.

Therefore, "What keeps thee, Hans?" sang an echo song
beneath the boy's whistling, and made him feel that his errand
was blest.

CHAPTER VII

HANS HAS HIS WAY

BROEK, with its quiet, spotless streets, its frozen rivulets,
its yellow brick pavements, and bright wooden houses,
was near by. It was a village where neatness and show were in
full blossom; but the inhabitants seemed to be either asleep or
dead.

Not a footprint marred the sanded paths, where pebbles and
sea-shells lay in fanciful designs. Every window-shutter was
closed as tightly as though air and sunshine were poison; and
the massive front doors were never opened. except on the occasion
of a wedding, christening, or a funeral.

Serene clouds of tobacco-smoke were floating through hidden
apartments, and children, who otherwise might have awakened
the place, were studying in out-of-the-way corners, or skating
upon the neighbouring canal. A few peacocks and wolves stood
in the gardens, but they had never enjoyed the luxury of flesh
and blood. They were cut out in growing box, and seemed
guarding the grounds with a sort of green ferocity. Certain
lively automata, ducks, women and sportsmen, were stowed
away in summer-houses, waiting for the spring-time, when they
could be wound up, and rival their owners in animation; and
the shining, tiled roofs, mosaic courtyards and polished house-
trimmings flashed up a silent homage to the sky, where never a
speck of dust could dwell.

Hans glanced toward the village, as he shook his silver
kwartjes, and wondered whether it were really true, as he had
often heard, that some of the people of Broek were so rich that
they used kitchen utensils of solid gold.

He had seen Mevrouw van Stoop's sweet cheeses in market,
and he knew that the lofty dame earned many a bright, silver
guilder in selling them. But did she set the cream to rise in
golden pans ? Did she use a golden skimmer ? When her cows
were in winter quarters, were their tails really tied up with
ribbons ?

These thoughts ran through his mind as he turned his face
toward Amsterdam, not five miles away, on the other side of
the frozen Y.[1] The ice upon the canal was perfect ; but his
wooden runners, so soon to be cast aside, squeaked a dismal
farewell, as he scraped and skimmed along.

When crossing the Y, whom should he see skating toward
him but the great Dr. Boekman, the most famous physician
and surgeon in Holland. Hans had never met him before, but
he had seen his engraved likeness in many of the shop windows
of Amsterdam. It was a face that one could never forget.
Thin and lank, though a born Dutchman, with stern, blue eyes,
and queer compressed lips, that seemed to say " no smiling permitted," he certainly was not a very jolly or sociable looking
personage, nor one that a well-trained boy would care to accost
unbidden.

But Hans *was* bidden, and that, too, by a voice he seldom
disregarded—his own conscience.

" Here comes the greatest doctor in the world," whispered the
voice, " God has sent him ; you have no right to buy skates when
you might, with the same money, purchase such aid for your
father ! "

The wooden runners gave an exultant squeak. Hundreds of
beautiful skates were gleaming and vanishing in the air above
him. He felt the money tingle in his fingers. The old doctor
looked fearfully grim and forbidding. Hans' heart was in his

[1] Pronounced EYE, an arm of the Zuider Zee.

throat, but he found voice enough to cry out, just as he was passing—

"Mynheer Boekman!"

The great man halted, and sticking out his thin under lip looked scowlingly about him.

Hans was in for it now.

"Mynheer," he panted, drawing close to the fierce-looking doctor, "I knew you could be none other than the famous Boekman. I have to ask a great favour."

"Humph!" muttered the doctor, preparing to skate past the intruder; "get out of the way—I've no money—never give to beggars."

"I am no beggar, Mynheer," retorted Hans, proudly, at the same time producing his mite of silver, with a grand air; "I wish to consult with you about my father. He is a living man, but sits like one dead. He cannot think. His words mean nothing—but he is not sick. He fell on the dykes."

"Hey? what?" cried the doctor, beginning to listen.

Hans told the whole story in an incoherent way, dashing off a tear once or twice as he talked, and finally ending with an earnest—

"Oh, do see him, Mynheer. His body is well—it is only his mind—I know this money is not enough; but take it, Mynheer, I will earn more—I know I will—oh! I will toil for you all my life, if you will but cure my father!"

What was the matter with the old doctor? A brightness like sunlight beamed from his face. His eyes were kind and moist; the hand that had lately clutched his cane, as if preparing to strike, was laid gently upon Hans' shoulder.

"Put up your money, boy, I do not want it—we will see your father. It is a hopeless case, I fear. How long did you say?"

"Ten years, Mynheer," sobbed Hans, radiant with sudden hope.

"Ah! a bad case; but I shall see him. Let me think. To-day I start for Leyden, to return in a week, then you may expect me. Where is it?"

"A mile south of Broek, Mynheer, near the canal. It is

only a poor, broken-down hut. Any of the children thereabout can point it out to your honour," added Hans, with a heavy sigh; "they are all half afraid of the place; they call it the idiot's cottage."

"That will do," said the doctor, hurrying on, with a bright backward nod at Hans; " I shall be there. A hopeless case," he muttered to himself; "but the boy pleases me. His eye is like my poor Laurens'. Confound it, shall I never forget that young scoundrel?" and, scowling more darkly than ever, the doctor pursued his silent way.

Again Hans was skating toward Amsterdam on the squeaking wooden runners; again his fingers tingled against the money in his pocket; again the boyish whistle rose unconsciously to his lips.

"Shall I hurry home," he was thinking, "to tell the good news, or shall I get the waffles and the new skates first? Whew! I think I'll go on!"

And so Hans bought the skates.

CHAPTER VIII

INTRODUCING JACOB POOT AND HIS COUSIN

HANS and Gretel had a fine frolic early on that Saint Nicholas' Eve. There was a bright moon, and their mother, though she believed herself to be without any hope of her husband's improvement, had been made so happy at the prospect of the meester's visit, that she had yielded to the children's entreaties for an hour's skating before bed-time.

Hans was delighted with his new skates, and in his eagerness to show Gretel how perfectly they "worked" did many things upon the ice, that caused the little maid to clasp her hands in solemn admiration. They were not alone, though they seemed quite unheeded by the various groups assembled upon the canal.

The two Van Holps, and Carl Schummel were there, testing

their fleetness to the utmost.   Out of four trials Peter Van Holp
had beaten three times.   Consequently Carl, never very amiable,
was in anything but a good humour.   He had relieved himself by
taunting young Schimmelpenninck, who, being smaller than the
others, kept meekly near them, without feeling exactly like one
of the party; but now a new thought seized Carl, or rather he
seized the new thought and made an onset upon his friends.

"I say, boys, let's put a stop to those young rag-pickers from
the idiot's cottage joining the race.   Hilda must be crazy to
think of it.   Katrinka Flack and Rychie Korbes are furious at
the very idea of racing with the girl; and for my part I don't
blame them.   As for the boy, if we've a spark of manhood in us
we will scorn the very idea of—— "

"Certainly we will ! " interposed Peter Van Holp, purposely
mistaking Carl's meaning, "who doubts it ?   No fellow with a
spark of manhood in him would refuse to let in two good skaters
just because they were poor ! "

Carl wheeled about savagely—

"Not so fast, master ! and I'd thank you not to put words in
other people's mouths.   You'd best not try it again."

"Ha ! ha ! " laughed little Voostenwalbert Schimmelpenninck,
delighted at the prospect of a fight, and sure that, if it should
come to blows, his favourite Peter could beat a dozen excitable
fellows like Carl.

Something in Peter s eye made Carl glad to turn to a weaker
offender.   He wheeled furiously upon Voost.

"What are you shrieking about, you little weasel ? You
skinny herring you—you little monkey with a long name for a
tail ! "

Half-a-dozen by-standers and by-skaters set up an applauding
shout at this brave witticism ; and Carl, feeling that he had
fairly vanquished his foes, was restored to partial good humour.
He, however, prudently resolved to defer plotting against
Hans and Gretel until some time when Peter should not be
present.

Just then, his friend, Jacob Poot, was seen approaching.
They could not distinguish his features at first ; but as he was

the stoutest boy in the neighbourhood there could be no mistaking his form.

"Hollo! here comes Fatty!" exclaimed Carl, "and there's some one with him, a slender fellow, a stranger."

"Ha! ha! that's like good bacon," cried Ludwig; "a streak of lean and a streak of fat."

"That's Jacob's English cousin," put in Master Voost, delighted at being able to give the information; "that's his English cousin, and, oh! he's got such a funny little name,— BEN DOBBS. He's going to stay with him until after the grand race."

All this time the boys had been spinning, turning, "rolling," and doing other feats upon their skates, in a quiet way, as they talked; but now they stood still, bracing themselves against the frosty air as Jacob Poot and his friend drew near.

"This is my cousin, boys," said Jacob rather out of breath— "Benjamin Dobbs. He's a John Bull, and he's going to be in the race."

All crowded, boy-fashion, about the newcomers. Benjamin soon made up his mind that the Hollanders, notwithstanding their queer gibberish, were a fine set of fellows.

If the truth must be told, Jacob had announced his cousin as "Benchamin Dopps," and called him a "Shon Pull," but as I translate every word of the conversation of our young friends, it is no more than fair to mend their little attempts at English. Master Dobbs felt at first decidedly awkward among his cousin's friends. Though most of them had studied English and French, they were shy about attempting to speak either, and he made very funny blunders when he tried to converse in Dutch. But the fun of skating glides over all barriers of speech. Through this, Ben soon felt that he knew the boys well; and when Jacob (with a sprinkling of French and English for Ben's benefit) told of a grand project they had planned, his cousin could now and then put in a "ja," or a nod, in quite a familiar way.

The project *was* a grand one, and there was to be a fine opportunity for carrying it out; for, besides the allotted holiday of the Festival of Saint Nicholas, four extra days were to be allowed for a general cleaning of the school-house.

Jacob and Ben had obtained permission to go on a long skating journey—no less a one than from Broek to the Hague, the capital of Holland, a distance of nearly fifty miles! [1]

"And now, boys," added Jacob, when he had told the plan, "who will go with us?"

"I will! I will!" cried the boys eagerly.

"And so will I!" ventured little Voostenwalbert.

"Ha! ha!" laughed Jacob, holding his fat sides, and shaking his puffy cheeks, "*you* go? Such a little fellow as you? Why, youngster, you haven't left off your pads yet!"

Now in Holland very young children wear a thin, padded cushion around their heads, surmounted with a framework of whalebone and ribbon, to protect them in case of a fall; and it is the dividing line between babyhood and childhood when they leave it off. Voost had arrived at this dignity several years before; consequently Jacob's insult was rather too great for endurance.

"Look out what you say!" he squeaked. "Lucky for you when you can leave off *your* pads—you're padded all over!"

"Ha! ha!" roared all the boys except Master Dobbs, who could not understand. "Ha! ha!" — and the good-natured Jacob laughed more than any.

"It ish my fat—yaw—he say I bees pad mit fat!" he explained to Ben.

So a vote was passed unanimously in favour of allowing the now popular Voost to join the party, if his parents would consent.

"Good-night!" sang out the happy youngster, skating homeward with all his might.

"Good-night!"

"We can stop at Haarlem, Jacob, and show your cousin the big organ," said Peter van Holp, eagerly, "and at Leyden, too, where there's no end to the sights; and spend a day and night

---

[1] Throughout this narrative distances are given in English statute miles of 5280 feet. The Dutch mile is more than four times as long as ours.

at the Hague, for my married sister, who lives there, will be delighted to see us; and the next morning we can start for home."

"All right!" responded Jacob, who was not much of a talker.

Ludwig had been regarding his brother with enthusiastic admiration.

"Hurrah for you, Pete! It takes you to make plans! Mother'll be as full of it as we are when we tell her we can take her love direct to sister Van Gend. My! but it's cold," he added,—"cold enough to take a fellow's head off his shoulders. We'd better go home."

"What if it is cold, old Tender-skin?" cried Carl, who was busily practising a step which he called the "double edge." "Great skating we should have by this time, if it was as warm as it was last December. Don't you know if it wasn't an extra cold winter, and an early one into the bargain, we couldn't go?"

"I know it's an extra cold night, anyhow," said Ludwig. "Whew! I'm going home!"

Peter Van Holp took out a bulgy gold watch, and holding it toward the moonlight, as well as his benumbed fingers would permit, called out—

"Hollo! it's nearly eight o'clock! Saint Nicholas is about by this time, and I, for one, want to see the little ones stare. Good-night!"

"Good-night!" cried one and all,—and off they started, shouting, singing, and laughing as they flew along.

Where were Gretel and Hans?

Ah! how suddenly joy sometimes comes to an end!

They had skated about an hour, keeping aloof from the others —quite contented with each other—and Gretel had exclaimed, "Ah, Hans, how beautiful! how fine! to think that we both have skates! I tell you the stork brought us good-luck!"— when they heard something!

It was a scream—a very faint scream! No one else upon the canal observed it, but Hans knew its meaning too well. Gretel saw him turn white in the moonlight as he hastily tore off his skates.

"The father!" he cried, "he has frightened our mother!" and Gretel ran after him toward the house as rapidly as she could.

CHAPTER IX

THE FESTIVAL OF SAINT NICHOLAS

BEFORE the Christmas tree began to flourish in the home-life of our country, a certain "right jolly old elf," with "eight tiny reindeer," used to drive his sleigh-load of toys up to our house-tops, and then bound down the chimney to fill the stockings so nopefully hung by the fireplace. His friends called him Santa Claus, and those who were most intimate ventured to say "Old Nick." It was said that he originally came from Holland. Doubtless he did ; but, if so, he certainly, like many other foreigners, changed his ways very much after landing upon our shores. In Holland, Saint Nicholas is a veritable saint, and often appears in full costume, with his embroidered robes, glittering with gems and gold, his mitre, his crozier, and his jewelled gloves. In Holland, Saint Nicholas visits earth on the 5th December, a time especially appropriated to him. Early on the morning of the 6th he distributes his candies, toys, and treasures, then vanishes for a year.

Christmas day is devoted by the Hollanders to church rites and pleasant family visiting. It is on Saint Nicholas' Eve that their young people become half wild with joy and expectation. To some of them it is a sorry time, for the saint is very candid, and if any of them have been bad during the past year, he is quite sure to tell them so. Sometimes he carries a birch rod under his arm, and advises the parents to give them scoldings in place of confections, and floggings instead of toys.

It was well that the boys hastened to their abodes on that bright winter evening, for in less than an hour afterwards, the saint made his appearance in half the homes of Holland. He visited the king's palace, and in the self-same moment appeared

in Annie Bouman's comfortable home.   Probably one of our
silver half-dollars would have purchased all that his saintship
left at the peasant Bouman's ; but a florin's worth will sometimes
do for the poor what hundreds of pounds may fail to do for the
rich ; it makes them happy and grateful, fills them with new
peace and love.

Hilda van Gleck's little brothers and sisters were in a high
state of excitement that night.   They had been admitted into
the grand parlour ; they were dressed in their best, and had
been given two cakes apiece at supper.   Hilda was as joyous as
any.   Why not ?   Saint Nicholas would never cross a girl of
fourteen from his list, just because she was tall and looked
almost like a woman.   On the contrary, he would probably
exert himself to do honour to such an august-looking damsel.
Who could tell ?   So she sported and laughed and danced as
gaily as the youngest, and was the soul of all their merry games.
Father, mother, and grandmother looked on approvingly ; so
did grandfather, before he spread his large red handkerchief over
his face, leaving only the top of his skull-cap visible.   This
kerchief was his ensign of sleep.

Earlier in the evening all had joined in the fun.   In the
general hilarity there had seemed to be a difference only in bulk
between grandfather and the baby.   Indeed a shade of solemn
expectation, now and then flitting across the faces of the younger
members, had made them seem rather more thoughtful than
their elders.

Now the spirit of fun reigned supreme.   The very flames
danced and capered in the polished grate.   A pair of prim
candles that had been staring at the astral lamp began to wink
at other candles far away in the mirrors.   There was a long bell-
rope suspended from the ceiling in the corner, made of glass
beads netted over a cord nearly as thick as your wrist.   It
generally hung in the shadow and made no sign ; but to-night it
twinkled from end to end.   Its handle of crimson glass sent
reckless dashes of red at the papered wall, turning its dainty
blue stripes into purple.   Passers-by halted to catch the merry
laughter, floating through curtain and sash into the street ; then

skipped on their way with a startled consciousness that the
village was wide awake. At last matters grew so uproarious
that the grandsire's red kerchief came down from his face
with a jerk. What decent old gentleman could sleep in such
a racket! Mynheer Van Gleck regarded his children with
astonishment. The baby even showed symptoms of hysterics.
It was high time to attend to business. Madame suggested that
if they wished to see the good Saint Nicholas, they should sing
the same loving invitation that had brought him the year before.

The baby stared and thrust his fist into his mouth as Mynheer
put him down upon the floor. Soon he sat erect, and looked
with a sweet scowl at the company. With his lace and
embroideries, and his crown of blue ribbon and whalebone (for
he was not quite past the tumbling age), he looked like the king
of the babies.

The other children, each holding a pretty willow basket,
formed at once in a ring, and moved slowly around the little
fellow, lifting their eyes, meanwhile, for the saint to whom they
were about to address themselves was yet in mysterious quarters.

Madame commenced playing softly upon the piano ; soon
the voices rose—gentle youthful voices—rendered all the sweeter
for their tremor.

> Welcome, friend! Saint Nicholas, welcome!
> Bring no rod for us, to-night!
> While our voices bid thee welcome,
> Every heart with joy is light!
>
>> Tell us every fault and failing,
>> We will bear thy keenest railing;
>> So we sing—so we sing—
>> Thou shalt tell us everything!
>
> Welcome, friend! Saint Nicholas, welcome!
> Welcome to this merry band!
> Happy children greet thee, welcome!
> Thou art gladd'ning all the land!
>
>> Fill each empty hand and basket,
>> 'Tis thy little ones who ask it;
>> So we sing—so we sing—
>> Thou wilt bring us everything!

During the chorus, sundry glances, half in eagerness, half in dread, had been cast towards the polished folding-doors. Now a loud knocking was heard. The circle was broken in an instant. Some of the little ones, with a strange mixture of fear and delight, pressed against their mother's knee. Grandfather bent forward, with his chin resting upon his hand; grandmother lifted her spectacles; Mynheer van Gleck, seated by the fireplace, slowly drew his meerschaum from his mouth, while Hilda and the other children settled themselves beside him in an expectant group.

The knocking was heard again.

"Come in," said Madame, softly.

The door slowly opened, and Saint Nicholas, in full array, stood before them. You could have heard a pin drop! Soon he spoke. What a mysterious majesty in his voice! what kindliness in his tones!

"Karel van Gleck, I am pleased to greet thee, and thy honoured vrouw Kathrine, and thy son and his good vrouw Annie!

"Children, I greet ye all! Hendrick, Hilda, Broom, Katy, Huygens, and Lucretia! And thy cousins, Wolfert, Diedrich, Mayken, Voost, and Katrina! Good children ye have been, in the main, since I last accosted ye. Diedrich was rude at the Haarlem fair last fall, but he has tried to atone for it since. Mayken has failed of late in her lessons, and too many sweets and trifles have gone to her lips, and too few stivers to her charity-box. Diedrich, I trust, will be a polite, manly boy for the future, and Mayken will endeavour to shine as a student. Let her remember, too, that economy and thrift are needed in the foundation of a worthy and generous life. Little Katy has been cruel to the cat more than once. Saint Nicholas can hear the cat cry when its tail is pulled. I will forgive her if she will remember from this hour that the smallest dumb creatures have feeling, and must not be abused."

As Katy burst into a frightened cry, the saint graciously remained silent until she was soothed.

"Master Broom," he resumed, "I warn thee that boys who

are in the habit of putting snuff upon the foot-stove of the school-mistress may one day be discovered and receive a flogging—— "

Master Broom coloured and stared in great astonishment.

" But thou art such an excellent scholar, I shall make thee no further reproof.

" Thou, Hendrick, didst distinguish thyself in the archery match last spring, and hit the Doel,[1] though the bird was swung before it to unsteady thine eye. I give thee credit for excelling in manly sport and exercise—though I must not unduly countenance thy boat-racing, since it leaves thee too little time for thy proper studies.

" Lucretia and Hilda shall have a blessed sleep to-night. The consciousness of kindness to the poor, devotion in their souls, and cheerful, hearty obedience to household rule will render them happy.

" With one and all I avow myself well content. Goodness, industry, benevolence, and thrift have prevailed in your midst. Therefore, my blessing upon you—and may the New Year find all treading the paths of obedience, wisdom, and love. To-morrow you shall find more substantial proofs that I have been in your midst. Farewell ! "

With these words came a great shower of sugar-plums upon a linen sheet spread out in front of the doors. A general scramble followed. The children fairly tumbled over each other in their eagerness to fill their baskets. Madame cautiously held the baby down in their midst, till the chubby little fists were filled. Then the bravest of the youngsters sprang up and burst open the closed doors—in vain they peered into the mysterious apartment—Saint Nicholas was nowhere to be seen.

Soon there was a general rush to another room, where stood a table, covered with the finest and whitest of linen damask. Each child, in a flutter of excitement, laid a shoe upon it. The door was then carefully locked, and its key hidden in the mother's bedroom. Next followed good-night kisses, a grand family procession to the upper floor, merry farewells at

---

[1] Bull's-eye.

bedroom-doors—and silence, at last, reigned in the Van Gleck mansion.

Early the next morning the door was solemnly unlocked and opened in the presence of the assembled household, when lo ! a sight appeared proving Saint Nicholas to be a saint of his word !

Every shoe was filled to overflowing, and beside each stood many a coloured pile. The table was heavy with its load of presents—candies, toys, trinkets, books, and other articles. Every one had gifts, from grandfather down to the baby.

Little Katy clapped her hands with glee, and vowed, inwardly, that the cat should never know another moment's grief.

Hendrick capered about the room, flourishing a superb bow and arrows over his head. Hilda laughed with delight as she opened a crimson box and drew forth its glittering contents. The rest chuckled and said "Oh !" and "Ah !" over their treasures, very much as we did here on last Christmas day.

With her glittering necklace in her hands, and a pile of books in her arms, Hilda stole towards her parents and held up her beaming face for a kiss. There was such an earnest, tender look in her bright eyes, that her mother breathed a blessing as she leaned over her.

"I am delighted with this book, thank you, father," she said, touching the top one with her chin. "I shall read it all day long."

"Ay, sweetheart," said Mynheer, "you cannot do better. There is no one like Father Cats. If my daughter learns his 'Moral Emblems' by heart, the mother and I may keep silent. The work you have there is the 'Emblems'—his best work. You will find it enriched with rare engravings from Van de Venne."

"Old Father Cats, my child, was a great poet, not a writer of plays like the Englishman Shakespeare, who lived in his time. I have read them in the German, and very good they are—very, very good—but not like Father Cats. Cats sees no daggers in the air ; he has no white women falling in love with dusky Moors ; no young fools sighing to be a lady's glove ; no crazy princes mistaking respectable old gentlemen for rats. No, no. He writes only sense. It is great wisdom in little bundles —a bundle for every day of your life. You can guide a state with Cats' poems, and you can put a little baby to sleep with his pretty songs. He was one of the greatest men of Holland. When I take you to the Hague I will show you the Kloosterkerk where he lies buried. *There* was a man for you to study, my sons! he was good through and through. What did he say?

> "O Lord, let me obtain this from Thee
> To live with patience, and to die with pleasure!"[1]

"Did patience mean folding his hands? No, he was a lawyer, statesman, ambassador, farmer, philosopher, historian, and poet. He was keeper of the Great Seal of Holland! He was a—Bah! there is too much noise here, I cannot talk"— and Mynheer, looking with astonishment into the bowl of his meerschaum—for it had "gone out"—nodded to his vrouw and left the apartment in great haste.

The fact is, his discourse had been accompanied throughout with a subdued chorus of barking dogs, squeaking cats, and bleating lambs, to say nothing of a noisy ivory cricket, that the baby was whirling with infinite delight. At the last, little Huygens, taking advantage of the increasing loudness of Mynheer's tones, had ventured a blast on his new trumpet, and Wolfert had hastily attempted an accompaniment on the drum. This had brought matters to a crisis, and well for the little creatures that it had. The saint had left no ticket for them to attend a lecture on Jacob Cats. It was not an appointed part of the ceremonies. Therefore when the youngsters saw that the mother looked neither frightened nor offended, they gathered new courage. The grand chorus rose triumphant, and frolic and joy reigned supreme.

Good Saint Nicholas! For the sake of the young Hollanders, I, for one, am willing to acknowledge him, and defend his reality against all unbelievers.

---

[1] O Heere laat my dat van uwen hand verwerven,
Te leven met gedult, en met vermaak te sterven.

Carl Schummel was quite busy during that day, assuring little children confidentially, that not Saint Nicholas, but their own fathers and mothers, had produced the oracle and loaded the tables.   But *we* know better than that.

And yet if this were a saint, why did he not visit the Brinker cottage that night?   Why was that one home, so dark and sorrowful, passed by?

CHAPTER X

WHAT THE BOYS SAW AND DID IN AMSTERDAM

"ARE we all here?" cried Peter, in high glee, as the party assembled upon the canal early the next morning, equipped for their skating journey.   "Let me see.   As Jacob has made me captain, I must call the roll.   Carl Schummel.   You here?"

"Ya!"

"Jacob Poot!"

"Ya!"

"Benjamin Dobbs!"

"Ya-a!"

"Lambert van Mounen!"

"Ya!"

"Ludwig van Holp!"

"Ya!"

"Voostenwalbert Schimmelpenninck!"

No answer.

"Ah! the little rogue has been kept at home.   Now, boys, it's just eight o'clock—glorious weather, and the Y is as firm as a rock—we'll be at Amsterdam in thirty minutes.   One, Two, Three, START!"

True enough, in less than half an hour they had crossed a dyke of solid masonry, and were in the very heart of the great metropolis of the Netherlands—a walled city of ninety-five islands and nearly two hundred bridges.   Although Ben had been there twice since his arrival in Holland, he saw much to excite wonder; but his Dutch comrades, having lived near by all their lives, considered it the most matter-of-course place in the world. Everything interested Ben; the tall houses with their forked chimneys and gable ends facing the street; the merchants' warerooms, perched high up under the roofs of their dwellings, with long, arm-like cranes hoisting and lowering goods past the household windows; the grand public buildings erected upon wooden piles driven deep into the marshy ground; the narrow streets; the canals everywhere crossing the city; the bridges; the locks; the various costumes, and, strangest of all, shops and dwellings crouching close to the fronts of the churches, sending their long, disproportionate chimneys far upward along the sacred walls.

If he looked up, he saw tall, leaning houses, seeming to pierce the sky with their shining roofs; if he looked down, there was the queer street, without crossing or curb—nothing to separate the cobble-stone pavement from the footpath of brick; and if he rested his eyes half way, he saw complicated little mirrors fastened upon the outside of nearly every window, so arranged that the inmates of the houses could observe all that was going on in the street, or inspect whoever might be knocking at the door, without being seen themselves.

Sometimes a dog-cart, heaped with wooden ware, passed him; then a donkey bearing a pair of panniers filled with crockery or glass; then a sled driven over the bare cobble-stones (the runners kept greased with a dripping oil rag so that it might run easily); and then, perhaps, a showy, but clumsy family-carriage, drawn by the brownest of Flanders horses, swinging the whitest of snowy tails.

The city was in full festival array. Every shop was gorgeous in honour of Saint Nicholas. Captain Peter was forced, more than once, to order his men away from the tempting show-windows, where everything that is, has been, or can be thought of in the way of toys was displayed. Holland is famous for this branch of manufacture. Every possible thing is copied in miniature for the benefit of the little ones; the intricate

mechanical toys that a Dutch youngster tumbles about in stolid
unconcern would create a stir in our Patent office.   Ben laughed
outright at some of the mimic fishing boats.   They were so
heavy and stumpy, so like the queer craft that he had seen
about Rotterdam.   The tiny trekschuiten, however, only a foot
or two long, and fitted out, complete, made his heart ache—he
so longed to buy one at once for his little brother in England.
He had no money to spare, for, with true Dutch prudence, the
party had agreed to take with them merely the sum required
for each boy's expenses, and to consign the purse to Peter for
safe keeping.   Consequently Master Ben concluded to devote
all his energies to sight seeing, and to think as seldom as
possible of little Robby.

He made a hasty call at the Marine School, and envied the
sailor-students their full-rigged brig and their sleeping-berths
swung over their trunks or lockers; he peeped into the Jews'
Quarter of the city, where the rich diamond cutters and squalid
old-clothes' men dwell, and wisely resolved to keep away from it;
he also enjoyed hasty glimpses of the four principal avenues of
Amsterdam—the Prinsen gracht, Keizers gracht, Heeren gracht
and Singel.   These are semi-circular in form, and the first three
average more than two miles in length.   A canal runs through
the centre of each, with a well-paved road on either side, lined
with stately buildings.   Rows of naked elms, bordering the canal,
cast a network of shadows over its frozen surface; and everything was so clean and bright that Ben told Lambert it seemed
to him like petrified neatness.

Fortunately the weather was cold enough to put a stop to
the usual street-flooding, and window-washing, or our young
excursionists might have been drenched more than once.   Sweep-
ing, mopping, and scrubbing form a passion with Dutch house-
wives, and to soil their spotless mansions is considered scarcely
less than a crime.   Everywhere a hearty contempt is felt for
those who neglect to rub the soles of their shoes to a polish
before crossing the door-sill; and, in certain places, visitors are
expected to remove their heavy shoes before entering.

Sir William Temple, in his Memoirs of "What passed in

Christendom from 1672 to 1679," tells a story of a pompous magistrate going to visit a lady of Amsterdam. A stout Holland lass opened the door, and told him in a breath that the lady was at home and that his shoes were not very clean. Without another word, she took the astonished man up by both arms, threw him across her back, carried him through two rooms, set him down at the bottom of the stairs, seized a pair of slippers that stood there and put them upon his feet. Then, and not until then, she spoke, telling him that her mistress was on the floor above, and that he might go up.

While Ben was skating, with his friends, upon the crowded canals of the city, he found it difficult to believe that the sleepy Dutchmen he saw around him, smoking their pipes so leisurely, and looking as though their hats might be knocked off their heads without their making any resistance, were capable of those outbreaks that had taken place in Holland—that they were really fellow-countrymen of the brave, devoted heroes of whom he had read in Dutch history.

As his party skimmed lightly along he told Van Mounen of a burial-riot which in 1696 had occurred in that very city, where the women and children turned out, as well as the men, and formed mock funeral processions through the town, to show the burgomasters that certain new regulations, with regard to burying the dead, would not be acceded to—how at last they grew so unmanageable, and threatened so much damage to the city that the burgomasters were glad to recall the offensive law.

"There's the corner," said Jacob, pointing to some large buildings, "where, about fifteen years ago, the great corn-houses sank down in the mud. They were strong affairs, and set up on good piles, but they had over seventy thousand hundredweight of corn in them ; and that was too much."

It was a long story for Jacob to tell, and he stopped to rest.

"How do you know there were seventy thousand hundred-weight in them?" asked Carl, sharply; "you were in your swaddling clothes then."

"My father knows all about it," was Jacob's suggestive reply.

Rousing himself with an effort, he continued—"Ben likes pictures. Show him some."

"All right," said the captain.

"If we had time, Benjamin," said Lambert van Mounen in English, "I should like to take you to the City Hall or *Stadhuis*. There are building-piles for you! It is built on nearly fourteen thousand of them, driven seventy feet into the ground. But what I wish you to see there is the big picture of Van Speyk blowing up his ship—great picture."

"Van *who*?" asked Ben.

"Van Speyk. Don't you remember? He was in the height of an engagement with the Belgians, and when he found that they had the better of him and would capture his ship, he blew it up, and himself too, rather than yield to the enemy."

"Wasn't that Van Tromp?"

"Oh, no. Van Tromp was another brave fellow. They've a monument to him down at Delft Haven—the place where the Pilgrims took ship for America."

"Well, what about Van Tromp? He was a great Dutch admiral; wasn't he?"

"Yes, he was in more than thirty sea-fights. He beat the Spanish fleet and an English one, and then fastened a broom to his mast-head to show that he had swept the English from the sea. Takes the Dutch to beat, my boy!"

"Stop there!" cried Ben, "broom or no broom, the English conquered him at last. I remember all about it now. He was killed somewhere on the Dutch coast, in an engagement in which the British fleet was victorious. Too bad," he added, maliciously, "wasn't it?"

"Ahem! where are we?" exclaimed Lambert, changing the subject. "Hollo! the others are away ahead of us—all but Jacob. Whew! how fat he is! He'll break down before we're half way."

Ben, of course, enjoyed skating beside Lambert, who, though a staunch Hollander, had been educated near London, and could speak English as fluently as Dutch; but he was not sorry when Captain van Holp called out—

"Skates off! There's the Museum!"

It was open, and there was no charge on that day for admission. In they went, shuffling, as boys will, when they have a chance, just to hear the sound of their shoes on the polished floor.

This Museum is in fact a picture gallery, where some of the finest works of the Dutch masters are to be seen, besides nearly two hundred portfolios of rare engravings.

Ben noticed, at once, that some of the pictures were hung on panels fastened to the wall with hinges. These could be swung forward like a window-shutter, thus enabling the subject to be seen in the best light. The plan served them well in viewing a small group by Gerard Douw, called the "Evening School," enabling them to observe its exquisite finish, and the wonderful way in which the picture seemed to be lit through its own windows. Peter pointed out the beauties of another picture by Douw, called "The Hermit," and he also told them some interesting anecdotes of the artist, who was born at Leyden in 1613.

"Boys!" called Lambert, in a loud whisper, "come look at this Bear Hunt."

It was a fine painting by Paul Potter, a Dutch artist of the seventeenth century, who produced excellent works before he was sixteen years old. The boys admired it because the subject pleased them. They passed carelessly by the masterpieces of Rembrandt and Van der Helst, and went into raptures over an ugly picture by Van der Venne, representing a sea-fight between the Dutch and English. They also stood spell-bound before a painting of two little urchins, one of whom was taking soup and the other eating an egg. The principal merit in this work was that the young egg-eater had kindly slobbered his face with the yoke for their entertainment.

An excellent representation of the "Feast of Saint Nicholas" next had the honour of attracting them.

"Look, Van Mounen," said Ben to Lambert, "could anything be better than this youngster's face? He looks as if he *knows* he deserves a whipping, but hopes Saint Nicholas may not have found him out. That's the kind of painting *I* like; something that tells a story."

"Come, boys!" cried the captain, "ten o'clock, time we were off!"

They hastened to the canal.

"Skates on! Are you ready? ONE, TWO—hollo! where's Poot?"

Sure enough where *was* Poot?

A square opening had just been cut in the ice not ten yards off. Peter observed it, and, without a word, skated rapidly toward it.

All the others followed, of course.

Peter looked in. They all looked in; then stared anxiously at each other.

"Poot!" screamed Peter, peering into the hole again. All was still. The black water gave no sign; it was already glazing on top.

Van Mounen turned mysteriously to Ben.

"*Didn't he have a fit once?*"

"My goodness! yes!" answered Ben, in a great fright.

"Then, depend upon it, he's been taken with one in the Museum!"

The boys caught his meaning. Every skate was off in a twinkling, and off they scampered to the rescue.

Alas! They did indeed find poor Jacob in a fit—but it was a fit of sleepiness. There he lay in a recess of the gallery, snoring like a trooper! The chorus of laughter that followed this discovery brought an angry official to the spot.

"What now! None of this racket! Here, you beer-barrel, wake up!" and Master Jacob received a very unceremonious shaking.

The order to start was again given. Master Poot was wide awake at last. The ice was a little rough and broken just there, but every boy was in high spirits.

"Shall we go on by the canal or the river?" asked Peter.

"Oh, the river, by all means," said Carl. "It will be such fun; they say it is perfect skating all the way, but it's much farther!"

Jacob Poot instantly became interested.

"*I* vote for the canal!" he cried.

"Well, the canal it shall be," responded the captain, "if all are agreed."

"Agreed!" they echoed, in rather a disappointed tone—and Captain Peter led the way.

"All right—come on—we can reach Haarlem in an hour?"

CHAPTER XI

BIG MANIAS AND LITTLE ODDITIES

WHILE skating along at full speed, they heard the train from Amsterdam coming close behind them.

"Hollo!" cried Ludwig, glancing toward the railway line— "who can't beat a locomotive? Let's give it a race!"

The whistle screamed at the very idea—so did the boys— and at it they went.

For an instant the boys were ahead, hurrahing with all their might—only for an instant, but even *that* was something.

This excitement over, they began to travel more leisurely, and indulge in conversation and frolic. Sometimes they stopped to exchange a word with the guards who were stationed at certain distances along the canal. These men, in winter, attend to keeping the surface free from obstruction. After a snow-storm they are expected to sweep the feathery covering away before it hardens into a marble pretty to look at, but very unwelcome to skaters. Now and then the boys so far forgot their dignity as to clamber among the ice-bound canal-boats crowded together in a widened harbour off the canal, but the watchful guards would soon spy them out and order them down with a growl.

Nothing could be straighter than the canal upon which our party were skating, and nothing straighter than the long rows of willow trees that stood, bare and wispy, along the bank. On the opposite side, lifted high above the surrounding country, lay the

carriage road on top of the great dyke, built to keep the Haarlem
Lake within bounds; stretching out far in the distance until it
became lost in a point, was the glassy canal, with its many
skaters, its brown-winged ice-boats, its push-chairs, and its queer
little sleds, light as cork, flying over the ice by means of iron-
pronged sticks in the hands of the riders. Ben was in ecstacy
with the scene.

Ludwig van Holp had been thinking how strange it was that
the English boy should know so much of Holland. According
to Lambert's account, he knew more about it than the Dutch
did. This did not quite please our young Hollander. Suddenly
he thought of something that he believed would make the
"Shon Pull" open his eyes. He drew near Lambert with a
triumphant—

"Tell him about the tulips!"

Ben caught the word "*tulpen*."

"Oh! yes," said he eagerly, in English, "the Tulip Mania
—are you speaking of that? I have often heard it mentioned,
but know very little about it. It reached its height in
Amsterdam, didn't it?"

Ludwig moaned; the words were hard to understand, but
there was no mistaking the enlightened expression on Ben's
face. Lambert, happily, was quite unconscious of his young
countryman's distress as he replied—

"Yes, here and in Haarlem, principally; but the excitement
ran high all over Holland, and in England too, for that matter."

"Hardly in England,[1] I think," said Ben, "but I am not
sure, as I was not there at the time."

[1] Although the Tulip Mania did not prevail in England as in Holland,
the flower soon became an object of speculation, and brought very large
prices. In 1636, tulips were publicly sold on the Exchange of London.
Even as late as 1800, a common price was fifteen guineas for one bulb. Ben
did not know that in his own day a single tulip plant, called the "Fanny
Kemble," had been sold in London for more than seventy guineas.

Mr. Mackay, in his *Memoirs of Popular Delusions*, tells a funny story
of an English botanist, who happened to see a tulip bulb lying in the con-
servatory of a wealthy Dutchman. Ignorant of its value, he took out his
penknife, and, cutting the bulb in two, became very much interested in his
investigations. Suddenly the owner appeared and, pouncing furiously upon
him, asked him if he knew what he was doing. "Peeling a most extra-

"Ha! ha! that's true, unless you are over two hundred years old. Well, I tell you, sir, there was never anything like it before nor since. Why, persons were so crazy after tulip bulbs in those days that they paid their weight in gold for them."

"What! the weight of a man?" cried Ben, showing such astonishment in his eyes that Ludwig fairly capered.

"No, no, the weight of a *bulb*. The first tulip was sent here from Constantinople about the year 1560. It was so much admired that the rich people of Amsterdam sent to Turkey for more. From that time they grew to be the rage, and it lasted for years. Single roots brought from one to four thousand florins; and one bulb, the Semper Augustus, brought fifty-five hundred."

"That's more than four hundred guineas of our money," interposed Ben.

"Yes, and I know I'm right, for I read it in a translation from Beckman, only day before yesterday. Every one speculated in tulips; even the bargemen and rag-women, and chimney-sweeps. The richest merchants were not ashamed to share the excitement. People bought bulbs and sold them again at a tremendous profit without ever seeing them. It grew into a kind of gambling. Some became rich by it in a few days, and some lost everything they had. Land, houses, cattle, and even clothing went for tulips when people had no ready money. Ladies sold their jewels and finery to enable them to join in the fun. Nothing else was thought of. At last the States-General interfered. People began to see what geese they were making of themselves, and down went the price of tulips. Old tulip debts couldn't be collected. Creditors went to law, and the

---

ordinary onion," replied the philosopher. "An onion!" shouted the Dutchman. "Its an ADMIRAL VANDER EYK!" "Thank you," replied the traveller, immediately writing the name in his note-book. "Pray, are these very common in your country?" "Confound it all!" screamed the Dutchman; "come before the syndic and you shall see!" In spite of his struggles, the poor investigator, followed by an indignant mob, was taken through the streets to a magistrate. Soon he learned to his dismay that he had destroyed a bulb worth four thousand florins, nearly four hundred pounds. He was lodged in prison until securities could be procured for the payment of the sum.

law turned its back upon them; debts made in gambling were not binding, it said. Then there was a time ! Thousands of rich speculators reduced to beggary in an hour. As old Beckman says, 'the bubble was burst at last.'"

"Yes, and a big bubble it was," said Ben, who had listened with great interest. "By the way, did you know that the name Tulip came from a Turkish word signifying turban ?"

"I had forgotten that," answered Lambert, "but it's a capital idea. Just fancy a party of Turks in full headgear squatted upon a lawn ! Ha ! ha ! capital idea !"

"There," groaned Ludwig to himself, "he's been telling Lambert something wonderful about tulips. I knew it."

"The fact is," continued Lambert, "you can conjure up quite a human picture out of a tulip bed in bloom, especially when it is nodding and bobbing in the wind. Did you ever notice it ?"

"Not I. It strikes me, Van Mounen, that you Hollanders are prodigiously fond of the flower to this day."

"Certainly. You can't have a garden without them; prettiest flower that grows, I think. My uncle has a magnificent bed of the finest varieties at his summer-house on the other side of Amsterdam."

"I thought your uncle lived in the city ?"

"So he does; but his summer-house, or pavilion, is a few miles off. He has another one built out over the river. We passed near it when we entered the city. Everybody in Amsterdam has a pavilion somewhere, if he can."

For some time the party skated onwards along the canal, chatting merrily as they glided over the smooth ice. Ben, despite the exercise, began to feel his toes cold and asked Lambert if they might stop.

Lambert laughed.

"That's your English blood, Benjamin; I'm not cold. And look at the skaters here on the canal—they're red as roses, and happy as lords. Hollo ! good Captain van Holp," called out Lambert in Dutch, "what say you to stopping at yonder farm-house and warming our toes ?"

"Who is cold?" asked Peter, turning around.

"Benjamin Dobbs."

"Benjamin Dobbs shall be warmed," and the party was brought to a halt.

CHAPTER XII

ON THE WAY TO HAARLEM

THE low roof of the farm-house, covered with bright-red tiles, extended over the cow-stable, which, clean as could be, nestled close to the main building. A neat, peaceful-looking old woman sat at one window knitting. At the other could be discerned part of the profile of a fat figure that, pipe in mouth, sat behind the shining little panes and snowy curtain. In answer to Peter's subdued knock, a fair-haired, rosy-cheeked lass in holiday attire opened the upper half of the green door (which was divided across the middle) and inquired their errand.

"May we enter and warm ourselves, jufvrouw?" asked the captain, respectfully.

"Yes, and welcome," was the reply, as the lower half of the door swung softly towards its mate. Every boy before entering rubbed long and faithfully upon the rough mat, and each made his best bow to the old lady and gentleman at the windows. Ben was half inclined to think that these personages were automatic, like the moving figures in the garden at Broek; for they both nodded their heads slowly, in precisely the same way, and both went on with their employment as steadily and stiffly as though they worked by machinery. The old man puffed! puffed! and his vrouw clicked her knitting-needles, as if regulated by internal cog-wheels. Even the real smoke issuing from the motionless pipe gave no convincing proof that they were human.

But the rosy-cheeked maiden. Ah! how she bustled about. How she gave the boys polished high-backed chairs to sit upon, how she made the fire blaze up as if it were inspired; how she made Jacob Poot almost weep for joy by bringing forth a great square of gingerbread, and a stone jug of sour wine; how she laughed and nodded as the boys ate like wild animals on good behaviour, and how blank she looked when Ben politely but firmly refused to take any black bread and sour-krout! How she pulled off Jacob's mitten, which was torn at the thumb, and mended it before his eyes, biting off the thread with her white teeth, and saying, "Now it will be warmer," as she bit; and finally, how she shook hands with every boy in turn and (throwing a deprecating glance at the female automaton) insisted upon filling their pockets with gingerbread!

All this time the knitting-needles clicked on, and the pipe never missed a puff.

When the boys were fairly on their way again, they came in sight of Zwanenburg Castle, with its massive stone front, and its gateway towers, each surmounted with a sculptured swan.

"Halfweg,[1] boys," said Peter; "off with your skates."

"You see," explained Lambert to his companion, "the river is here five feet higher than the land—so we must have everything strong in the way of dykes and sluice-gates, or there would be wet work at once. The sluice arrangements here are supposed to be something special—we will walk over them, and you shall see enough to make you open your eyes.

"The lake at the other side of the dyke is full of the biggest eels you ever saw—I've caught them here, often—perfectly prodigious? I tell you they're sometimes a match for a fellow; they'd almost wriggle your arm from the socket if you were not on your guard. But you're not interested in eels, I perceive. The castle's a big affair. Isn't it?"

"Yes. What do those swans mean? Anything?" asked Ben, looking up at the stone gate-towers.

"The swan is held almost in reverence by us Hollanders. These give the building its name, Zwanenburg—swan-castle. That is all I know. This is a very important spot; for it is here that the wise ones hold council with regard to dyke matters.

[1] Half way.

The castle was once the residence of the celebrated Christiaan Brunings."

"What about *him*?" asked Ben.

"Peter could answer you better than I," said Lambert, "if you could only understand each other, or were not such cowards about leaving your mother-tongues. But I have often heard my grandfather speak of Brunings. He is never tired of telling us of the great engineer—how good he was, and how learned, and how, when he died, the whole country seemed to mourn as for a friend. He belonged to a great many learned societies, and was at the head of the State department entrusted with the care of the dykes, and other defences against the sea. There's no counting the improvements he made in dykes and sluices and water-mills, and all that kind of thing. We Hollanders, you know, consider our great engineers as the highest of public benefactors. Brunings died years ago; they've a monument to his memory in the cathedral of Haarlem. I have seen his portrait, and I tell you, Ben, he was right noble-looking. No wonder the castle looks so stiff and proud. It is something to have given shelter to such a man!"

"Yes, indeed," said Ben; "I wonder, Van Mounen, whether you or I will ever give any old building a right to feel proud. Heigho! there's a great deal to be done yet in this world, and some of us, who are boys now, will have to do it. Look to your shoe latchet, Van; it's unfastened."

CHAPTER XIII

A CATASTROPHE

IT was nearly one o'clock when Captain van Holp and his command entered the grand old city of Haarlem. They had skated nearly seventeen miles since morning, and were still as fresh as young eagles. From the youngest (Ludwig van Holp, who was just fourteen) to the eldest, no less a personage than the captain himself, a veteran of seventeen, there was but one opinion—that this was the greatest frolic of their lives. To be sure, Jacob Poot had become rather short of breath during the last mile or two, and perhaps he felt ready for another nap ; but there was enough jollity in him yet for a dozen. Even Carl Schummel, who had become very intimate with Ludwig during the excursion, forgot to be ill-natured. As for Peter, he was the happiest of the happy, and had sung and whistled so joyously while skating, that the staidest passers-by had smiled as they listened.

"Come, boys, it's nearly lunch-hour," he said, as they neared a coffee-house on the main street. "We must have something more solid than the pretty maiden's gingerbread." And the Captain plunged his hands into his pockets as if to say, "There's money enough here to feed an army ! "

" Hollo ! " cried Lambert, " what ails the man ? "

Peter, pale and staring, was clapping his hands upon his breast and sides— he looked like one suddenly becoming deranged.

" He's sick ! " cried Ben.

" No, he's lost something," said Carl.

Peter could only gasp, "The pocket-book ! with all our money in it—it's gone ! "

For an instant all were too much startled to speak.

Carl at last came out with a gruff—

"No sense in letting one fellow have all the money. I said so from the first. Look in your other pocket."

" I did—it isn't there."

" Open your under-jacket."

Peter obeyed mechanically. He even took off his hat and looked into it ; then thrust his hand desperately into every pocket.

"It's gone, boys," he said at last, in a hopeless tone. "No lunch for us, nor dinner neither. What is to be done ? We can't get on without money. If we were in Amsterdam I could get as much as we want, but there is not a man in Haarlem from whom I can borrow a stiver. Don't one of you know any one here who would lend us a few guilders ? "

Each boy looked into five blank faces. Then something like a smile passed around the circle; but it got sadly knotted up when it reached Carl.

"That wouldn't do," he said crossly; "I know some people here, rich ones, too, but father would flog me soundly if I borrowed a cent from anyone. He has 'AN HONEST MAN NEED NOT BORROW,' written over the gateway of his summer-house."

"Humph!" responded Peter, not particularly admiring the sentiment just at that moment.

The boys grew desperately hungry at once.

"It wash my fault," said Jacob, in a penitent tone, to Ben. "I say first, petter all de poys put zair pursh into Van Holp's monish."

"Nonsense, Jacob; you did it all for the best."

Ben said this in such a sprightly tone that the two Van Holps and Carl felt sure he had proposed a plan that would relieve the party at once.

"What? what? Tells us, Van Mounen," they cried.

"He says it is not Jacob's fault that the money is lost—that he did it for the best, when he proposed that Van Holp should put all of our money into his purse."

"Is that all?" said Ludwig, dismally; "he need not have made such a fuss in just saying *that*. How much money have we lost?"

"Don't you remember," said Peter. "We each put in exactly ten guilders. The purse had sixty guilders in it. I am the stupidest fellow in the world; little Schimmelpenninck would have made you a better captain. I could pommel myself for bringing such a disappointment upon you."

"Do it, then," growled Carl. "Pooh," he added, "we all know it was an accident, but that doesn't help matters. We must have money, Van Holp, even if you have to sell your wonderful watch."

"Sell my mother's birthday present! Never! I will sell my coat, my hat, anything but my watch."

"Come, come," said Jacob, pleasantly, "we are making too much of this affair. We can go home and start again in a day or two."

"*You* may be able to get another ten-guilder piece," said Carl, "but the rest of us will not find it so easy. If we go home, we stay home, you may depend."

Our captain, whose good nature had not yet forsaken him for a moment, grew indignant.

"Do you think I will let you suffer for my carelessness?" he exclaimed; "I have three times sixty guilders in my strong box at home!"

"Oh, I beg your pardon," said Carl hastily, adding, in a surlier tone, "well, I see no better way than to go back hungry."

"I see a better plan than that," said the captain.

"What is it?" cried all the boys.

"Why, to make the best of a bad business and go back pleasantly, and like men," said Peter, looking so gallant and handsome as he turned his frank face and clear blue eyes upon them, that they caught his spirit.

"Ho! for the captain," they shouted.

"Now, boys, we may as well make up our minds there's no place like Broek, after all, and that we mean to be there in two hours. Is that agreed to?"

"Agreed," cried all, as they ran to the canal.

"On with your skates! Are you ready? Here, Jacob, let me help you."

"Now. One, two, three—start!"

And the boyish faces that left Haarlem at that signal were nearly as bright as those that had entered it with Captain Peter half an hour before.

CHAPTER XIV

HANS

"DONDER and Blixin!" cried Carl angrily, before the party had skated twenty yards from the city gates, "if here isn't that wooden-skate ragamuffin in the patched

leather breeches.   That fellow is everywhere, confound him!
We'll be lucky," he added, in as sneering a tone as he dared
to assume, "if our captain doesn't order us to halt and shake
hands with him."

"Your captain is a terrible fellow," said Peter, pleasantly;
"but this is a false alarm, Carl—I cannot spy your bugbear
anywhere among the skaters—ah! there he is! why, what is
the matter with the lad?"

Poor Hans! His face was pale, his lips compressed. He
skated like one under the efforts of a fearful dream. Just as he
was passing, Peter hailed him:

"Good day, Hans Brinker?"

Hans' countenance brightened at once. "Ah! Mynheer,
is that you?   It is well we meet!"

"Just like his impertinence," hissed Carl Schummel, darting scornfully past his companions, who seemed inclined to
linger with their captain.

"I am glad to see you, Hans," responded Peter, cheerily;
"but you look troubled.   Can I serve you?"

"I have a trouble, Mynheer," answered Hans, casting
down his eyes. Then lifting them again with almost a happy
expression, he added, "but it is Hans who can help Mynheer
van Holp this time."

"How?" asked Peter, making, in his blunt Dutch way,
no attempt to conceal his surprise.

"By giving you this, Mynheer," and Hans held forth the
missing purse.

"Hurrah!" shouted the boys, taking their cold hands from
their pockets to wave them joyfully in the air. But Peter
said, "Thank you, Hans Brinker," in a tone that made Hans
feel as if the king had knelt to him.

The shout of the delighted boys reached the muffled ears
of the fine young gentleman who, under a full pressure of
pent-up wrath, was skating toward Amsterdam. Carl only
halted, and with his back toward his party wondered what on
earth had happened. There he stood, immovable, until, feeling
sure that nothing but the prospect of something to eat could

have made them hurrah so heartily, he turned and skated slowly toward his excited comrades.

Meantime Peter had drawn Hans aside from the rest.

"How did you know it was my purse?" he asked.

"You paid me three guilders yesterday, Mynheer, for making the white-wood chain, telling me that I must buy skates."

"Yes, I remember."

"I saw your purse then; it was of yellow leather."

"And where did you find it to-day?"

"I left my home this morning, Mynheer, in great trouble, and as I skated, I took no heed until I stumbled against some timber, and while I was rubbing my knee, I saw your purse nearly hidden under a log."

"That place! Ah, I remember now; just as we were passing it I pulled my handkerchief from my pocket, and probably flirted out the purse at the same time. It would have been gone but for you, Hans. Here"—pouring out the contents —"you must give us the pleasure of dividing the money with you——"

"No, Mynheer," answered Hans. He spoke quietly, without pretence, or any grace of manner, but Peter, somehow, felt rebuked, and put the silver back without a word.

"I like that boy, rich or poor," he thought to himself, then added aloud, "May I ask about this trouble of yours, Hans?"

"Ah, Mynheer, it is a sad case; but I have waited here too long. I am going to Leyden to see the great Doctor Boekman——"

"Doctor Boekman!" exclaimed Peter, in astonishment.

"Yes, Mynheer, and I have not a moment to lose. Good-day!"

"Stay, I am going that way. Come, my lads! Shall we return to Haarlem?"

"Yes," cried the boys eagerly, and off they started.

"Now," said Peter, drawing near Hans, both skimming the ice so easily and lightly as they skated on together, that they seemed scarce conscious of moving, "we are going to stop at

Leyden, and if you are going there only with a message to Doctor Boekman cannot I do the errand for you? The boys may be too tired to skate so far to-day, but I will promise to see him early to-morrow if he is to be found in the city."

"Ah, Mynheer, that would be serving me indeed; it is not the distance I dread, but leaving my mother so long."

"Is she ill?"

"No, Mynheer. It is the father. You may have heard it; how he has been without wit for many a year—ever since the great Schlossen mill was built; but his body has been well and strong. Last night the mother knelt upon the hearth to blow the peat (it is his only delight to sit and watch the live embers; and she will blow them into a blaze every hour of the day to please him). Before she could stir, he sprang upon her like a giant, and held her close to the fire, all the time laughing and shaking his head. I was on the canal; but I heard the mother scream and ran to her. The father had never loosened his hold, and her gown was smoking. I tried to deaden the fire, but with one hand he pushed me off. There was no water in the cottage or I could have done better; and all that time he laughed—such a terrible laugh, Mynheer —hardly a sound, but all in his face. I tried to pull her away, but that only made it worse; then—it was dreadful, but could I see the mother burn?—I beat him—beat him with a stool. He tossed me away. The gown was on fire. I *would* put it out. I can't remember well after that; I found myself upon the floor, and the mother was praying. It seemed to me that she was in a blaze, and all the while I could hear that laugh. My sister Gretel screamed out that he was holding the mother close to the very coals; *I* could not tell! Gretel flew to the closet and filled a porringer with the food he liked, and put it upon the floor. Then, Mynheer, he left the mother and crawled to it like a little child. She was not burnt, only a part of her clothing. Ah, how kind she was to him all night, watching and tending him. He slept in a high fever, with his hand pressed to his head. The mother says he has done that so much of late, as though he felt pain there. Ah, Mynheer, I did not mean to tell you. If the father was himself, he would not harm even a kitten."

For a moment the two boys moved on in silence—

"It is terrible," said Peter at last—"How is he to-day?"

"Very ill, Mynheer—— "

"Why go for Dr. Boekman, Hans? There are others in Amsterdam who could help him, perhaps; Boekman is a famous man, sought only by the wealthiest, and they often wait upon him in vain?"

"He *promised*, Mynheer,—he promised me yesterday to come to the father in a week; but now that the change has come we cannot wait—we think the poor father is dying. Oh! Mynheer, you can plead with him to come quick—he will not wait a whole week and our father dying—the good meester is so kind—— "

"*So kind!*" echoed Peter, in astonishment, "why he is known as the crossest man in Holland!"

"He looks so because he has no fat, and his head is busy, but his heart is kind, I know. Tell the meester what I have told you, Mynheer, and he will come."

"I hope so, Hans, with all my heart. You are in haste to turn homeward, I see. Promise me that should you need a friend, you will go to my mother, at Broek. Tell her I bade you see her; and, Hans Brinker—not as a reward, but as a gift —take a few of these guilders."

Hans shook his head resolutely.

"No, no, Mynheer—I cannot take it. If I could find work in Broek or at the South Mill I would be glad, but it is the same story everywhere—'wait till spring.'"

"It is well you speak of it," said Peter eagerly, "for my father needs help at once. Your pretty chain pleased him much. He said, 'That boy has a clean cut; he would be good at carving.' There is to be a carved portal to our new summer-house, and father will pay well for the job."

"God is good!" cried Hans in sudden delight. "Oh! Mynheer, that would be too much joy. I have never tried big work; but I can do it—I know I can."

"Well, tell my father you are the Hans Brinker of whom I spoke. He will be glad to serve you."

Hans stared in honest surprise.

"Thank you, Mynheer."

"Now, captain," shouted Carl, anxious to appear as good-humoured as possible, by way of atonement, "here we are in the midst of Haarlem, and no word from you yet—we await your orders, and we're as hungry as wolves."

Peter made a cheerful answer, and turned hurriedly to Hans.

"Come, get something to eat, and I will detain you no longer."

What a quick, wistful look Hans threw upon him! Peter wondered that he had not noticed before that the poor boy was hungry.

"Ah, Mynheer, even now the mother may need me, the father may be worse—I must not wait. May God care for you,"—and, nodding hastily, Hans turned his face homeward and was gone.

"Come, boys," sighed Peter, "now for our tiffin!"

CHAPTER XV

HOMES

IT must not be supposed that our young Dutchmen had already forgotten the great skating-race which was to take place on the Twentieth. On the contrary, they had thought and spoken of it very often during the day. Even Ben, though he had felt more like a traveller than the rest, had never once, through all the sight-seeing, lost a certain vision of silver skates which, for a week past, had haunted him night and day.

Like a true "John Bull," as Jacob had called him, he never doubted that his English fleetness, English strength, English everything, could at any time enable him, on the ice, to put all Holland to shame, and the rest of the world, too, for that matter. Ben certainly was a superb skater. He had enjoyed not half the opportunities for practising that had fallen to his new comrades; but he had improved his share to the utmost; and was, besides, so strong of frame, so supple of limb. In short, such a tight, trim, quick, graceful fellow in every way, that he had taken to skating as naturally as a chamois to leaping, or an eagle to soaring.

Only to the heavy heart of poor Hans had the vision of the Silver Skates failed to appear during that starry winter night, and the brighter sunlit day.

Even Gretel had seen them flitting before her as she sat beside her mother through those hours of weary watching—not as prizes to be won, but as treasures passing hopelessly beyond her reach.

Rychie, Hilda, and Katrinka—why they had scarcely known any other thought than "the race! the race! It will come off on the Twentieth!"

These three girls were friends. Though of nearly the same age, talent, and station, they were as different as girls could be.

Hilda Van Gleck you already know—a warm-hearted, noble girl of fourteen. Rychie Korbes was beautiful to look upon, far more sparkling and pretty than Hilda, but not half so bright and sunny within. Clouds of pride, of discontent and envy, had already gathered in her heart, and were growing bigger and darker every day. Of course these often relieved themselves very much after the manner of other clouds; but who saw the storms and the weeping? Only her maid, or her father, mother, and little brother—those who loved her better than all. Like other clouds, too, hers often took queer shapes, and what was really but mist and vapoury fancy, assumed the appearance of monster wrongs, and mountains of difficulty. To her mind, the poor peasant girl Gretel was not a human being, a God-created creature like herself—she was only something that meant poverty, rags, and dirt.

Carl was too much like her, within, to be an earnest admirer, and perhaps he suspected the clouds. He, being deep and

surly, and always uncomfortably in earnest, of course preferred
the lively Katrinka, whose nature was made of a hundred
tinkling bells.   She was a coquette in her infancy, a coquette in
her childhood, and now a coquette in her school-days.   Without
a thought of harm, she coquetted with her studies, her duties,
even her little troubles.   They shouldn't know when they
bothered her, not they.   She coquetted with her mother, her
pet lamb, her baby brother, even with her own golden curls —
tossing them back as if she despised them.   Every one liked
her, but who could love her?   She was never in earnest.   A
pleasant face, a pleasant heart, a pleasant manner—these only
satisfy for an hour.   Poor, happy Katrinka! such as she, tinkle,
tinkle so merrily through their early days; but Life is so apt to
coquette with them in turn, to put all their sweet bells out of
tune, or to silence them one by one !

How different were the homes of these three girls from the
tumbling old cottage where Gretel dwelt.   Rychie lived in a
beautiful house near Amsterdam, where the carved sideboards
were laden with services of silver, and where silken tapestries
hung in folds from ceiling to floor.

Hilda's father owned the largest mansion in Broek.   Its
glittering roof of polished tiles, and its boarded front, painted
in half-a-dozen various colours, were the admiration of the
neighbourhood.

Katrinka's home, not a mile distant, was the finest of Dutch
country-seats.   The garden was so stiffly laid out in little paths
and patches that the birds might have mistaken it for a great
Chinese puzzle with all the pieces spread out ready for use.
But in summer it was beautiful; the flowers made the best of
their stiff quarters, and, when the gardener was not watching,
glowed and bent and twined about each other in the prettiest
way imaginable.   Such a tulip bed !   Why, the Queen of the
Fairies would never care for a grander city in which to hold her
court ! but Katrinka preferred the bed of pink and white
hyacinths.   She loved their freshness and fragrance, and the
light-hearted way in which their bell-shaped blossoms swung in
the breeze.

Carl was both right and wrong when he said that Katrinka and Rychie were furious at the very idea of the peasant Gretel joining in the race. He had heard Rychie declare it was "disgraceful, shameful, TOO BAD!" which in Dutch, as in English, is generally the strongest expression an indignant girl can use; and he had seen Katrinka nod her pretty head, and heard her sweetly echo "shameful, too bad!" as nearly like Rychie as tinkling bells can be like the voice of real anger. This had satisfied him. He never suspected that had Hilda, not Rychie, first talked with Katrinka upon the subject, the bells would have jingled as willing an echo. She would have said, "Certainly, let her join us," and would have skipped off thinking no more about it. But *now* Katrinka with sweet emphasis pronounced it a shame that a goose-girl, a forlorn little creature like Gretel, should be allowed to spoil the race.

Rychie, being rich and powerful (in a schoolgirl way), had other followers, besides Katrinka, who were induced to share her opinions because they were either too careless or too cowardly to think for themselves.

Poor little Gretel! Her home was sad and dark enough now. Raff Brinker lay moaning upon his rough bed, and his vrouw, forgetting and forgiving everything, bathed his forehead, his lips, weeping and praying that he might not die. Hans, as we know, had started in desperation for Leyden to search for Dr. Boekman, and induce him, if possible, to come to their father at once. Gretel, filled with a strange dread, had done the work as well as she could, wiped the rough brick floor, brought peat to build up the slow fire, and melted ice for her mother's use. This accomplished, she seated herself upon a low stool near the bed, and begged her mother to try and sleep a while.

"You are so tired," she whispered; "not once have you closed your eyes since that dreadful hour last night. See, I have straitened the willow bed in the corner, and spread everything soft upon it I could find, so that the mother might lie in comfort. Here is your jacket. Take off that pretty dress; I'll fold it away very careful, and put it in the big chest before you go to sleep."

Dame Brinker shook her head without turning her eyes from her husband's face.

"I can watch, mother," urged Gretel, "and I'll wake you every time the father stirs. You are so pale, and your eyes are so red—oh, mother, *do*!"

The child pleaded in vain. Dame Brinker would not leave her post.

Gretel looked at her in troubled silence, wondering whether it were very wicked to care more for one parent than for the other—and sure, yes, quite sure, that she dreaded her father, while she clung to her mother with a love that was almost idolatry.

"Hans loves the father so well," she thought, "why cannot I? Yet I could not help crying when I saw his hand bleed that day, last month, when he snatched the knife—and now, when he moans, how I ache, ache all over. Perhaps I love him, after all, and God will see I am not such a bad, wicked girl as I thought. Yes, I love the poor father—almost as Hans does—not quite, for Hans is stronger and does not fear him. Oh, will that moaning go on for ever and ever! Poor mother, how patient she is; *she* never pouts, as I do, about the money that went away so strange. If he only could, just for one instant, lift his eyes and look at us, as Hans does, and tell us where mother's guilders went, I would not care for the rest—yes, I would care—I don't want the poor father to die, to be all blue and cold like Annie Bouman's little sister—I *know* I don't —dear God, I don't want father to die."

Her thoughts merged into a prayer. When it ended, the poor child scarcely knew. Soon she found herself watching a little pulse of light at the side of the fire, beating faintly but steadily, showing that somewhere in the dark pile there was warmth and light that would overspread it at last. A large earthen cup filled with burning peat stood near the bedside; Gretel had placed it there to "stop the father's shivering," she said. She watched it as it sent a glow around the mother's form, tipping her faded skirt with light, and shedding a sort of newness over the threadbare bodice. It was a relief to Gretel to see the lines in that weary face soften as the firelight flickered gently across it.

Next she counted the window-panes, broken and patched as they were; and finally, after tracing every crack and seam in the walls, fixed her gaze upon a carved shelf made by Hans. The shelf hung as high as Gretel could reach; it held a large leather-covered Bible, with brass clasps—a wedding present to Dame Brinker from the family at Heidelberg.

"Ah, how handy Hans is! If he were here he could turn the father some way, so the moans would stop. Dear! dear! if this sickness lasts, we shall never skate any more. I must send my new skates back to the beautiful lady. Hans and I will not see the race "—and Gretel's eyes, that had been dry before, grew full of tears.

"Never cry, child," said her mother soothingly. "This sickness may not be as bad as we think. The father has lain this way before."

Gretel sobbed now.

"Oh, mother, it is not that alone—you do not know all—I am very, very bad and wicked!"

"You, Gretel! you so patient and good!" and a bright, puzzled look beamed for an instant upon the child. "Hush, lovey, you'll wake him."

Gretel hid her face in her mother's lap, and tried not to cry.

Her little hand, so thin and brown, lay in the coarse palm of her mother, creased with many a hard day's work. Rychie would have shuddered to touch either, yet they pressed warmly upon each other. Soon Gretel looked up, with a dull, homely look, and said in a trembling voice—

"The father tried to burn you—he did—I saw him, and he was *laughing* !"

"Hush, child!"

The mother's words came so suddenly and sharply, that Raff Brinker, dead as he was to all that was passing round him, twitched slightly upon the bed.

Gretel said no more, but plucked drearily at the jagged edge of a hole in her mother's holiday gown. It had been burned there—well for Dame Brinker that the gown was woollen.

CHAPTER XVI

HAARLEM—THE BOYS HEAR VOICES

REFRESHED and rested, our boys came forth from the coffee-house just as the big clock in the Square, after the manner of certain Holland time-keepers, was striking TWO with its half-hour bell, for half-past TWO.

The captain was absorbed in thought, at first, for Hans Brinker's sad story still echoed in his ears. Not until Ludwig rebuked him with a laughing "Wake up, grandfather!" did he reassume his position as gallant boy-leader of his band.

"Ahem! this way, young gentlemen!"

They were walking through the streets of the city, not on a curbed *side-walk*, for such a thing is rarely to be found in Holland, but on the brick pavement that lay on the borders of the cobble-stone carriage-way without breaking its level expanse.

Haarlem, like Amsterdam, was gayer than usual in honour of St. Nicholas.

A strange figure was approaching them. It was a small man dressed in black, with a short cloak; he wore a wig and a cocked hat, from which a long crape streamer was flying.

"Who comes here?" cried Ben; "what a queer-looking object!"

"That's the aanspreeker," said Lambert; "some one is dead."

"Is that the way men dress in mourning in this country?"

"Oh, no. The aanspreeker attends funerals, and it is his business, when any one dies, to notify all the friends and relatives."

"What a strange custom."

"Well," said Lambert, "I see another man has lately been born to the world to fill up the vacant place."

Ben stared.   " How do you know that ? "

" Don't you see that pretty red pincushion hanging on yonder door ? " asked Lambert, in return.

" Yes."

" Well, that's a boy."

" A boy ! what do you mean ? "

" I mean that here in Haarlem whenever a boy is born, the parents have a red pincushion put out at the door.   If our young friend had been a girl instead of a boy the cushion would have been white.   In some places they have much more fanciful affairs, all trimmed with lace, and even among the very poorest houses you will see a bit of ribbon or even a string tied on the door-latch—— "

" Look ! " almost screamed Ben, " there *is* a white cushion, at the door of that double-jointed house with the funny roof."

" I don't see any house with a funny roof."

" Oh, of course not," said Ben ; " I forget you're a native ; but all the roofs are queer to me, for that matter.   I mean the house next to that green building."

" True enough—there's a girl !   I tell you what, captain," called out Lambert, slipping easily into Dutch, " we must get out of this street as soon as possible.   It's full of babies ! They'll set up a squall in a moment."

The captain laughed.   " I shall take you to hear better music than that," he said ; " we are just in time to hear the organ of St. Bavon.   The church is open to-day."

" What, the great Haarlem organ ? " asked Ben ; " that will be a treat indeed.   I have often read of it, with its tremendous pipes, and its *vox humana* [1] that sounds like a giant singing."

" The same," answered Lambert van Mounen.

Peter was right.   The church was open, though not for religious services.   Some one was playing upon the organ. As the boys entered, a swell of sound rushed forth to meet them.   It seemed to bear them, one by one, into the shadows of the building.

[1] An organ stop which produces an effect resembling the HUMAN VOICE.

Louder and louder it grew until it became like the din and roar of some mighty tempest, or like the ocean surging upon the shore. In the midst of the tumult a tinkling bell was heard; another answered, then another, and the storm paused as if to listen. The bells grew bolder; they rang out loud and clear. Other deep-toned bells joined in; they were tolling in solemn concert—ding, dong! ding, dong! The storm broke forth again with redoubled fury—gathering its distant thunder. The boys looked at each other, but did not speak. It was growing serious. What was that? *Who* screamed? *What* screamed—that terrible, musical scream? Was it man or demon? Or was it some monster shut up behind that carved brass frame—behind those great silver columns—some despairing monster begging, screaming for freedom? It was the Vox Humana!

At last an answer came,—soft, tender, loving, like a mother's song. The storm grew silent; hidden birds sprang forth filling the air with glad, ecstatic music, rising higher and higher until the last faint note was lost in the distance.

The Vox Humana was stilled; but in the glorious hymn of thanksgiving that now arose, one could almost hear the throbbing of a human heart. What did it mean? That man's imploring cry should in time be met with a deep content? That gratitude would give us freedom? To Peter and Ben it seemed that the angels were singing. Their eyes grew dim, and their souls dizzy with a strange joy. At last, as if borne upward by invisible hands, they were floating away on the music, all fatigue forgotten, and with no wish but to hear for ever those beautiful sounds—when suddenly Van Holp's sleeve was pulled impatiently and a gruff voice beside him asked—

"How long are you going to stay here, captain, blinking at the ceiling like a sick rabbit? It's high time we started."

"Hush!" whispered Peter, only half aroused.

"Come, man! let's go," said Carl, giving the sleeve a second pull.

Peter turned reluctantly; he would not detain the boys

against their will. All but Ben were casting rather reproachful glances upon him.

"Well, boys," he whispered, "we will go. Softly now."

"That's the greatest thing I've seen or heard since I've been in Holland!" cried Ben, enthusiastically, as soon as they reached the open air. "It's glorious!"

Ludwig and Carl laughed slyly at the English boy's *wartaat*, or gibberish; Jacob yawned; Peter gave Ben a look that made him instantly feel that he and Peter were not so very different after all, though one hailed from Holland and the other from England; and Lambert, the interpreter, responded with a brisk—

"You may well say so. I believe there are other organs nowadays that are said to be as fine; but for years and years this organ of St. Bavon was the grandest in the world."

"Do you know how large it is?" asked Ben. "I noticed that the church itself was prodigiously high, and that the organ filled the end of the great aisle almost from floor to roof."

"That's true," said Lambert, "and how superb the pipes looked — just like grand columns of silver. They're only for show, you know; the *real* pipes are behind them, some big enough for a man to crawl through, and some smaller than a baby's whistle. Well, for size, the church is higher than Westminster Abbey, to begin with, and, as you say, the organ makes a tremendous show even then. Father told me last night that it is one hundred and eight feet high, fifty feet broad, and has over five thousand pipes; it has sixty-four *stops*, if you know what they are, *I* don't, and three key-boards."

"Good for you," said Ben. "You have a fine memory. *My* head is a perfect colander for figures; they slip through as fast as they're poured in. But other facts and historical events stay behind—that's some consolation."

"There we differ," returned Van Mounen. "I'm great on names and figures; but history, take it altogether, seems to me to be the most hopeless kind of a jumble."

Meantime Carl and Ludwig were having a discussion concerning some square wooden monuments they had observed in the interior of the church. Ludwig declared that each bore the name of the person buried beneath, and Carl insisted that they had no names, but only the heraldic arms of the deceased painted on a black ground, with the date of the death in gilt letters.

"I ought to know," said Carl, "for I walked across to the east side, to look for the cannon-ball which mother told me was embedded there. It was fired into the church, in the year fifteen hundred and something, by those rascally Spaniards, while the services were going on. There it was in the wall, sure enough, and while I was walking back, I noticed the monuments. I tell you they haven't a sign of a name upon them."

"Ask Peter," said Ludwig, only half convinced.

"Carl is right," replied Peter, who, though conversing with Jacob, had overheard their dispute. "Well, Jacob, as I was saying, Handel, the great composer, chanced to visit Haarlem, and of course he at once hunted up this famous organ. He gained admittance, and was playing upon it with all his might, when the regular organist chanced to enter the building. The man stood awe-struck ; he was a good player himself, but he had never heard such music before. 'Who is there?' he cried ; 'if it is not an angel, it must be Handel!' When he discovered that it *was* the great musician, he was still more mystified. 'But how is this?' said he. 'You have done impossible things ; no ten fingers on earth can play the passages you have given ; human hands couldn't control all the keys and stops!' 'I know it,' said Handel, coolly; 'and for that reason I was forced to strike some notes with the end of my nose.' Donder ! just think how the old organist must have stared !"

"Hey ! what?" exclaimed Jacob, startled, when Peter's animated voice suddenly became silent.

"Haven't you heard me, you rascal?" was the indignant rejoinder.

"Oh, yes—no—the fact is—I heard you at first—I'm awake now ; but I do believe I've been walking beside you half asleep," stammered Jacob, with such a doleful, bewildered look on his face, that Peter could not help laughing.

CHAPTER XVII

THE MAN WITH FOUR HEADS

AFTER leaving the church, the boys stopped near by in the open market-place, to look at the bronze statue of Laurens Janzoon Coster, who is believed by the Dutch to have been the inventor of printing. This is disputed by those who award the same honour to Johannes Gutenberg of Mayence; while many maintain that Faustus, a servant of Coster, stole his master's wooden types on a Christmas eve, when the latter was at church, and fled with his booty, and his secret, to Mayence. Coster was a native of Haarlem, and the Hollanders are naturally anxious to secure the credit of the invention for their illustrious townsman. Certain it is, that the first book he printed is kept by the city in a silver case wrapped in silk, and is shown with great caution as a most precious relic.

Of course Lambert and his English friend fully discussed this subject. They also had rather a warm argument concerning another invention. Lambert declared that the honour of giving both the telescope and microscope to the world lay between Metius and Jonsen, both Hollanders; while Ben as stoutly insisted that Roger Bacon, an English monk of the thirteenth century, "wrote out the whole thing, perfect description of microscopes and telescopes too, long before either of those other fellows were born."

On one subject, however, they both agreed: that the art of curing and pickling herrings was discovered by William Beukles of Holland, and that the country did perfectly right in honouring him as a national benefactor, for its wealth and importance had been in a great measure due to its herring trade.

Soon afterward, while passing a cobbler's shop, Ben exclaimed—

"Hollo! Lambert, here is the name of one of your greatest

men over a cobbler's stall? Boerhaave—if it were only Herman Boerhaave instead of Hendrick, it would be complete."

Lambert knit his brows reflectively, as he replied—

"Boerhaave—Boerhaave—the name is perfectly familiar; I remember, too, he was born in 1668, but the rest is all gone, as usual. There have been so many famous Hollanders, you see, it is impossible for a fellow to know them all. What was he? Did he have two heads? or was he one of your great, natural swimmers like Marco Polo?"

"He had *four* heads," answered Ben, laughing, "for he was a great physician, naturalist, botanist, and chemist. I am full of him just now, for I read his life a few weeks ago."

"Pour out a little, then," said Lambert; "only walk faster; we shall lose sight of the other boys."

"Well," resumed Ben, quickening his pace and looking with great interest at everything going on in the crowded street, "this Dr. Boerhaave was a great anspewker."

"A great *what*?" roared Lambert.

"Oh, I beg pardon; I was thinking of that man over there, with the cocked hat. He's an anspewker, isn't he?"

"Yes. He's an aanspreeker, if that is what you mean to say. But what about your friend with the four heads?"

"Well, as I was going to say, the doctor was left a penniless orphan at sixteen, without education or friends."

"Jolly beginning!" interposed Lambert.

"Now, don't interrupt. He was a poor friendless orphan at sixteen, but he was so persevering and industrious, so determined to gain knowledge, that he made his way, and in time became one of the most learned men of Europe. All the—how comically persons do dress here, to be sure! Just look at those men and women with their sugar-loaf hats; and see this woman ahead of us with a straw-bonnet like a scoop-shovel, tapering to a point in the back. Did ever you see anything so funny? And those tremendous wooden shoes too. I declare she's a beauty!"

"Oh, they are only back-country folk," said Lambert, rather impatiently. "You might as well let old Boerhaave drop, or else shut your eyes——"

"Ha! ha! Well, I was *going* to say—All the big men of his day sought out this great professor. Even Peter the Great, when he came over to Holland from Russia to learn ship-building, attended his lectures regularly. By that time Boerhaave was professor of medicine and chemistry and botany in the University of Leyden. He had grown to be very wealthy as a practising physician; but he used to say that the poor were his best patients, because God would be their paymaster. All Europe learned to love and honour him. In short, he became so famous that a certain mandarin of China addressed a letter 'To the illustrious Boerhaave, physician in Europe,' and the letter found its way to him without any difficulty."

"My goodness! That is what I call being a public character. The boys have stopped. How now, Captain van Holp, where next?"

"We propose to move on," said Van Holp; "there is nothing to see at this season in the Bosch—the Bosch is a noble wood, Benjamin, a grand Park where they have most magnificent trees, protected by law—do you understand?"

"Ya!" nodded Ben, as the captain proceeded—

"Unless you all desire to visit the Museum of Natural History, we may go on the grand canal again. If we had more time it would be pleasant to take Benjamin up the Blue Stairs."

"What are the Blue Stairs, Lambert?" asked Ben.

"They are the highest point of the Dunes. You have a grand view of the ocean from there, besides a fine chance to see how wonderful these Dunes are. One can hardly believe that the wind could ever heap up sand in so remarkable a way. But we have to go through Bloemendal to get there—not a very pretty village, and some distance from here. What do you say?"

"Oh, I am ready for anything. For my part, I would rather steer direct for Leyden, but we'll do as the captain says—hey, Jacob?"

"Ya, dat ish goot," said Jacob, who felt decidedly more like taking another nap, than ascending the Blue Stairs.

The captain was in favour of going to Leyden.

"It's four long miles from here. (Full sixteen of your

English miles, Benjamin.)   We have no time to lose if you wish
to reach there before midnight.   Decide quickly, boys—Blue
Stairs or Leyden?"

"Leyden," they answered—and were out of Haarlem in a
twinkling, admiring the lofty, tower-like windmills and pretty
country-seats as they left the city behind them.

"If you really wish to see Haarlem," said Lambert to Ben,
after they had skated a while in silence, "you should visit it in
summer.   It is the greatest place in the world for beautiful
flowers.   The walks around the city are superb ; and the 'Wood,'
with its miles of noble elms, all in full feather, is something to
remember.   You need not smile, old fellow, at my saying, 'full
feather'—I was thinking of waving plumes, and got my words
mixed up a little.   But a Dutch elm beats everything ; it is the
noblest tree on earth, Ben—if you except the English oak——"

"Ay," said Ben, solemnly, "*if* you except the English oak"
—and for some moments he could scarcely see the canal, because
Robby and Jenny kept bobbing in the air before his eyes.

CHAPTER XVIII

FRIENDS IN NEED

MEANTIME, the other boys were listening to Peter's account
of an incident which had long ago occurred[1] in a part of
the city where stood an ancient castle, whose lord had tyrannised
over the burghers of the town to such an extent that they
surrounded his castle and laid siege to it.   Just at the last
extremity, when the haughty lord felt that he could hold out
no longer, and was preparing to sell his life as dearly as
possible, his lady appeared on the ramparts, and offered to
surrender everything, provided she was permitted to bring out
and retain, as much of her most precious household goods as
she could carry upon her back.   The promise was given—and
forth came the lady from the gateway, bearing her husband

[1] Sir Thomas Carr's *Tour through Holland.*

upon her shoulders. The burghers' pledge preserved him from the fury of the troops, but left them free to wreak their vengeance upon the castle.

"Do you *believe* that story, Captain Peter?" asked Carl, in an incredulous tone.

"Of course, I do; it is historical. Why should I doubt it?"

"Simply because no woman could do it—and, if she could, she wouldn't. That is *my* opinion."

"And *I* believe there are many who *would*. That is, to save any one they really cared for," said Ludwig.

Jacob, who, in spite of his fat and sleepiness, was of rather a sentimental turn, had listened with deep interest.

"That is right, little fellow," he said, nodding his head approvingly; "I believe every word of it. I shall never marry a woman who would not be glad to do as much for *me*."

"Heaven help her!" cried Carl, turning to gaze at the speaker; "why, Poot, three *men* couldn't do it!"

"Perhaps not," said Jacob, quietly—feeling that he had asked rather too much of the future Mrs. Poot. "But she must be *willing*, that is all."

"Ay," responded Peter's cheery voice, "willing heart makes nimble foot—and who knows, but it may make strong arms also."

"Pete," asked Ludwig, changing the subject, "did you tell me last night that the painter Wouverman was born in Haarlem?"

"Yes, and Jacob Ruysdael and Berghem too. I like Berghem, because he was always good natured—they say he always sang while he painted, and though he died nearly two hundred years ago, there are traditions still afloat concerning his pleasant laugh. He was a great painter, and he had a wife who was as cross as could be."

"They balanced each other finely," said Ludwig; "he was kind and she was cross. But, Peter, before I forget it, wasn't that picture of St. Hubert and the Horse painted by Wouverman? You remember father showed us an engraving from it last night."

"Yes, indeed; there is a story connected with that picture."

"Tell us!" cried two or three, drawing closer to Peter as they skated on.

"Wouverman," began the captain, oratorically, "was born in 1620, just four years before Berghem. He was a master of his art, and especially excelled in painting horses. Strange as it may seem, people were so long finding out his merits, that, even after he had arrived at the height of his excellence, he was obliged to sell his pictures for very paltry prices. The poor artist became completely discouraged, and, worse than all, was over head and ears in debt. One day he was talking over his troubles with his father-confessor, who was one of the few who recognised his genius. The priest determined to assist him, and accordingly lent him six hundred guilders, advising him at the same time to demand a better price for his pictures. Wouverman did so, and in the meantime paid his debts. Matters brightened with him at once. Everybody appreciated the great artist who painted such costly pictures. He grew rich. The six hundred guilders were returned, and in gratitude Wouverman sent also a work which he had painted, representing his benefactor as Saint Hubert kneeling before his horse—the very picture, Ludwig, of which we were speaking last night."

"So! so!" exclaimed Ludwig, with deep interest, "I must take another look at the engraving as soon as we get home."

At that same hour, while Ben was skating with his companions beside the Holland dyke, Robby and Jenny stood in their pretty English school-house, ready to join in the duties of their reading-class.

"Commence! Master Robert Dobbs," said the teacher, "page 242 ; now, sir, mind every stop."

And Robby, in a quick childish voice, roared forth at school-room pitch—

"LESSON 62.—THE HERO OF HAARLEM

"Many years ago, there lived in Haarlem, one of the principal cities of Holland, a sunny-haired boy of gentle disposition. His father was a *sluicer*—that is, a man whose business it was to open and close the sluices, or large oaken gates, that are placed at regular distances across the entrances of the canals, to regulate the amount of water that shall flow into them.

"The sluicer raises the gates more or less according to the quantity of water required, and closes them carefully at night, in order to avoid all possible danger of an over supply running into the canal, or the water would soon overflow it and inundate the surrounding country. As a great portion of Holland is lower than the level of the sea, the waters are kept from flooding the land, only by means of strong dykes, or barriers, and by means of these sluices, which are often strained to the utmost by the pressure of the rising tides. Even the little children in Holland know that constant watchfulness is required to keep the rivers and ocean from overwhelming the country, and that a moment's neglect of the sluicer's duty may bring ruin and death to all."

["Very good," said the teacher; "now Susan."]

"One lovely autumn afternoon, when the boy was about eight years' old, he obtained his parents' consent to carry some cakes to a blind man who lived out in the country, on the other side of the dyke. The little fellow started on his errand with a light heart, and, having spent an hour with his grateful old friend, he bade him farewell and started on his homeward walk.

"Trudging stoutly along by the canal, he noticed how the autumn rains had swollen the waters. Even while humming his careless, childish song, he thought of his father's brave old gates and felt glad of their strength, for, thought he, 'if *they* gave way, where would father and mother be? These pretty fields would be all covered with the angry waters—father always calls them the *angry* waters; I suppose he thinks they are mad at him for keeping them out so long.' And with these thoughts just flitting across his brain, the little fellow stooped to pick the pretty blue flowers that grew along his way. Sometimes he stopped to throw some feathery seed-ball in the air, and watch it as it floated away; sometimes he listened to the stealthy rustling of a rabbit, speeding through the grass, but oftener he smiled as he recalled the happy light he had seen arise on the weary, listening face of his blind old friend."

["Now, Henry," said the teacher, nodding to the next little reader.]

"Suddenly the boy looked around him in dismay. He had not noticed that the sun was setting : now he saw that his long shadow on the grass had vanished. It was growing dark, he was still some distance from home, and in a lonely ravine, where even the blue flowers had turned to grey. He quickened his footsteps ; and with a beating heart recalled many a nursery tale of children belated in dreary forests. Just as he was bracing himself for a run, he was startled by the sound of trickling water. Whence did it come ? He looked up and saw a small hole in the dyke through which a tiny stream was flowing. Any child in Holland will shudder at the thought of *a leak in the dyke* ! The boy understood the danger at a glance. That little hole, if the water were allowed to trickle through, would soon be a large one, and a terrible inundation would be the result.

"Quick as a flash he saw his duty. Throwing away his flowers, the boy clambered up the heights, until he reached the hole. His chubby little finger was thrust in, almost before he knew it. The flowing was stopped ! 'Ah !' he thought, with a chuckle of boyish delight, 'the angry waters must stay back now ! Haarlem shall not be drowned while *I* am here !'

"This was all very well at first, but the night was falling rapidly ; chill vapours filled the air. Our little hero began to tremble with cold and dread. He shouted loudly ; he screamed 'come here ! come here !' but no one came. The cold grew more intense, a numbness, commencing in the tired little finger, crept over his hand and arm, and soon his whole body was filled with pain. He shouted again, 'Will no one come ? Mother ! mother !' Alas, his mother, good, practical soul, had already locked the doors, and had fully resolved to scold him on the morrow, for spending the night with blind Jansen without her permission. He tried to whistle, perhaps some straggling boy might heed the signal ; but his teeth chattered so, it was impossible. Then he called on God for help ; and the answer came, through a holy resolution—'I will stay here till morning.'"

["Now, Jenny Dobbs," said the teacher. Jenny's eyes were glistening, but she took a long breath and commenced :]

"The midnight moon looked down upon that small solitary form, sitting upon a stone, half-way up the dyke. His head was bent but he was not asleep, for every now and then one restless hand rubbed feebly the outstretched arm that seemed fastened to the dyke—and often the pale, tearful face turned quickly at some real or fancied sound.

"How can we know the sufferings of that long and fearful watch—what falterings of purpose, what childish terrors came over the boy as he thought of the warm little bed at home, of his parents, his brothers, and sisters, then looked into the cold, dreary night! If he drew away that tiny finger, the angry waters, grown angrier still, would rush forth, and never stop until they had swept over the town. No, he would hold it there till daylight—if he lived! He was not very sure of living. What did this strange buzzing mean? and then the knives that seemed pricking and piercing him from head to foot? He was not certain now that he could draw his finger away, even if he wished to.

"At daybreak a clergyman, returning from the bedside of a sick parishioner, thought he heard groans as he walked along on the top of the dyke. Bending, he saw, far down on the side, a child apparently writhing with pain.

"'In the name of wonder, boy,' he exclaimed, 'what are you doing there?'

"'I am keeping the water from running out,' was the simple answer of the little hero. 'Tell them to come quick.'

"It is needless to add that they did come quickly and that——"

["Jenny Dobbs," said the teacher, rather impatiently, "if you cannot control your feelings so as to read distinctly, we will wait until you recover yourself."

"Yes, sir!" said Jenny, quite startled.]

It was strange; but at that very moment, Ben, far over the sea, was saying to Lambert—

"The noble little fellow! I have frequently met with an

account of the incident, but I never knew, till now, that it was really true."

"True! Of course it is," said Lambert, kindling. "I have given you the story just as mother told it to me, years ago. Why, there is not a child in Holland who does not know it. And, Ben, you may not think so, but that little boy represents the spirit of the whole country. Not a leak can show itself anywhere either in its politics, honour, or public safety, that a million fingers are not ready to stop it, at any cost."

"Whew!" cried Master Ben, "big talking that!"

"It's *true* talk anyway," rejoined Lambert, so very quietly that Ben wisely resolved to make no further comment.

CHAPTER XIX

ON THE CANAL

THE skating season had commenced unusually early; our boys were by no means alone upon the ice. The afternoon was so fine, that men, women, and children, bent upon enjoying the holiday, had flocked to the Grand Canal from far and near. Saint Nicholas had evidently remembered the favourite pastime; shining new skates were everywhere to be seen. Whole families were skimming their way to Haarlem or Leyden or the neighbouring villages. The ice seemed fairly alive. Ben noticed the erect, easy carriage of the women, and their picturesque variety of costume. There were the latest fashions, fresh from Paris, floating past dingy, moth-eaten garments that had seen service through two generations; coal-scuttle bonnets perched over freckled faces bright with holiday smiles; stiff muslin caps, with wings at the sides, flapping beside cheeks rosy with health and contentment; furs, too, encircling the whitest of throats; and scanty garments fluttering below faces ruddy with exercise. In short, every quaint and comical mixture of dry-goods and flesh that Holland could furnish seemed sent to enliven the scene.

There were belles from Leyden, and fishwives from the border villages; cheese-women from Gouda, and prim matrons from beautiful country-seats on the Haarlemmer Meer. Grey-headed skaters were constantly to be seen; wrinkled old women, with baskets upon their heads; and plump little toddlers on skates clutching at their mothers' gowns. Some women carried their babies upon their backs, firmly secured with a bright shawl. The effect was pretty and graceful as they darted by, or sailed slowly past, now nodding to an acquaintance, now chirruping, and throwing soft baby-talk, to the muffled little ones they carried.

Boys and girls were chasing each other, and hiding behind the one-horse sleds, that, loaded high with peat or timber, pursued their cautious way along the tract marked out as "safe." Beautiful, queenly women were there, enjoyment sparkling in their quiet eyes. Sometimes a long file of young men, each grasping the coat of the one before him, flew by with electric speed; and sometimes the ice squeaked under the chair of some gorgeous old dowager, or rich burgomaster's lady, who, very red in the nose, and sharp in the eyes, looked liked a scare-thaw invented by old Father Winter for the protection of his skating grounds. The chair would be heavy with footstoves and cushions, to say nothing of the old lady. Mounted upon shining runners it slid along, pushed by the sleepiest of servants, who, looking neither to the right nor the left, bent himself to his task while she cast direful glances upon the screaming little rowdies who invariably acted as body-guard.

As for the men, they were pictures of placid enjoyment. Some were attired in ordinary citizens' dress; but many looked odd enough with their short woollen coats, wide breeches, and big silver buckles. These seemed to Ben like little boys who had, by a miracle, sprung suddenly into manhood, and were forced to wear garments that their astonished mothers had altered in a hurry. He noticed, too, that nearly all the men had pipes as they passed him, whizzing and smoking like so many locomotives. There was every variety of pipes, from those of common clay to the most expensive meerschaums mounted in silver and gold. Some were carved into extraordinary and fantastic shapes, representing birds, flowers, heads, bugs, and dozens of other things; some resembled the "Dutchman's pipe" that grows in the American woods; some were red, and many were of a pure snowy white; but the most respectable were those which were ripening into a shaded brown. The deeper and richer the brown, of course, the more honoured the pipe, for it was a proof that the owner, if honestly shading it, was deliberately devoting his manhood to the effort. What pipe would not be proud to be the object of such a sacrifice?

For a while, Ben skated on in silence. There was so much to engage his attention that he almost forgot his companions. Part of the time he had been watching the ice-boats as they flew over the great Haarlemmer Meer (or Lake), the frozen surface of which was now plainly visible from the canal. These boats had very large sails, much larger in proportion than those of ordinary vessels, and were set upon a triangular frame, furnished with an iron "runner" at each corner,—the widest part of the triangle crossing the bow, and its point stretching beyond the stern. They had rudders for guiding, and brakes for arresting their progress, and were of all sizes and kinds, from small, rough affairs, managed by a boy, to large and beautiful ones, filled with gay pleasure parties, and manned by competent sailors, who, smoking their stumpy pipes, reefed and tacked and steered with great solemnity and precision.

Some of the boats were painted and gilded in gaudy style, and flaunted gay pennons from their mast-heads; others, white as snow, with every spotless sail rounded by the wind, looked like swans borne onward by a resistless current. It seemed to Ben as, following his fancy, he watched one of these in the distance, that he could almost hear its helpless, terrified cry, but he soon found that the sound arose from a nearer and less romantic cause—from an ice-boat not fifty yards from him, using its brakes to avoid a collision with a peat-sled.

It was a rare thing for these boats to be upon the canal, and their appearance generally caused no little excitement among skaters, especially among the timid; but to-day every ice-boat in the country seemed afloat, or rather aslide, and the canal had its full share.

Ben, though delighted at the sight, was often startled at the swift approach of the resistless, high-winged things, threatening to dart in any and every possible direction. It required all his energies to keep out of the way of the passers-by, and to prevent those screaming little urchins from upsetting him with their sleds. Once he halted to watch some boys who were making a hole in the ice, preparatory to using their fishing spears. Just as he concluded to start again, he found himself suddenly bumped into an old lady's lap. Her push-chair had come upon him from the rear. The old lady screamed, the servant who was propelling her gave a warning hiss. In another instant Ben found himself apologising to empty air—the indignant old lady was far ahead.

This was a slight mishap compared with one that now threatened him. A huge ice-boat, under full sail, came tearing down the canal, almost paralysing Ben with the thought of instant destruction. It was close upon him. He saw its gilded prow, heard the schipper shout, felt the great boom fairly whizz over his head, was blind, deaf, and dumb all in an instant, then opened his eyes, to find himself spinning some yards behind its great skate-like rudder. It had passed within an inch of his shoulder, but he was safe !—safe to see England again.

Lambert chided him roundly.

"I thought it was all over with you, you careless fellow ! Why don't you look where you are going ? Not content with sitting on all the old ladies' laps, you must make a Juggernaut of every ice-boat that comes along. We shall have to hand you over to the aansprekers yet, if you don't look out ! "

"Please don't," said Ben, with mock humility—then seeing how pale Lambert's lips were, added in a low tone :

"I do believe I *thought* more in that one moment, Van Mounen, than in all the rest of my past life."

There was no reply, and for a while the two boys skated on in silence.

Soon a faint sound of distant bells reached their ears.

" Hark ! " said Ben, " what is that ? "

" The carillons," replied Lambert. "They are trying the bells in the chapel of yonder village. Ah ! Ben, you should hear the chimes of the ' New Church ' at Delft ; they are superb. Nearly five hundred sweet-toned bells, and one of the best carilloneurs of Holland to play upon them. Hard work, though; they say the fellow often has to go to bed from positive exhaustion after his performances. You see, the bells are attached to a kind of keyboard, something like they have on pianofortes. There are also a set of pedals for the feet. When a brisk tune is going on, the player looks like a kicking frog fastened to his seat with a skewer."

" For shame," said Ben, indignantly.

Peter had, for the present, exhausted his stock of Haarlem anecdotes, and now, having nothing to do but to skate, he and his three companions were hastening to " catch up " with Lambert and Ben.

"That English lad is fleet enough," said Peter ; " if he were a born Hollander, he could do no better. Hollo ! Here you are, Van Mounen ; why, we hardly hoped for the honour of meeting you again. Who were you flying from in such haste ? "

"Snails," retorted Lambert. " What kept you ? "

" We have been talking, and, beside, we halted once to give Poot a chance to rest."

" He begins to look rather worn out," said Lambert in a low voice.

Just then a beautiful ice-boat with reefed sail, and flying streamers, swept leisurely by. Its deck was filled with children, muffled up to their chins. Looking at them from the ice, you could see only smiling little faces imbedded in bright-coloured, woollen wrappings. They were singing a chorus in honour of Saint Nicholas. The music, starting in the discord of a hundred childish voices, floated, as it rose into exquisite harmony :—

> Friend of sailors, and of children !
>   Double claim have we,
> As in youthful joy we're sailing,
>   O'er a frozen sea !
>   Nicholas ! Saint Nicholas !
>   Let us sing to thee.

While through wintry air we're rushing,
   As our voices blend,
Are you near us? Do you hear us,
   Nicholas, our friend?
             Nicholas! Saint Nicholas!
             Love can never end.

Sunny sparkles, bright before us,
   Chase away the cold!
Hearts where sunny thoughts are welcome
   Never can grow old—
             Nicholas! Saint Nicholas!—
             Never can grow old.

Pretty gift and loving lesson,
   Festival and glee,
Bid us thank thee as we're sailing
   O'er the frozen sea—
             Nicholas! Saint Nicholas!
             So we sing to thee!

CHAPTER XX

JACOB POOT CHANGES THE PLAN

THE last note died away in the distance. Our boys, who in their vain efforts to keep up with the boat, had felt that they were skating backward, turned to look at one another.

"How beautiful that was!" exclaimed Van Mounen.

"Just like a dream!" said Ludwig.

Jacob drew close to Ben, giving his usual approving nod as he spoke:—

"Dat ish goot. Dat ish te pest vay. *I* shay petter to take to Leyden mit a poat!"

"Take a boat!" exclaimed Ben, in dismay. "Why, man, our plan was to *skate*, not to be carried like little children."

"But!" retorted Jacob, "dat ish no little—no papies—to go for poat!"

The boys laughed, but exchanged uneasy glances. It would

be great fun to jump on an ice-boat, if they had a chance ; but to abandon so shamefully their grand undertaking—who could think of such a thing ?

An animated discussion arose at once.

Captain Peter brought his party to a halt.

"Boys," said he, "it strikes me that we should consult Jacob's wishes in this matter. He started the excursion, you know!"

"Pooh!" sneered Carl, throwing a contemptuous glance at Jacob ; "who's tired? We can rest all night at Leyden."

Ludwig and Lambert looked anxious and disappointed. It was no slight thing to lose the credit of having skated all the way from Broek to the Hague, and back again ; but both agreed that Jacob should decide the question.

Good-natured, tired Jacob! He read the popular sentiment at a glance.

"Oh! no," he said, in Dutch. "I was joking. We will skate, of course."

The boys gave a delighted shout, and started on again with renewed vigour.

All but Jacob. He tried his best not to seem fatigued, and, by not saying a word, saved his breath and energy for the great business of skating. But in vain. Before long, the stout body grew heavier and heavier — the tottering limbs weaker and weaker. Worse than all, the blood, anxious to get as far as possible from the ice, mounted to the puffy, good-natured cheeks, and made the roots of his thin, yellow hair glow into a fiery red.

This kind of work is apt to summon Vertigo, of whom good Hans Andersen writes—the same who hurls daring young hunters from the mountains, or spins them from the sharpest heights of the glaciers, or catches them as they tread the stepping-stones of the mountain torrent.

Vertigo came, unseen, to Jacob. After tormenting him a while, with one touch sending a chill from head to foot, with the next, scorching every vein with fever, she made the canal rock and tremble beneath him, the white sails bow and spin as they passed, then cast him heavily upon the ice.

"Hollo!" cried Van Mounen. "There goes Poot!"

Ben sprang hastily forward.

"Jacob! Jacob, are you hurt?"

Peter and Carl were lifting him. The face was white enough now. It seemed like a dead face—even the good-natured look was gone.

A crowd collected. Peter unbuttoned the poor boy's jacket, loosened his red tippet, and blew between the parted lips.

"Stand off, good people!" he cried, "give him air!"

"Lay him down," called out a woman from the crowd.

"Stand him upon his feet," shouted another.

"Give him wine," growled a stout fellow who was driving a loaded sled.

"Yes, yes! give him wine!" echoed everybody.

Ludwig and Lambert shouted in concert:

"Wine! wine! Who has wine!"

A sleepy-eyed Dutchman began to fumble mysteriously under the heaviest of blue jackets, saying as he did so:

"Not so much noise, young masters, not so much noise! The boy was a fool to faint off like a girl."

"Wine, quick!" cried Peter, who, with Ben's help, was rubbing Jacob from head to foot.

Ludwig stretched forth his hand imploringly toward the Dutchman, who with an air of great importance was still fumbling beneath the jacket.

"*Do* hurry! He will die! Has any one else any wine?"

"He *is* dead!" said an awful voice from among the by-standers.

This startled the Dutchman.

"Have a care!" he said, reluctantly drawing forth a small blue flask, "this is schnaps. A little is enough."

A little *was* enough. The paleness gave way to a faint flush. Jacob opened his eyes, and, half bewildered, half ashamed, feebly tried to free himself from those who were supporting him.

There was no alternative now for our party but to have their exhausted comrade carried, in some way, to Leyden. As for expecting him to skate any more that day, the thing was impossible. In truth, by this time each boy began to entertain secret yearnings towards ice-boats, and to avow a Spartan resolve not to desert Jacob. Fortunately a gentle, steady breeze was setting southward. If some accommodating schipper [1] would but come along, matters would not be quite so bad after all.

Peter hailed the first sail that appeared; the men in the stern would not even look at him. Three drays on runners came along, but they were already loaded to the utmost. Then an ice-boat, a beautiful, tempting little one, whizzed past like an arrow. The boys had just time to stare eagerly at it when it was gone. In despair, they resolved to prop up Jacob with their strong arms, as well as they could, and take him to the nearest village.

At that moment a very shabby ice-boat came in sight. With but little hope of success, Peter hailed it, at the same time taking off his hat and flourishing it in the air.

The sail was lowered, then came the scraping sound of the brake, and a pleasant voice called out from the deck:

"What now?"

"Will you take us on?" cried Peter, hurrying with his companions as fast as he could, for the boat was "bringing to" some distance ahead; "will you take us on?"

"We'll pay for the ride!" shouted Carl.

The man on board scarcely noticed him except to mutter something about its not being a trekschuit. Still looking toward Peter, he asked:

"How many?"

"Six."

"Well, it's Nicholas' Day—up with you! Young gentleman sick?" (nodding towards Jacob).

"Yes—broken down—skated all the way from Broek," answered Peter. "Do you go to Leyden?"

"That's as the wind says. It's blowing that way now. Scramble up!"

Poor Jacob! if that willing Mrs. Poot had only appeared just

[1] Skipper. Master of a small trading vessel—a pleasure-boat or ice-boat.

then, her services would have been invaluable. It was as much
as the boys could do to hoist him into the boat. All were in at
last. The schipper, puffing away at his pipe, let out the sail,
lifted the brake, and sat in the stern with folded arms.

"Whew! How fast we go!" cried Ben; "this is something
like! Feel better, Jacob?"

"Much petter, I tanks you."

"Oh, you'll be as good as new in ten minutes. This makes
a fellow feel like a bird."

Jacob nodded, and blinked his eyes.

"Don't go to sleep, Jacob; it's too cold. You might never
wake up, you know. Persons often freeze to death in that way."

"I no sleep," said Jacob, confidently—and in two minutes he
was snoring.

Carl and Ludwig laughed.

"We must wake him!" cried Ben, "it is dangerous I tell
you,—Jacob! J-a-a-c——"

Captain Peter interfered, for three of the boys were helping
Ben for the fun of the thing.

"Nonsense! don't shake him! Let him alone, boys. One
never snores like that when one's freezing. Cover him up with
something. Here, this cloak will do; hey, schipper?" and he
looked toward the stern for permission to use it.

The man nodded.

"There," said Peter, tenderly adjusting the garment, "let
him sleep. He will be frisky as a lamb when he wakes. How
far are we from Leyden, schipper?"

"Not more 'n a couple of pipes," replied a voice, rising from
smoke like the genii in fairy tales (puff! puff!)—"likely not
more 'n one an' a half (puff! puff!)—if this wind holds!"
(puff! puff! puff!)

"What is the man saying, Lambert?" asked Ben, who was
holding his mittened hands against his cheeks to ward off the
cutting air.

"He says we're about two pipes from Leyden. Half the
boors here on the canal measure distances by the time it takes
them to finish a pipe."

" How ridiculous."

"See here, Benjamin Dobbs," retorted Lambert, growing unaccountably indignant at Ben's quiet smile ; " see here, you've a way of calling every other thing you see on *this* side of the German ocean, ' ridiculous.' It may suit *you*, this word, but it don't suit *me*. When you want anything ridiculous just remember your English custom of making the Lord Mayor of London, at his installation, count the nails in a horse-shoe to prove *his learning*."

"Who told you we had any such custom as that ? " cried Ben, looking grave in an instant.

"Why, I *know* it—no use of any one telling me. It's in all the books—and it's true. It strikes me," continued Lambert, laughing in spite of himself, " that you have been kept in happy ignorance of a good many ridiculous things on *your* side of the map."

"Humph ! " exclaimed Ben, trying not to smile, " I'll inquire into that Lord Mayor business when I get home. There must be some mistake. B-r-r-roooo ! How fast we're going. This is glorious ! "

It was a grand sail, or ride, I scarce know which to call it ; perhaps " fly " would be the best word ; for the boys felt very much as Sinbad did when, tied to the roc's leg, he darted through the clouds ; or as Bellerophon felt when he shot through the air on the back of his winged horse Pegasus. Sailing, riding, or flying, whichever it was, everything was rushing past, backward—and before they had time to draw a long breath, Leyden itself, with its high-peaked roofs, flew half-way to meet them.

When the city came in sight it was high time to waken the sleeper. That feat accomplished, Peter's prophecy came to pass. Master Jacob was quite restored and in excellent spirits.

The schipper made a feeble remonstrance when Peter, with hearty thanks, endeavoured to slip some silver pieces into his tough, brown palm.

" Ye see, young master," said he, drawing away his hand, " the regular line o' trade 's *one* thing, and a favour 's another."

"I know it," said Peter, "but those boys and girls of yours will want sweets when you get home. Buy them some in the name of Saint Nicholas."

The man grinned. "Ay, true enough, I've young 'uns in plenty, a clean boat-load of them. You are a sharp young master at guessing."

This time, the knotty hand hitched forward again, quite carelessly, it seemed, but its palm was upward. Peter hastily dropped in the money and moved away.

The sail soon came tumbling down. Scrape, scrape went the brake, scattering an ice shower round the boat.

"Good-bye, schipper!" shouted the boys, seizing their skates and leaping from the deck one by one, "many thanks to you!"

"Good-bye! good-b—— Hold! here! stop! I want my coat."

Ben was carefully assisting his cousin over the side of the boat.

"What is the man shouting about? Oh, I know; you have his wrapper round your shoulders!"

"Dat ish true," answered Jacob, half-jumping, half-tumbling down upon the framework; "dat ish vot make him sho heavy."

"Made *you* so heavy, you mean, Poot?"

"Ya, made you sho heavy—dat ish true," said Jacob, innocently, as he worked himself free from the big wrapper; "dere now you hands it mit him straits way, and tells him I voz much tanks for dat."

"Ho! for an inn!" cried Peter, as they stepped into the city. "Be brisk, my fine fellows!"

CHAPTER XXI

MYNHEER KLEEF AND HIS BILL OF FARE

THE boys soon found an unpretending establishment near the Breedstraat (Broad Street), with a funnily-painted lion over the door. This was the ROODE LEEUW, or Red Lion, kept by

one Huygens Kleef, a stout Dutchman, with short legs and a
very long pipe.

By this time they were in a ravenous condition. The tiffin,
taken at Haarlem, had served only to give them an appetite, and
this had been heightened by their exercise, and swift sail upon
the canal.

"Come, mine host, give us what you can!" cried Peter, rather
pompously.

"I can give you anything—everything," answered Mynheer
Kleef, performing a difficult bow.

"Well, give us sausage and pudding."

"Ah, mynheer, the sausage is all gone.   There is no pudding."

"Salmagundi, then, and plenty of it."

"That is out also, young master."

"Eggs, and be quick."

"Winter eggs are *very* poor eating," answered the innkeeper,
puckering his lips, and lifting his eyebrows.

"No eggs?   Well, caviare."

The Dutchman raised his fat hands :

"Caviare!   That is made of gold!   Who has caviare to
sell?"

Peter had sometimes eaten it at home.   He knew that it was
made of the roes of the sturgeon, and certain other large fish,
but he had no idea of its cost.

"Well, mine host, what have you?"

"What have I?   Everything.   I have rye-bread, sour-krout,
potato-salad, and the fattest herring in Leyden."

"What do you say, boys?" asked the captain.   "Will that
do?"

"Yes," cried the famished youths, "if he'll only be quick."

Mynheer moved off like one walking in his sleep, but soon
opened his eyes wide at the miraculous manner in which his
herring were made to disappear.   Next came, or rather went,
potato-salad, rye-bread, and coffee ; then Utrecht water flavoured
with orange, and, finally, slices of dry gingerbread.   This last
delicacy was not on the regular bill of fare ; but Mynheer Kleef,
driven to extremes, solemnly produced it from his own private

stores, and gave only a placid blink when his voracious young travellers started up, declaring they had eaten enough.

"I should think so!" he exclaimed internally, but his smooth face gave no sign.

Softly rubbing his hands, he asked—

"Will your worships have beds?"

"Will your worships have beds?" mocked Carl. "What do you mean? Do we look sleepy?"

"Not at all, master; but I would cause them to be warmed and aired. None sleep under damp sheets at the Red Lion."

"Ah, I understand. Shall we come back here to sleep, captain?"

Peter was accustomed to finer lodgings; but this was a frolic.

"Why not?" he replied. "We can fare excellently here."

"Your worship speaks only the truth," said mynheer, with great deference.

"How fine to be called 'your worship,'" laughed Ludwig aside to Lambert, while Peter replied—

"Well, mine host, you may get the rooms ready by nine."

"I have one beautiful chamber, with three beds, that will hold all of your worships," said Mynheer Kleef, coaxingly.

"That will do."

"Whew," whistled Carl, when they reached the street.

Ludwig started. "What now?"

"Nothing—only Mynheer Kleef of the Red Lion little thinks how we shall make things spin in that same room to-night. We'll set the bolsters flying!"

"Order!" cried the captain. "Now, boys, I must seek this great Dr. Boekman before I sleep. If he is in Leyden, it will be no great task to find him, for he always puts up at the Golden Eagle when he comes here. I wonder that you did not all go to bed at once; still, as you are awake, what say you to walking with Ben up by the Museum or the Stadhuis?"

"Agreed," said Ludwig and Lambert; but Jacob preferred to go with Peter. In vain Ben tried to persuade him to remain at the inn and rest. He declared that he never felt "petter," and wished of all things to take a look at the city, for it was his first "stop mit Leyden."

"Oh it will not harm him," said Lambert. "How long the day has been—and what glorious sport we have had. It hardly seems possible that we left Broek only this morning."

Jacob yawned :

"I have enjoyed it well," he said ; "but it seems to me at least a week since we started."

Carl laughed, and muttered something about "twenty naps."

"Here we are at the corner. Remember, we all meet at the Red Lion at eight," said the captain, as he and Jacob walked away.

CHAPTER XXII

THE RED LION BECOMES DANGEROUS

THE boys were glad to find a blazing fire awaiting them upon their return to the Red Lion. Carl and his party were there first. Soon afterward Peter and Jacob came in. They had inquired in vain concerning Dr. Boekman. All they could ascertain was that he had been seen in Haarlem that morning.

"As for his being in Leyden," the landlord of the Golden Eagle had said to Peter, "the thing is impossible. He always lodges here when in town. By this time there would be a crowd at my door waiting to consult him. Bah ! people make such fools of themselves ! "

"He is called a great surgeon," said Peter.

"Yes, the greatest in Holland. But what of that ? What of being the greatest pill-choker and knife-slasher in the world ? The man is a bear. Only last month on this very spot, he called me *a pig*, before three customers ! "

"No ! " exclaimed Peter, trying to look surprised and indignant.

"Yes, master—A PIG," repeated the landlord, puffing at his

pipe with an injured air. "Bah! if he did not pay fine prices and bring customers to my house, I would sooner see him in the Vleit canal than give him lodgment."

Perhaps mine host felt that he was speaking too openly to a stranger, or it may be he saw a smile lurking in Peter's face, for he added sharply—

"Come, now, what more do you wish? Supper? Beds?"

"No, mynheer, I am but searching for Dr. Boekman."

"Go find him. He is not in Leyden."

Peter was not to be put off so easily. After receiving a few more rough words, he succeeded in obtaining permission to leave a note for the famous surgeon, or rather, he *bought* from his amiable landlord the privilege of writing it there, and a promise that it should be promptly delivered when Dr. Boekman arrived. This accomplished, Peter and Jacob returned to the Red Lion.

This inn had once been a fine house, the home of a rich burgher; but, having grown old and shabby, it had passed through many hands, until finally it had fallen into the possession of Mynheer Kleef. He was fond of saying, as he looked up at its dingy, broken walls—"Mend it, and paint it, and there's not a prettier house in Leyden." It stood six stories high from the street. The first three were of equal breadth but of various heights, the last three were in the great, high roof, and grew smaller and smaller like a set of double steps until the top one was lost in a point. The roof was built of short, shining tiles, and the windows, with their little panes, seemed to be scattered irregularly over the face of the building, without the slightest attention to outward effect. But the public room on the ground-floor was the landlord's joy and pride. He never said "Mend it, and paint it," there, for everything was in the highest condition of Dutch neatness and order. If you will but open your mind's eye you may look into the apartment.

Imagine a large, bare room, with a floor that seemed to be made of squares cut out of glazed earthern pie-dishes, first a yellow piece, then a red, until the whole looked like a vast checker-board. Fancy a dozen high-backed wooden chairs standing around; then a great hollow chimney-place all aglow with its blazing fire, reflected a hundred times in the polished steel fire-dogs; a tiled hearth, tiled sides, tiled top, with a Dutch sentence upon it; and over all, high above one's head, a narrow mantelshelf, filled with shining brass candlesticks, pipe-lighters and tinder-boxes. Then see in one end of the room, three pine tables; in the other, a closet and a deal dresser. The latter is filled with mugs, dishes, pipes, tankards, earthern and glass bottles, and is guarded at one end by a brass-hooped keg standing upon long legs. Everything dim with tobacco smoke, but otherwise clean as soap and sand can make it. Next picture two sleepy, shabby-looking men, in wooden shoes, seated near the glowing fireplace, hugging their knees and smoking short, stumpy pipes; Mynheer Kleef walking softly and heavily about, clad in leather knee-breeches, felt shoes, and a green jacket wider than it is long; then throw a heap of skates in the corner, and put six tired, well-dressed boys, in various attitudes, upon the wooden chairs, and you will see the coffee-room of the Red Lion just as it appeared at nine o'clock on the evening of December 6, 184–. For supper, gingerbread again; slices of Dutch sausage; rye-bread sprinkled with aniseed; pickles; a bottle of Utrecht water, and a pot of very mysterious coffee. The boys were ravenous enough to take all they could get, and pronounce it excellent. Ben made wry faces, but Jacob declared he had never eaten a better meal. After they had laughed and talked a while, and counted their money by way of settling a discussion that arose concerning their expenses, the captain marched his company off to bed, led on by a greasy pioneer-boy who carried skates and a candlestick instead of an axe.

One of the ill-favoured men by the fire had shuffled toward the dresser, and was ordering a mug of beer, just as Ludwig, who brought up the rear, was stepping from the apartment.

"I don't like that fellow's eye," he whispered to Carl; "he looks like a pirate, or something of that kind."

"Looks like a granny!" answered Carl in sleepy disdain.

Ludwig laughed uneasily.

"Granny or no granny," he whispered, "I tell you he looks just like one of those men in the 'voetspoelen.'"

"Pooh!" sneered Carl, "I knew it. That picture was too much for you. Look sharp now, and see if yon fellow with the candle doesn't look like the other villain."

"No, indeed, his face is as honest as a Gouda cheese. But, I say, Carl, that really was a horrid picture."

"Humph! What did you stare at it so long for?"

"I couldn't help it."

By this time the boys had reached the "beautiful room with three beds in it." A dumpy little maiden with long ear-rings met them at the doorway, dropt them a courtesy, and passed out. She carried a long-handled thing that resembled a frying-pan with a cover.

"I am glad to see that," said Van Mounen to Ben.

"What?"

"Why, the warming-pan. It's full of hot ashes, she's been heating our beds."

"Oh! a warming-pan, eh! Much obliged to her, I'm sure," said Ben, too sleepy to make any further comment.

It was a cold, cheerless room, a fire had been newly kindled in the burnished stove, and seemed to shiver even while it was trying to burn. The windows, with their funny little panes were bare and shiny, and the cold, waxed floor looked like a sheet of yellow ice. Three rush-bottomed chairs stood stiffly against the wall, alternating with three narrow wooden bedsteads, that made the room look like the deserted ward of an hospital. At any other time the boys would have found it quite impossible to sleep in pairs, especially in such narrow quarters; but to-night they lost all fear of being crowded, and longed only to lay their weary bodies upon the feather beds that lay lightly upon each cot. Had the boys been in Germany, instead of Holland, they might have been covered also by a bed of down or feathers. This peculiar form of luxury was at that time adopted only by wealthy or eccentric Hollanders.

Ludwig had not quite lost his friskiness; but the other boys, after one or two feeble attempts at pillow-firing, composed themselves for the night with the greatest dignity. Nothing like fatigue for making boys behave themselves.

"Good-night, boys!" said Peter's voice, from under the covers.

"Good-night," called back everybody but Jacob, who already lay snoring beside the captain.

"I say," shouted Carl, after a moment, "don't sneeze, anybody. Ludwig's in a fright!"

"No such thing," retorted Ludwig, in a smothered voice. Then there was a little whispered dispute, which was ended by Carl saying—

"For *my* part, I don't know what fear is. But you really are a timid fellow, Ludwig."

Ludwig grunted sleepily, but made no further reply.

It was the middle of the night. The fire had shivered itself to death, and, in place of its gleams, little squares of moonlight lay upon the floor, slowly, slowly shifting their way across the room. Something else was moving also, but they did not see it. Sleeping boys keep but a poor look-out. During the early hours of the night, Jacob Poot had been gradually but surely winding himself with all the bedcovers. He now lay like a monster chrysalis beside the half-frozen Peter, who, accordingly, was skating with all his might over the coldest, bleakest of dreamland icebergs.

Something else, I say, besides the moonlight, was moving across the bare, polished floor—moving, not quite so slowly, but quite as stealthily.

Wake up, Ludwig! The voetspoelen pirate is growing real!

No. Ludwig does not waken, but he moans in his sleep.

Does not Carl hear it—Carl, the brave, the fearless?

No. Carl is dreaming of the race.

And Jacob? Van Mounen? Ben?

Not they. They, too, are dreaming of the race; and Katrinka is singing through their dreams—laughing, flitting past them. Now and then a wave from the great organ surges through their midst.

Still the thing moves, slowly, slowly.

Peter! Captain Peter, there is danger!

Peter heard no call; but, in his dream, he slid a few thousand feet from one iceberg to another, and the shock awoke him.

Whew! How cold he was! He gave a hopeless, desperate tug at the chrysalis. In vain; sheet, blanket, and spread were firmly wound about Jacob's inanimate form. Peter looked drowsily toward the window.

"Clear moonlight," he thought; "we shall have pleasant weather to-morrow. Hollo! what's that?"

He saw the moving thing, or rather something black, crouching upon the floor, for it had halted as Peter stirred.

He watched in silence.

Soon it moved again, nearer and nearer. It was a man crawling upon hands and feet!

The captain's first impulse was to call out; but he took an instant to consider matters.

The creeper had a shining knife in one hand. This was ugly; but Peter was naturally self-possessed. When the head turned, Peter's eyes were closed as if in sleep; but at other times nothing could be keener, sharper, than the captain's gaze.

Closer, closer crept the robber. His back was very near Peter now. The knife was laid softly upon the floor; one careful arm reached forth stealthily to drag the clothes from the chair by the captain's bed—the robbery was commenced.

Now was Peter's time! Holding his breath, he sprang up and leaped with all his strength upon the robber's back, stunning the rascal with the force of the blow. To seize the knife was but a second's work. The robber began to struggle, but Peter sat like a giant astride the prostrate form.

"If you stir," said the brave boy, in as terrible a voice as he could command, "stir but one inch, I will plunge this knife into your neck. Boys! boys! wake up!" he shouted, still pressing down the black head, and holding the knife at pricking distance; "give us a hand! I've got him! I've got him!"

"Up, boys!" cried Peter, never budging. "Ludwig! Lambert! Thunder! Are you all dead?"

Dead! not they. Van Mounen and Ben were on their feet in an instant.

"Hey? What now?" they shouted.

"I've got a robber here," said Peter, coolly. "(Lie still, you scoundrel, or I'll slice your head off!) Now, boys, cut out your bed-cord—plenty of time—he's a dead man if he stirs."

Peter felt that he weighed a thousand pounds. So he did, with that knife in his hand. The man growled and swore, but dared not move.

Ludwig was up by this time. He had a great jack-knife, the pride of his heart, in his breeches pocket. It could do good service now. They bared the bedstead in a moment. It was laced backward and forward with a rope.

"I'll cut it," cried Ludwig, sawing away at the knot; "hold him tight, Pete!"

"Never fear!" answered the captain, giving the robber a warning prick.

The boys were soon pulling at the rope like good fellows. It was out at last—a long, stout piece.

"Now, boys," commanded the captain, "lift up his rascally arms! Cross his hands over his back! That's right—excuse me for being in the way—tie them tight!"

"Yes, and his feet, too, the villain!" cried the boys, in great excitement, tying knot after knot with Herculean jerks.

The prisoner changed his tone.

"Oh—oh!" he moaned, "spare a poor sick man—I was but walking in my sleep."

"Ugh!" grunted Lambert, still tugging away at the rope, "asleep, were you? well, we'll wake you up."

The man muttered fierce oaths between his teeth—then cried in a piteous voice, "Unbind me, good young masters! I have five little children at home. By Saint Bavon I swear to give you each a ten-guilder piece if you will but free me!"

"Ha! ha!" laughed Peter.

"Ha! ha!" laughed the other boys.

Then came threats—threats that made Ludwig fairly shudder, though he continued to bind and tie with redoubled energy.

"Hold up, mynheer housebreaker!" said Van Mounen in a warning voice. "That knife is very near your throat. If you make the captain nervous, there is no telling what may happen."

The robber took the hint, and fell into a sullen silence.

Just at this moment Poot stirred upon the bed and sat erect.

"What's the matter?" he asked, without opening his eyes.

"Matter!" echoed Ludwig, half trembling, half laughing; "get up, Jacob. Here's work for you! Come sit on this fellow's back while we get into our clothes, we're half perished."

"What fellow? Donder!"

"Hurrah for Poot!" cried all the boys, as Jacob, sliding quickly to the floor, bed-clothes and all, took in the state of affairs at a glance, and sat heavily beside Peter on the robber's back.

Oh, didn't the fellow groan then!

"No use in holding him down any longer, boys," said Peter, rising, but bending as he did so to draw a pistol from the man's belt. "You see I've been keeping guard over this pretty little weapon for the last ten minutes. It's cocked, and the least wriggle might have set it off. No danger now. I must dress myself. You and I, Lambert, will go for the police. I'd no idea it was so cold."

"Where is Carl?" asked one of the boys.

They looked at one another. Carl certainly was not among them.

"Oh!" cried Ludwig, frightened at last, "where is he? Perhaps he's had a fight with the robber, and got killed."

"Not a bit of it," said Peter, quietly, as he buttoned his stout jacket. "Look under the beds."

They did so. Carl was not there.

Just then they heard a commotion on the stairway. Ben hastened to open the door. The landlord almost tumbled in, he was armed with a big blunderbuss. Two or three lodgers followed; then the daughter, with an upraised frying-pan in one hand, and a candle in the other; and, behind her, looking pale and frightened, the gallant Carl!

"There's your man, mine host," said Peter, nodding toward the prisoner.

Mine host raised his blunderbuss, the girl screamed, and Jacob, more nimble than usual, rolled quickly from the robber's back.

"Don't fire," cried Peter; "he is tied, hand and foot. Let's roll him over, and see what he looks like."

Carl stepped briskly forward, with a blustering "Yes. *We'll* turn him over in a way he won't like. Lucky we've caught him!"

"Ha! ha!" laughed Ludwig, "where were you, Master Carl?"

"Where was I?" retorted Carl, angrily; "why, I went to give the alarm, to be sure!"

All the boys exchanged glances; but they were too happy and elated to say anything ill-natured. Carl certainly was bold enough now. He took the lead while three others aided him in turning the helpless man.

While the robber lay, face up, scowling and muttering, Ludwig took the candlestick from the girl's hand.

"I must have a good look at the beauty," he said, drawing closer, but the words were no sooner spoken than he turned pale, and started so violently that he almost dropped the candle.

"THE VOETSPOELEN!" he cried; "why, boys, it's the man who sat by the fire!"

"Of course it is," answered Peter, "we counted our money before him like simpletons. But what have we to do with voetspoelen, brother Ludwig? A month in jail is punishment enough."

The landlord's daughter had left the room. She now ran in, holding up a pair of huge wooden shoes. "See, father," she cried, "here are his great ugly boots. It's the man that we put in the next room after the young masters went to bed. Ah! it

was wrong to send the poor young gentlemen up here, so far out
of sight and sound."

"The scoundrel!" hissed the landlord, "he has disgraced my
house. I go for the police at once!"

In less than fifteen minutes two drowsy-looking officers were
in the room. After telling Mynheer Kleef that he must appear
early in the morning with the boys, and make his complaint
before a magistrate, they marched off with their prisoner.

One would think the captain and his band could have slept
no more that night; but the morning has not yet been found
that can prevent youth and an easy conscience from drifting
down the river of dreams. The boys were too much fatigued to
let so slight a thing as capturing a robber bind them to wakeful-
ness. They were soon in bed again, floating away to strange
scenes made of familiar things. Ludwig and Carl had spread
their bedding upon the floor. One had already forgotten the
voetspoelen, the race—everything; but Carl was wide-awake.
He heard the carrilons ringing out their solemn nightly music,
and the watchman's noisy clapper putting in discord at the
quarter-hours; he saw the moonshine glide away from the
window, and the red morning light come pouring in, and all the
while he kept thinking—

"Pooh! what a goose I have made of myself!"

Carl Schummel alone, with none to look or to listen, was not
quite so grand a fellow as Carl Schummel strutting about in his
boots.

CHAPTER XXIII

BEFORE THE COURT

YOU may believe the landlord's daughter bestirred herself to
prepare a good meal for the boys next morning. Mynheer
had a Chinese gong that could make more noise than a dozen of
breakfast bells. Its hideous reveille clanging through the house
generally startled the drowsiest lodgers into activity, but the
maiden would not allow it to be sounded this morning.

"Let the brave young gentlemen sleep," she said to the greasy kitchen-boy; "they shall be warmly fed when they waken."

It was ten o'clock when Captain Peter and his band came straggling down one by one.

"A pretty hour," said mine host, gruffly. "It is high time we were before the court. Fine business this for a respectable inn. You will testify truly, young masters, that you found most excellent fare and lodgment at the Red Lion?"

"Of course we will," answered Carl, saucily, "and pleasant company, too, though they visit at rather unseasonable hours."

A stare and a "humph!" was all the answer Mynheer made to this, but the daughter was more communicative. Shaking her ear-rings at Carl, she said sharply—

"Not so very pleasant either, master traveller, if one could judge by the way *you* ran away from it!"

"Impertinent creature!" hissed Carl, under his breath, as he began busily to examine his skate-straps. Meantime the kitchen-boy, listening outside at the crack of the door, doubled himself with silent laughter.

After breakfast the boys went to the Police Court, accompanied by Huygens Kleef and his daughter. Mynheer's testimony was principally to the effect that such a thing as a robber at the Red Lion had been unheard of until last night; and as for the Red Lion, it was a most respectable inn—as respectable as any house in Leyden. Each boy, in turn, told all he knew of the affair, and identified the prisoner in the box as the same man who entered their room in the dead of night. Ludwig was surprised to find that the robber was a man of ordinary size— especially after he had described him, under oath, to the Court as a tremendous fellow, with great square shoulders, and legs of prodigious weight. Jacob swore that he was awakened by the robber kicking and thrashing upon the floor; and, immediately afterward, Peter and the rest (feeling sorry that they had not explained the matter to their sleepy comrade) testified that the man had not moved a muscle from the moment the point of the dagger touched his throat, until, bound from head to foot, he was rolled over for inspection. The landlord's daughter made

one boy blush, and all the court smile, by declaring that "if it
hadn't been for that handsome young gentleman there " (pointing
to Peter), "they might have all been murdered in their beds ;
for the dreadful man had a great, shining knife, almost as long
as your honour's arm," and *she* believed "the handsome young
gentleman had struggled hard enough to get it away from him,
but he was too modest, bless him ! to say so."

Finally, after a little questioning and cross-questioning from
the public prosecutor, the witnesses were dismissed, and the
robber was handed over to the consideration of the Criminal
Court.

"The scoundrel !" said Carl, savagely, when the boys reached
the street, "he ought to be sent to jail at once. If I had been
in your place, Peter, I certainly should have killed him outright !"

"He was fortunate, then, in falling into gentler hands," was
Peter's quiet reply. "It appears he has been arrested before
under a charge of house-breaking. He did not succeed in robbing
this time, but he broke the door-fastenings, and that I believe
makes a burglary in the eye of the law. He was armed with a
knife, too, and that makes it worse for him, poor fellow !"

"Poor fellow !" mimicked Carl; "one would think he was
your brother !"

"So he is my brother, and yours, too, Carl Schummel, for
that matter," answered Peter, looking into Carl's eye. "We cannot say what we might have become under other circumstances.
We have been bolstered up from evil since the hour we were
born. A happy home and good parents might have made that
man a fine fellow instead of what he is. God grant that the
law may cure and not crush him !"

"Amen to that !" said Lambert, heartily, while Ludwig van
Holp looked at his brother in such a bright, proud way, that
Jacob Poot, who was an only son, wished from his heart that the
little form buried in the old church at home had lived to grow
up beside him.

"Humph !" said Carl, "it's very well to be saintly and forgiving, and all that sort of thing, but I'm naturally hard. All

these fine ideas seem to rattle off of me like hailstones—and it's nobody's business, either, if they do."

Peter recognised a touch of good feeling in this clumsy concession; holding out his hand, he said, in a frank, hearty tone—

"Come, lad, shake hands, and let us be good friends even if we don't exactly agree on all questions."

"We do agree better than you think," sulked Carl, as he returned Peter's grasp.

"All right," responded Peter, briskly; "now Van Mounen, we await Benjamin's wishes. Where would he like to go?"

"To the Egyptian Museum," answered Lambert, after holding a brief consultation with Ben.

"That is on the Breede Straat. To the Museum let it be. Come, boys!"

CHAPTER XXIV

THE BELEAGUERED CITIES

"THIS open square before us," said Lambert, as he and Ben walked on together, "is pretty in summer, with its shady trees. They call it the Ruine. Years ago it was covered with houses, and the Rapenburg canal, here, ran through the street. Well, one day a barge loaded with forty thousand pounds of gunpowder, bound for Delft, was lying alongside, and the bargemen took a notion to cook their dinner on the deck; and before any one knew it, sir, the whole thing blew up, killing lots of persons and scattering about three hundred houses to the winds."

"What!" exclaimed Ben, "did the explosion destroy three hundred houses!"

"Yes, sir, my father was in Leyden at the time. He says it was terrible. The explosion occurred just at noon, and was like a volcano. All this part of the town was on fire in an instant, buildings tumbling down, and men, women, and children groaning under the ruins. The king himself came to the city and acted nobly, father says, staying out in the streets all night, encouraging the survivors in their efforts to arrest the fire, and rescue as many as possible from under the heaps of stone and rubbish. Through his means a collection for the benefit of the sufferers was raised throughout the kingdom, besides a hundred thousand guilders paid out of the treasury. Father was only nineteen years old then; it was in 1807, I believe, but he remembers it perfectly. A friend of his, Professor Luzac, was among the killed. They have a tablet erected to his memory, in Saint Peter's Church, further on—the queerest thing you ever saw—with an image of the professor carved upon it, representing him just as he looked when he was found after the explosion."

"What a strange idea! Isn't Boerhaave's monument in Saint Peter's also?"

"I cannot remember. Perhaps Peter knows."

The captain delighted Ben by saying that the monument was there, and that he thought they might be able to see it during the day.

"Lambert," continued Peter, "ask Ben if he saw Van der Werf's portrait at the Town Hall last night?"

"No," said Lambert, "I can answer for him. It was too late to go in. I say, boys, it is really wonderful how much Ben knows. Why, he has told me a volume of Dutch history already. I'll wager he has the siege of Leyden at his tongue's end."

"His tongue must burn then," interposed Ludwig, "for if Bilderdyk's account is true, it was a pretty hot affair."

Ben was looking at them with an inquiring smile.

"We are speaking of the siege of Leyden," explained Lambert.

"Oh, yes," said Ben, eagerly, "I had forgotten all about it. This was the very place. Let's give old Van der Werf three cheers. Hur—— "

Van Mounen uttered a hasty "hush!" and explained that, patriotic as the Dutch were, the police would soon have something to say if a party of boys cheered in the street at mid-day.

"What! not cheer Van der Werf?" cried Ben, indignantly.

"One of the greatest chaps in history! Only think! Didn't he hold out against those murderous Spaniards for months and months! There was the town, surrounded on all sides by the enemy; great black forts sending fire and death into the very heart of the city—but no surrender! Every man a hero—women, and children, too, brave and fierce as lions—provisions giving out, the very grass from between the paving-stones gone—till people were glad to eat horses and cats, and dogs and rats. Then came the Plague—hundreds dying in the streets—but no surrender! Then when they could bear no more—when the people, brave as they were, crowded about Van der Werf in the public square begging him to give up; what did the noble old burgomaster say? —'I have sworn to defend this city, and with God's help, *I mean to do it*! If my body can satisfy your hunger, take it, and divide it among you—but expect no surrender so long as I am alive.' Hurrah! hur—— "

Ben was getting uproarious; Lambert, playfully clapped his hand over his friend's mouth. The result was one of those quick india-rubber scuffles fearful to behold, but delightful to human nature in its polliwog state.

"Vat wash te matter, Pen?" asked Jacob, hurrying forward.

"Oh! nothing at all," panted Ben, "except that Van Mounen was afraid of starting an English riot in this orderly town. He stopped my cheering for old Van der—— "

"Ya! ya—it ish no goot to sheer—to make te noise for dat —you vill shee old Van der Does's likeness mit te Stadhuis."

"See old Van der Does? I thought it was Van der Werf's picture they had there."

"Ya," responded Jacob, "Van der Werf—vell, vot of it! both ish just ash goot."

"Yes, Van der Does was a noble old Dutchman, but he was not Van der Werf. I know he defended the city like a brick, and—— "

"Now vot for you shay dat, Penchamin? He no defend te citty mit breek, he fight like good soltyer mit his guns. You like make te fun mit effrysinks Tutch."

"No! no! no! I said he defended the city *like* a brick.

That is very high praise, I would have you understand. We English call even the Duke of Wellington a brick."

Jacob looked puzzled; but his indignation was already on the ebb:

"Vell, it ish no matter. I no tink, before, soltyer mean breek, but it ish no matter."

Ben laughed good-naturedly, and, seeing that his cousin was tired of talking in English, he turned to his friend of the two languages—

"Van Mounen! they say the very carrier-pigeons that brought news of relief to the besieged city are somewhere here in Leyden. I really should like to see them. Just think of it! At the very height of the trouble if the wind didn't turn, and blow in the waters, and drown hundreds of the Spaniards, and enable the Dutch boats to sail in right over the land with men and provisions to the very gates of the city. The pigeons, you know, did great service, in bearing letters to and fro. I have read somewhere that they were reverently cared for from that day, and, when they died, they were stuffed, and placed for safe keeping in the Town Hall. We must be sure to have a look at them."

Van Mounen laughed. "On that principle, Ben, I suppose when you go to Rome you'll expect to see the identical goose who saved the Capitol. But it will be easy enough to see the pigeons. They are in the same building with Van der Werf's portrait. Which was the greatest defence, Ben, the siege of Leyden or the siege of Haarlem?"

"Well," replied Ben, thoughtfully, "Van der Werf is one of my heroes; we all have our historical pets, you know; but I really think the siege of Haarlem brought out a braver, more heroic resistance even than the Leyden one; besides they set the Leyden sufferers an example of courage and fortitude, for their turn came first."

"I don't know much about the Haarlem siege," said Lambert, "except that it was in 1573. Who beat?"

"The Spaniards," said Ben. "The Dutch had stood out for months. Not a man would yield, nor a woman either for that matter. They shouldered arms and fought gallantly beside their husbands and fathers. Three hundred of them did duty under Kanau Hesselaer, a great woman, and brave as Joan of Arc. All this time the city was surrounded by the Spaniards under Frederic of Toledo, son of that beauty, the Duke of Alva. Cut off from all possible help from without, there seemed to be no hope for the inhabitants, but they shouted defiance over the city walls. They even threw bread into the enemy's camps to show that they were not afraid of starvation. Up to the last they held out bravely, waiting for the help that never could come—growing bolder and bolder until their provisions were exhausted. Then it was terrible. In time hundreds of famished creatures fell dead in the streets, and the living had scarcely strength to bury them. At last, they made the desperate resolution, that rather than perish by lingering torture, the strongest would form in a square, placing the weakest in the centre, and rush in a body to their death, with the faint chance of being able to fight their way through the enemy. The Spaniards received a hint of this, and, believing there was nothing the Dutch would not dare to do, they concluded to offer terms."

"High time I should think."

"Yes; with falsehood and treachery they soon obtained an entrance into the city, promising protection and forgiveness to all except those whom the citizens themselves would acknowledge as deserving of death."

"You don't say so !" said Lambert, quite interested; "that ended the business, I suppose."

"Not a bit of it," returned Ben, "for the Duke of Alva had already given his son orders to show mercy to none."

"Ah ! there was where the great Haarlem massacre came in. I remember now. You can't wonder that the Hollanders dislike Spain when you read of the way they were butchered by Alva and his hosts, though I admit that our side sometimes retaliated terribly. But, as I have told you before, I have a very indistinct idea of historical matters. Everything is utter confusion—from the Flood to the Battle of Waterloo. One thing is plain, however, the Duke of Alva was about the worst specimen of a man that ever lived."

"That gives only a faint idea of him," said Ben; "but I hate to think of such a wretch. What if he *had* brains, and military skill, and all that sort of thing! Give me such men as Van der Werf, and—what now?"

"Why," said Van Mounen, who was looking up and down the street in a bewildered way, "we've walked right past the Museum, and I don't see the boys. Let us go back."

CHAPTER XXV

LEYDEN

THE boys met at the Museum, and were soon engaged in examining its extensive collection of curiosities, receiving a new insight into Egyptian life, ancient and modern. Ben and Lambert had often visited the British Museum, but that did not prevent them from being surprised at the richness of the Leyden collection. There were household utensils, wearing apparel, weapons, musical instruments, sarcophagi, and mummies of men, women, and cats, ibexes, and other creatures. They saw a massive gold armlet that had been worn by an Egyptian king at a time when some of these same mummies, perhaps, were nimbly treading the streets of Thebes; and jewels and trinkets such as Pharaoh's daughter wore, and the children of Israel borrowed when they departed out of Egypt.

There were other interesting relics, from Rome and Greece, and some curious Roman pottery which had been discovered in digging near the Hague—relics of the days when the countrymen of Julius Cæsar had settled there. Where have they not settled? I, for one, would hardly be astonished if relics of the ancient Romans should some day be found deep under the grass growing round the Bunker-hill monument.

When the boys left this Museum, they went to another, and

saw a wonderful collection of fossil animals, skeletons, birds, minerals, precious stones, and other natural specimens ; but as they were not learned men, they could only walk about and stare, enjoy the little knowledge of natural history they possessed, and wish with all their hearts they had acquired more. Even the skeleton of the mouse puzzled Jacob. What wonder ? He was not used to seeing the cat-fearing little creatures running about in their bones—and how could he ever have imagined their necks to be so queer ?

Besides the Museum of Natural History, there was Saint Peter's Church to be visited, containing Professor Luzac's memorial, and Boerhaave's monument of white and black marble, with its urn and carved symbols of the four ages of life, and its medallion of Boerhaave, adorned with his favourite motto, "Simplex sigillum veri." They also obtained admittance to a tea-garden, which in summer was a favourite resort of the citizens, and passing naked oaks and fruit-trees, ascended a high mound which stood in the centre. This was the site of a round tower now in ruins, said by some to have been built by Hengist the Anglo-Saxon king, and by others to have been the castle of one of the ancient counts of Holland.

As the boys walked about on the top of its stone wall, they could get but a poor view of the surrounding city. The tower stood higher when, more than two centuries ago, the inhabitants of beleaguered Leyden, shouted to the watcher on its top their wild, despairing cries, "Is there any help ? Are the waters rising ? What do you see ?"

And for months he could only answer, "No help. I see around us nothing but the enemy."

Ben pushed these thoughts away ; and resolutely looking down into the bare tea-garden, filled it in imagination with gay summer groups. He tried to forget old battle-clouds, and picture only curling wreaths of tobacco smoke, rising from among men, women, and children enjoying their tea and coffee in the open air. But a tragedy came in spite of him.

Poot was bending over the edge of the high wall. It would be just like him to grow dizzy and tumble off. Ben turned impatiently away. If the fellow, with his weak head, knew no better than to be venturesome, why, let him tumble. Horror! what meant that heavy, crashing sound?

Ben could not stir. He could only gasp.

"Jacob!"

"Jacob!" cried another startled voice and another. Ready to faint, Ben managed to turn his head. He saw a crowd of boys on the edge of the wall opposite—but Jacob was not there!

"Good Heaven!" he cried, springing forward, "where is my cousin?"

The crowd parted. It was only four boys after all. There sat Jacob in their midst, holding his sides, and laughing heartily.

"Did I frighten you all?" he said, in his native Dutch; "well, I will tell you how it was. There was a big stone lying on the wall, and I put my—my foot out just to push it a little, you see; and the first thing I knew down went the stone all the way to the bottom, and left me sitting here on top with both my feet in the air. If I had not thrown myself back at that moment, I certainly should have rolled over after the stone. Well, it is no matter. Help me up, boys."

"You are hurt, Jacob!" said Ben, seeing a shade of seriousness pass over his cousin's face as they lifted him to his feet.

Jacob tried to laugh again. "Oh, no—I feels little hurt ven I stant up, but it ish no matter."

The monument to Van der Werf in the Hooglandsche Kerk was not accessible that day; but the boys spent a few pleasant moments in the Stadhuis or Town Hall, a long irregular structure, somewhat in the Gothic style, uncouth in architecture, but picturesque from age. It's little steeple, tuneful with bells, seemed to have been borrowed from some other building, and hastily clapped on as a finishing touch.

Ascending the grand staircase, the boys soon found themselves in rather a gloomy apartment, containing the masterpiece of Lucas Van Leyden, or Hugens, a Dutch artist, born three hundred and seventy years ago, who painted well when he was ten years of age, and became distinguished in art when only fifteen. This picture, called The Last Judgment, considering the remote age in which it was painted, is truly a remarkable production. The boys, however, were less interested in tracing out the merits of the work than they were in the fact of its being a triptych—that is, painted on three divisions, the two outer ones swung on hinges so as to close, when required, over the main portion.

The historical pictures by Harel de Moor and other famous Dutch artists interested them for a while, and Ben had to be almost pulled away from the dingy old portrait of Van der Werf.

The Town Hall, as well as the Egyptian Museum, is on the Breede Straat, the longest and finest street in Leyden. It has no canal running through it, and the houses, painted in every variety of colour, have a picturesque effect as they stand with their gable ends to the street. Some are very tall, with half of their height in their step-like roofs ; others crouch before the public edifices and churches. Being clean, spacious, well-shaded, and adorned with many elegant mansions, it compares favourably with the finer portions of Amsterdam. It is kept scrupulously neat ; many of the gutters are covered with boards that open like trap-doors ; and it is supplied with pumps surmounted with shining brass ornaments kept scoured and bright at the public cost. The city is intersected by numerous waterroads formed by the river Rhine, there grown sluggish, fatigued by its long travel ; but more than one hundred and fifty stone bridges re-unite the dissevered streets. The same world-renowned river, degraded from the beautiful, free-flowing Rhine, serves as a moat around the rampart that surrounds Leyden, and is crossed by drawbridges at the imposing gateways that give access to the city. Fine broad promenades, shaded by noble trees, border the canals, and add to the retired appearance of the houses behind, heightening the effect of scholastic seclusion that seems to pervade the place.

Ben, as he scanned the buildings on the Rapenburg canal,

was somewhat disappointed in the appearance of the great University of Leyden. But when he recalled its history,—how, attended with all the pomp of a grand civic display, it had been founded by the Prince of Orange, as a tribute to the citizens for the bravery displayed during the siege; when he remembered the great men in religion, learning, and science, who had once studied there, and thought of the hundreds of students now sharing the benefits of its classes and its valuable scientific museums,—he was quite willing to forego architectural beauty, though he could not help feeling that no amount of it could have been misplaced on such an institution.

Peter and Jacob regarded the building with even a deeper, more practical interest, for they were to enter it as students in the course of a few months.

"Poor Don Quixote would have run a hopeless tilt in this part of the world," said Ben, after Lambert had been pointing out some of the oddities and beauties of the suburbs; "it is all windmills. You remember his terrific contest with one, I suppose?"

"No," said Lambert, bluntly.

"Well, I don't either—that is, not definitely. But there was something of that kind in his adventures, and if there wasn't, there should have been. Look at them, how frantically they whirl their great arms! just the thing to excite the crazy knight to mortal combat. It bewilders one to look at them; help me to count all those we can see, Van Mounen. I want a big item for my note-book"; and after a careful reckoning, superintended by all the party, Master Ben wrote in pencil— "Saw, Dec.—, 184-, ninety-eight windmills within full view of Leyden."

He would have been glad to visit the old brick mill in which the painter Rembrandt was born; but he abandoned the project upon learning that it would take them out of their way. Few boys, as hungry as Ben was by this time, would hesitate long between Rembrandt's home a mile off and tiffin close by. Ben chose the latter.

After tiffin, they rested awhile, and then—took another,

which, for form sake, they called dinner. After dinner the
boys sat warming themselves at the inn—all but Peter, who
occupied the time in another fruitless search for Dr. Boekman.

This over, the party once more prepared for skating. They
were thirteen miles from the Hague, and not as fresh as when
they had left Broek early on the previous day; but they were
in good spirits, and the ice was excellent.

CHAPTER XXVI

THE PALACE AND THE WOOD

AS the boys skated onward, they saw a number of fine
country seats, all decorated and surrounded according to
the Dutchest of Dutch taste, but impressive to look upon, with
their great, formal houses, elaborate gardens, square hedges, and
wide ditches—some crossed by a bridge, having a gate in the
middle to be carefully locked at night. These ditches, everywhere traversing the landscape, had long ago lost their summer
film, and now shone under the sunlight like trailing ribbons of
glass.

The boys travelled bravely, all the while performing the surprising feat of producing gingerbread from their pockets and
causing it to vanish instantly.

Twelve miles were passed. A few more long strokes would
take them to the Hague, when Van Mounen proposed that they
should vary their course, by walking into the city through the
Bosch.

"Agreed!" cried one and all, and their skates were off in a
twinkling.

The Bosch is a grand park or wood, nearly two miles long,
containing the celebrated House in the Wood—*Huis in't Bosch*
—sometimes used as a royal residence.

This building, though plain outside for a palace, is elegantly
furnished within, and finely frescoed—that is, the walls and

ceiling are covered with groups and designs painted directly upon them while the plaster was fresh. Some of the rooms are tapestried with Chinese silk, beautifully embroidered. One contains a number of family portraits, among them a group of royal children, who in time were orphaned by a certain axe which figures very frequently in European history. These children were painted many times by the Dutch artist Van Dyck, who was court-painter to their father, Charles the First of England. Beautiful children they were! what a deal of trouble the English nation would have been spared had they been as perfect in heart and soul as they were in form!

The park surrounding the palace is charming, especially in summer, for flowers and birds make it bright as fairyland. Long rows of magnificent oaks rear their proud heads, conscious that no profaning hand will ever bring them low. In fact, the Wood has for ages been held as an almost sacred spot. Children are never allowed to meddle with its smallest twig; the axe of the woodman has never resounded there. Even war and riot have passed it reverently, pausing for a moment in their devastating way. Philip of Spain, while he ordered Dutchmen to be mowed down by hundreds, issued a mandate that not a bough of the beautiful Wood should be touched; and once, when in a time of great necessity the State was about to sacrifice it to assist in filling a nearly-exhausted treasury, the people rushed to the rescue, and nobly contributed the required amount rather than that the Bosch should fall.

What wonder, then, that the oaks have a grand, fearless air? Birds from all Holland have told them how, elsewhere, trees are cropped and bobbed into shape, but *they* are untouched. Year after year they expand in unclipped luxuriance and beauty; their wide-spreading foliage, alive with song, casts a cool shade over lawn and pathway, or bows to its image in the sunny ponds.

Meanwhile, as if to reward the citizens for allowing her to have her way for once, Nature departs from the invariable level, wearing gracefully the ornaments that have been reverently bestowed upon her: so the lawn slopes in a velvety green; the paths wind in and out ; flower-beds glow and send forth perfume ; and ponds and sky look at each other in mutual admiration.

Even on that winter day the Bosch was beautiful. Its trees were bare, but beneath them still lay the ponds, every ripple smoothed into glass. The blue sky was bright overhead, and, as it looked down through the thicket of boughs, it saw another blue sky, not nearly so bright, looking up from the dim thicket under the ice.

Never had the sunset appeared more beautiful to Peter than when he saw it exchanging farewell glances with the windows and shining roofs of the city before him. Never had the Hague itself seemed more inviting. He was no longer Peter van Holp, going to visit a great city, nor a fine young gentleman bent on sight-seeing ; he was a knight, an adventurer, travel-soiled and weary, a Hop-o'-my-Thumb grown large, a Fortunatus approaching the enchanted castle where luxury and ease awaited him— for his own sister's house was not half-a-mile away.

"At last, boys," he cried, in high glee, "we may hope for a royal resting-place—good beds, warm rooms, and something fit to eat. I never realised before what a luxury such things are. Our lodgings at the Red Lion have made us appreciate our own homes."

CHAPTER XXVII

THE MERCHANT-PRINCE AND THE SISTER-PRINCESS

WELL might Peter feel that his sister's house was like an enchanted castle. Large and elegant as it was, a spell of quiet hung over it. The very lion crouching at its gate seemed to have been turned into stone through magic. Within, it was guarded by Genii, in the shape of red-faced servants, who sprang silently forth at the summons of bell or knocker. There was a cat also, who appeared as knowing as any Puss-in-Boots ; and a brass gnome in the hall whose business it was to stand with outstretched arms ready to receive sticks and umbrellas. Safe

within the walls bloomed a Garden of Delight, where the flowers
firmly believed it was summer, and a sparkling fountain was
laughing merrily to itself because Jack Frost could not find it.
There was a Sleeping Beauty, too, just at the time of the boys'
arrival; but when Peter, like a true prince, flew lightly up the
stairs, and kissed her eyelids, the enchantment was broken.
The princess became his own good sister, and the fairy castle
just one of the finest, most comfortable houses of the Hague.

As may well be believed, the boys received the heartiest of
welcomes. After they had conversed awhile with their lively
hostess, one of the genii summoned them to a grand repast in a
red-curtained room, where floor and ceiling shone like polished
ivory, and the mirrors suddenly blossomed into rosy-cheeked
boys as far as the eye could reach.

They had caviare now, and salmagundi, and sausage and
cheese, besides salad and fruit and biscuit and cake. How the
boys could partake of such a medley was a mystery to Ben; for
the salad was sour, and the cake was sweet; the fruit was dainty,
and the salmagundi heavy with onions and fish. But, while he
was wondering, he made a hearty meal, and was soon absorbed
in deciding which he really preferred, the coffee or the anisette
cordial. It was delightful, too, this taking one's food from
dishes of frosted silver and liqueur glasses from which Titania
herself might have sipped. The young gentleman afterward
wrote to his mother that pretty and choice as things were at
home, he had never known what cut glass, china, and silver
services were until he visited the Hague.

Of course Peter's sister soon heard of all the boys' adventures.
How they had skated over forty miles and seen rare sights on
the way; how they had lost their purse and found it again;
how one of the party had fallen and given them an excuse for a
grand sail in an ice-boat; how, above all, they had caught a
robber, and so for a second time saved their slippery purse.

"And now, Peter," said the lady, when the story was finished,
"you must write at once to tell the good people of Broek that
your adventures have reached their height—that you and your
fellow-travellers have all been taken prisoners."

The boys looked startled.

"Indeed, I shall do no such thing," laughed Peter; "we must leave to-morrow at noon."

But the sister had already decided differently, and a Holland lady is not to be easily turned from her purpose. In short she held forth such strong temptations, and was so bright and cheerful, and said so many coaxing and unanswerable things, both in English and Dutch, that the boys were all delighted when it was settled that they should remain at the Hague for at least two days.

Next the grand skating-race was talked over. Mevrouw van Gend gladly promised to be present on the occasion—"I shall witness your triumph, Peter," she said, "for you are the fastest skater I ever knew."

Peter blushed and gave a slight cough, as Carl answered for him—

"Ah, Mevrouw, he is swift; but all the Broek boys are fine skaters—even the rag-pickers"—and he thought bitterly of poor Hans.

The lady laughed. "That will make the race all the more exciting," she said; "but I shall wish each of you to be the winner."

At this moment her husband Mynheer van Gend came in, and the enchantment falling upon the boys was complete.

The invisible fairies of the household at once clustered about them, whispering that Jasper van Gend had a heart as young and fresh as their own, and if he loved anything in this world, more than industry, it was sunshine and frolic. They hinted also something about his having a heart full of love and a head full of widsom, and finally gave the boys to understand that when Mynheer said a thing he meant it.

Therefore his frank "Well now, this is pleasant," as he shook hands with them all, made the boys feel quite at home and as happy as squirrels.

There were fine paintings in the drawing-room and exquisite statuary, and portfolios filled with rare Dutch engravings; besides many beautiful and curious things from China and Japan.

The boys felt that it would require a month to examine all the treasures of the apartment.

Ben noticed with pleasure English books lying upon the table. He saw also, over the carved, upright piano, life-sized portraits of William of Orange and his English queen—a sight that, for a time, brought England and Holland side by side in his heart. William and Mary have left a halo round the English throne to this day—he the truest patriot that ever served an adopted country, she the noblest wife that ever sat upon a British throne, up to the time of Victoria and Albert the Good. As Ben looked at the pictures, he remembered accounts he had read of King William's visit to the Hague in the winter of 1691. He who sang the Battle of Ivry had not yet told the glowing story of that day, but Ben knew enough of it to fancy that he could almost hear the shouts of the delighted populace as he looked from the portraits to the street, which at this moment was aglow with a bonfire, kindled in a neighbouring square.

That royal visit was one never to be forgotten. For two years William of Orange had been monarch of a foreign land, his head working faithfully for England, but his whole heart yearning for Holland. Now, when he sought its shores once more, the entire nation bade him welcome. Multitudes flocked to the Hague to meet him—"many thousands came sliding or skating along the frozen canals from Amsterdam, Rotterdam, Leyden, Haarlem, Delft."[1] All day long the festivities of the capital were kept up, the streets were gorgeous with banners, evergreen arches, trophies, and mottoes of welcome and emblems of industry. William saw the deeds of his ancestors and scenes of his own past life depicted on banners and tapestries along the streets. At night superb fireworks were displayed upon the ice. Its glassy surface was like a mirror. Sparkling fountains of light sprang up from below to meet the glittering cascades leaping upon it. Then a feathery fire of crimson and green shook millions of rubies and emeralds into the ruddy depths of the ice; and all this time the people were shouting, "God bless William of Orange! long live the king!" They were half mad

[1] Macaulay's *History of England.*

with joy and enthusiasm. William, their own prince, their stadtholder, had become the ruler of three kingdoms; he had been victorious in council and in war, and now in his hour of greatest triumph had come as a simple guest to visit them. The king heard their shouts with a beating heart. It is a great thing to be beloved by one's country. His English courtiers complimented him upon his reception. "Yes," said he, "but the shouting is nothing to what it would have been if Mary had been with me."

While Ben was looking at the portraits, Mynheer van Gend was giving the boys an account of a recent visit to Antwerp. As it was the birthplace of Quentin Matsys, the blacksmith, who for love of an artist's daughter studied until he became a great painter, the boys asked their host if he had seen any of Matsys' works.

"Yes, indeed," he replied, "and excellent they are. His famous triptych in a chapel of the Antwerp cathedral, with the Descent from the Cross on the centre panel, is especially fine; but I confess I was more interested in his well."

"What well, Mynheer?" asked Ludwig.

"One in the heart of the city, near this same cathedral, whose lofty steeple is of such delicate workmanship that the French Emperor said it reminded him of Mechlin lace. The well is covered with a gothic canopy surmounted by the figure of a knight in full armour. It is all of metal, and proves that Matsys was an artist at the forge as well as at the easel; indeed, his great fame is mainly derived from his miraculous skill as an artificer in iron."

Next, Mynheer showed the boys some exquisite Berlin castings, which he had purchased in Antwerp. They were *iron jewellery*, and very delicate—beautiful medallions designed from rare paintings, bordered with fine tracery and open work—worthy, he said, of being worn by the fairest lady of the land. Consequently the necklace was handed, with a bow and a smile, to the blushing Mevrouw van Gend.

Something in the lady's aspect, as she bent her bright young face over the gift, caused Mynheer to add earnestly—

"I can read your thoughts, sweetheart."

She looked up in playful defiance.

"Ah! now I am sure of them. You were thinking of those noble-hearted women, but for whom Prussia might have fallen. I know it by that proud light in your eye."

"The proud light in my eye plays me false, then," she answered; "I had no such grand matter in my mind. To confess the simple truth, I was only thinking how lovely this necklace would be with my blue brocade."

"So! so!" exclaimed the rather crest-fallen spouse.

"But I *can* think of the other, Jasper, and it will add a deeper value to your gift. You remember the incident, do you not, Peter—how, when the French were invading Prussia, and for lack of means the country was unable to defend itself against the enemy, the women turned the scale by pouring their plate and jewels into the public treasury?"

"Aha!" thought Mynheer, as he met his vrouw's kindling glance. "The proud light is there now, in earnest."

Peter remarked maliciously that the women had still proved true to their vanity on that occasion, for jewellery they would have. If gold or silver were wanted by the kingdom, they would relinquish it and use iron, but they could not do without their ornaments.

"What of that?" said the vrouw, kindling again. "It is no sin to love beautiful things, if you adapt your material to circumstances. All *I* have to say is, the women saved their country, and, indirectly, introduced a very important branch of manufacture. Is not that so, Jasper?"

"Of course it is, sweetheart," said Mynheer; "but Peter needs no word of mine to convince him that all the world over, women have never been found wanting in their country's hour of trial, though (bowing to Mevrouw) his own countrywomen stand foremost in the records of female patriotism and devotion."

Then turning to Ben, the host talked with him in English of the fine old Belgian city. Among other things, he told the origin of its name. Ben had been taught that Antwerp was derived from *ae'nt werf* (on the wharf), but Mynheer van Gend gave him a far more interesting derivation.

It appears that about three thousand years ago, a great giant, named Antigonus, lived on the river Scheld, on the site of the present city of Antwerp. This giant claimed half the merchandise of all navigators who passed his castle. Of course some were inclined to oppose this simple regulation. In such cases, Antigonus, by way of teaching them to practise better manners next time, cut off and threw into the river the right hands of the merchants. Thus hand-werpen (or hand-throwing) changed to Antwerp, came to be the name of the place. The escutcheon or arms of the city has two hands upon it : what better proof than this could one have of the truth of the story, especially when one wishes to believe it !

The giant was finally conquered and thrown into the Scheld by a hero called Brabo, who in turn gave a name to the district known as Brabant. Since then the Dutch merchants have travelled the river in peace ; but I, for one, thank old Antigonus for giving the city so romantic an origin.

When Mynheer van Gend had related in two languages this story of Antwerp, he was tempted to tell other legends—some in English, some in Dutch—and so the moments, borne upon the swift shoulders of gnomes and giants, glided rapidly away toward bedtime.

It was hard to break up so pleasant a party, but the Van Gend household moved with the regularity of clockwork. There was no lingering at the threshold when the cordial "Good-night !" was spoken. Even while our boys were mounting the stairs, the invisible household fairies again clustered around them, whispering that system and regularity had been chief builders of the master's prosperity.

Beautiful chambers with three beds in them were not to be found in this mansion. Some of the rooms contained two, but each visitor slept alone. Before morning, the motto of the party evidently was, "every boy his own chrysalis," and Peter, at least, was not sorry to have it so.

Tired as he was, Ben, after noting a curious bell-rope in the corner, began to examine his bed-clothes. Each article filled him with astonishment — the exquisitely fine pillow-spread trimmed with costly lace, and embroidered with a gorgeous crest and initial, the *dekbed* cover (a great silk bag, large as the bed, stuffed with swan's down), and the pink satin quilts, embroidered with garlands of flowers. He could scarcely sleep for thinking what a queer little bed it was, so comfortable and pretty, too, with all its queerness. In the morning he examined the top coverlet with care, for he wished to send home a description of it in his next letter. It was a Japanese spread, marvellous in texture as well as in its variety of brilliant colouring, and worth, as Ben afterwards learned, not less than fifty guineas.

The floor was of polished wooden mosaic, nearly covered with a rich carpet, bordered with thick, black fringe. Another room displayed a margin of satin-wood around the carpet. Hung with tapestry, its walls of crimson silk were topped with a gilded cornice which shot down gleams of light far into the polished floor.

Over the doorway of the room in which Jacob and Ben slept was a bronze stork, who, with outstretched neck, held a lamp to light the guests into the apartment. Between the two narrow beds of carved white-wood and ebony, stood the household treasure of the Van Gends, a massive oaken chair, upon which the Prince of Orange had once sat during a council meeting. Opposite stood a quaintly carved clothes-press, waxed and polished to the utmost, and filled with precious stores of linen ; beside it a table holding a large Bible, whose great golden clasps looked poor compared with its solid, ribbed binding, made to outlast six generations.

There was a ship model on the mantelshelf, and over it hung an old portrait of Peter the Great, who, you know, once gave the dockyard cats of Holland a fine chance to look at a king, which is one of the special prerogatives of cats. Peter, though Czar of Russia, was not too proud to work as a common shipwright in the dockyards of Saardam and Amsterdam, that he might be able to introduce among his countrymen Dutch improvements in shipbuilding. It was this willingness to be thorough in even the smallest beginnings that earned for him the title of Peter the Great.

Peter the little (comparatively speaking) was up first the next morning; knowing the punctual habits of his brother-in-law, he took good care that none of the boys should oversleep themselves. A hard task he found it to wake Jacob Poot; but, after pulling that young gentleman out of bed, and, with Ben's help, dragging him about the room for awhile, he succeeded in arousing him.

While Jacob was dressing, and moaning within him, because the felt slippers, provided him as a guest, were too tight for his swollen feet, Peter wrote to inform their friends at Broek of the safe arrival of his party at the Hague. He also begged his mother to send word to Hans Brinker, that Dr. Boekman had not yet reached Leyden, but that a letter containing Hans' message had been left at the hotel where the doctor always lodged during his visits to the city. "Tell him, also," wrote Peter, "that I shall call there again as I pass through Leyden." The poor boy seemed to feel sure that "the meester" would hasten to save his father, but we, who know the gruff old gentleman better, may be confident he will do no such thing. It would be a kindness to send a visiting physician from Amsterdam to the cottage at once, if Jufrouw[1] Brinker will consent to receive any but the great king of the meesters, as Dr. Boekman certainly is.

"You know, mother," added Peter, "that I have always considered sister Van Gend's house as rather quiet and lonely; but I assure you, it is not so now. Sister says, our presence has warmed it for the whole winter. Brother Van Gend is very kind to us all. He says we make him wish that he had a houseful of boys of his own. He has promised to let us ride on his noble black horses. They are gentle as kittens, he says, if one have but a firm touch at the rein. Ben, according to

[1] In Holland, women of the lower grades of society do not take the title of Mrs. (or Mevrouw) when they marry, as with us. They assume their husband's name, but are still called Miss Jufvrouw, pronounced Yuffrow.

Jacob's account, is a glorious rider, and your son Peter is not a very bad hand at the business; so we two are to go out together this morning mounted like knights of old. After we return, brother Van Gend says he will lend Jacob his English pony and obtain three extra horses; and all of the party are to trot about the city, in a grand cavalcade, led on by him. He will ride the black horse which father sent him from Friesland. My sister's pretty roan, with the long white tail, is lame, and she will ride none other; else she would accompany us. I could scarce close my eyes last night after sister told me of the plan. Only the thought of poor Hans Brinker and his sick father checked me—but for that I could have sung for joy. Ludwig has given us a name already—the Broek Cavalry. We flatter ourselves that we shall make an imposing appearance, especially in single file. . . ."

The Broek Cavalry were not disappointed. Mynheer van Gend readily procured good horses; and all the boys could ride, though none were as perfect horsemen (or horseboys) as Peter and Ben. They saw the Hague to their hearts' content; and the Hague saw them—expressing its approbation, loudly, through the mouths of small boys and cart-dogs; silently, through bright eyes that, not looking very deeply into things, shone as they looked at the handsome Carl, and twinkled with fun as a certain portly youth with shaking cheeks rode past, "bumpetty, bumpetty, bump!"

On their return, the boys pronounced the great porcelain stove in the family sitting-room a decidedly useful piece of furniture, for they could gather round it and get warm without burning their noses or bringing on chilblains. It was so very large that, though hot nowhere, it seemed to send out warmth by the houseful. Its pure white sides and polished brass rings made it a pretty object to look upon, notwithstanding the fact that our ungrateful Ben, while growing thoroughly warm and comfortable beside it, concocted a satirical sentence for his next letter, to the effect that a stove in Holland must of course resemble a great tower of snow, or it wouldn't be in keeping with the oddity of the country.

To describe all the boys saw and did on that day and the next would render this little book a formidable volume indeed. They visited the brass-cannon foundry, saw the liquid fire poured into moulds, and watched the smiths who, half-naked, stood in the shadow, like demons playing with flame. They admired the grand public buildings and massive private houses, the elegant streets and noble Bosch—pride of all beauty-loving Hollanders. The palace with its brilliant mosaic floors, its frescoed ceilings and gorgeous ornaments, filled Ben with delight; he was surprised that some of the churches were so very plain—elaborate sometimes in external architecture, but bare and bleak within, with their blank, white-washed walls.

If there were no printed record, the churches of Holland would almost tell her story. I will not enter into the subject here, except to say that Ben—who had read of her struggles and wrongs, and of the terrible retribution she from time to time dealt forth—could scarcely tread a Holland town without mentally leaping horror-stricken over the bloody stepping-stones of its history. He could not forget Philip of Spain nor the Duke of Alva even while rejoicing in the prosperity that followed the Liberation. He looked in the meekest of Dutch eyes, for something of the fire that once lit the haggard faces of those desperate, lawless men, who, wearing with pride their title of "Beggars," which their oppressors had mockingly cast upon them, became the terror of land and sea. In Haarlem, he had wondered that the air did not still resound with the cries of Alva's three thousand victims. In Leyden, his heart had swelled in sympathy as he thought of the long procession of scarred and famished creatures who, after the siege, with Adrian van der Werf at their head, tottered to the great church to sing a glorious anthem because Leyden was free! He remembered that this was even before they had tasted the bread brought by the Dutch ships. They would praise God first, then eat. Thousands of trembling voices were raised in glad thanksgiving. For a moment, it swelled higher and higher—then suddenly changed to sobbing—not one of all the multitude could sing another note. But who shall say that the anthem, even to its very end, was not heard in heaven !

Here, in the Hague, other thoughts came to Ben. Of how Holland in later years unwillingly put her head under the French yoke, and how, galled and lashed past endurance, she had resolutely jerked it out again. He liked her for that. What nation of any spirit, thought he, could be expected to stand such work, paying all her wealth into a foreign treasury, and yielding up the flower of her youth under foreign conscription. It was not so very long ago, either, since English guns had been heard booming close by in the German Ocean ; well—all the fighting was over at last. Holland was a snug little monarchy now in her own right, and Ben, for one, was glad of it. Arrived at this charitable conclusion, he was prepared to enjoy to the utmost all the wonders of her capital ; he quite delighted Mynheer van Gend with his hearty and intelligent interest—so, in fact did all the boys, for a merrier, more observant party never went sight-seeing.

CHAPTER XXVIII

THROUGH THE HAGUE

THE picture gallery in the Maurits Huis,[1] one of the finest in the world, seemed only to have flashed by the boys during a two hours' visit, so much was there to admire and examine. As for the Royal Cabinet of curiosities, in the same building, they felt that they had but glanced at it, though they were there nearly half-a-day. It seemed to them that Japan had poured all her treasures within it walls. For a long period Holland, always foremost, in commerce, was the only nation allowed to have any intercourse with Japan. One can well forego a journey to that country if he can but visit the Museum at the Hague.

Room after room is filled with collections from the Hermit

---

[1] A building erected by Prince Maurice of Nassau.

Empire—costumes peculiar to various ranks and pursuits, articles of ornament, household utensils, weapons, armour, and surgical instruments. There is also an ingenious Japanese model of the island of Desina, the Dutch factory in Japan. It appears almost as the island itself would if seen through a reversed opera-glass, and makes one feel like a Gulliver coming unexpectedly upon a Japanese Lilliput. There you see hundreds of people in native costumes, standing, kneeling, stooping, reaching —all at work, or pretending to be—and their dwellings, even their very furniture, spread out before you, plain as day. In another room a huge tortoise-shell baby-house, fitted up in Dutch style and inhabited by dignified Dutch dolls, stands ready to tell you at a glance how people lived in Holland.

Gretel, Hilda, Katrinka, even the proud Rychie Korbes, would have been delighted with this; but Peter and his gallant band passed it by without a glance. The war implements had the honour of detaining them for an hour—such clubs, murderous krits or daggers, fire-arms, and about all, such wonderful Japanese swords, quite capable of performing the accredited Japanese feat of cutting a man in two at a single stroke!

There were Chinese and other oriental curiosities in the collection. Native historical relics, too, upon which our young Dutchmen gazed very soberly, though they were secretly proud to show them to Ben.

There was a model of the cabin at Saardam in which Peter the Great lived during his short career as a shipbuilder. Also, wallets and bowls—once carried by the " Beggar " Confederates, who, uniting under the Prince of Orange, had freed Holland from the tyranny of Spain; the sword of Admiral Van Speyk, who about ten years before had perished in voluntarily blowing up his own ship; and Van Tromp's armour, with the marks of bullets upon it. Jacob looked around, hoping to see the broom which the plucky admiral fastened to his mast-head—but it was not there. The waistcoat which William Third [1] of England

---

[1] William, Prince of Orange, who became King of England, was a great-grandson of William the Silent, Prince of Orange, who was murdered by Geraerts (or Gerard), July 10, 1584.

wore during the last days of his life possessed great interest for
Ben; and one and all gazed with a mixture of reverence and
horror-worship at the identical clothing worn by William the
Silent when he was murdered at Delft by Balthazar Geraerts.
A tawny leather doublet and plain surcoat of grey cloth, a soft
felt hat, and a high neck-ruff, from which hung one of the
" Beggars' " medals—these were not in themselves very princely
objects, though the doublet had a tragic interest from its dark
stains and bullet-holes.   Ben could readily believe, as he
looked upon the garments, that the Silent Prince, true to his
greatness of character, had been exceedingly simple in his attire.
His aristocratic prejudices were, however, decidedly shocked
when Lambert told him of the way in which William's bride
first entered the Hague.

"The beautiful Louisa de Coligny, whose father and former
husband both had fallen at the massacre of St. Bartholomew,
was coming to be fourth wife to the Prince, and of course,"
said Lambert, "we Hollanders were too gallant to allow the
lady to enter the town on foot.   No, sir, we sent (or rather my
ancestors did) a clean, open post-waggon to meet her, with a
plank across it for her to sit upon ! "

"Very gallant, indeed ! " exclaimed Ben, with almost a sneer
in his polite laugh, "and she the daughter of an Admiral of
France."

"Was she ?   Upon my word I had nearly forgotten that.
But, you see, Holland had very plain ways in the good old
time ; in fact, we are a very simple, frugal people to this day.
The Van Gend establishment is a decided exception, you know."

" A very agreeable exception, I think," said Ben.

"Certainly, certainly.   But, between you and me, Mynheer
van Gend, though he has wrought his own fortunes, can afford
to be magnificent, and yet be frugal."

"Exactly so," said Ben, profoundly ; at the same time stroking his upper lip and chin, which latterly he believed had been
showing delightful and unmistakable signs of coming dignities.

While tramping on foot through the city, Ben often longed for
a good English side-walk.   Here, as in the other towns, there was

no curb, no raised pavement for foot-travellers; but the streets were clean and even, and all vehicles were kept scrupulously within a certain tract. Strange to say, there were nearly as many sleds as waggons to be seen, though there was not a particle of snow. The sleds went scraping over the bricks or cobble-stones; some provided with an apparatus in front for sprinkling water to diminish the friction, and some rendered less musical by means of a dripping oil-rag, which the driver occasionally applied to the runners.

Ben was surprised at the noiseless way in which Dutch labourers do their work. Even around the warehouses and docks there was no bustle, no shouting from one to another. A certain twitch of the pipe, or turn of the head, or, at most, a raising of the hand, seemed to be all the signal necessary. Entire loads of cheeses or herrings are pitched from cart or canal-boat into the warehouses without a word; but the passer-by must take his chance of being pelted, for a Dutchman seldom looks before or behind him while engaged at work.

Poor Jacob Poot, who seemed destined to bear all the mishaps of the journey, was knocked nearly breathless by a great cheese, which a fat Dutchman was throwing to a fellow-labourer; but he recovered himself, and passed on without evincing the least indignation.

Ben professed great sympathy on the occasion, but Jacob insisted that it was "notting."

"Then why did you screw your face so when it hit you?"

"What for screw mine face," repeated Jacob, soberly, "vy, it vash de—de "——

"The what?" insisted Ben, maliciously.

"Vy, de—de—vat you call dis, vat you taste mit de nose?"

Ben laughed.

"Oh, you mean the smell."

"Yesh. Dat ish it," said Jacob, eagerly—"it wash de shmell. I draw mine face for dat!"

"Ha! ha!" roared Ben, "that's a good one. A Dutch boy smell a cheese. You can never make me believe *that*!"

"Vell, it ish no matter," replied Jacob, trudging on beside

Ben in perfect good humour—"vait till you hit mit cheese—
dat ish all."

Soon he added pathetically—"Penchamin, I no likes be call
Tutch—dat ish no goot. I bees a Hollander."

Just as Ben was apologising, Lambert hailed him,

"Hold fast! Ben. Here is the Fish Market. There is not
much to be seen at this season. But we can take a look at
the storks if you wish."

Ben knew that storks were held in peculiar reverence in
Holland, and that the bird figured upon the arms of the capital.
He had noticed cart-wheels placed upon the roofs of Dutch
cottages to entice storks to settle upon them; he had seen
their huge nests, too, on many a thatched gable roof from
Broek to the Hague. But it was winter now. The nests were
empty. No greedy birdlings opened their mouths—or rather
their heads—at the approach of a great white-winged thing,
with outstretched neck and legs, bearing a dangling something
for their breakfast. The long-bills were far away, picking up
food on African shores; and before they would return in the
spring, Ben's visit to the land of dykes would be over.

Therefore he pressed eagerly forward, as Van Mounen led
the way through the fish-market, anxious to see if storks in
Holland were anything like the melancholy specimens he had
seen in the Zoological Gardens of London.

It was the same old story. A tamed bird is a sad bird,
say what you will. These storks lived in a sort of kennel,
chained by the feet like felons, though supposed to be honoured
by being kept at the public expense. In summer they were
allowed to walk about the market, where the fish-stalls were
like so many free dining-saloons to them. Untasted delicacies
in the form of raw fish and butcher's offals, lay about their
kennels now, but the city-guests preferred to stand upon one
leg, curving back their long neck, and leaning their head
sidewise, in a blinking reverie. How gladly they would have
changed their petted state for the busy life of some hard-
working stork mother, or father, bringing up a troublesome
family on the roof of a rickety old building, where flapping

windmills frightened them half to death every time they
ventured forth on a frolic.

Ben soon made up his mind, and rightly, too, that the
Hague, with its fine streets and public parks shaded with
elms, was a magnificent city. The prevailing costume was
like that of London or Paris, and his British ears were many
a time cheered by the music of British words. The shops
were different in many respects from those on Oxford Street
and the Strand, but they often were illumined by a printed
announcement that English was "spoken within." Others
proclaimed themselves to have London Stout for sale—and
one actually promised to regale its customers with ENGLISH
ROAST BEEF.

Over every possible shop-door was the never-failing placard,
"Tabak te Koop" (tobacco to be sold). Instead of coloured
glass globes in the windows, or high jars of leeches, the drug-
stores had a gaping Turk's head at the entrance—or, if the
establishment were particularly fine, a wooden mandarin, entire,
indulging in a full yawn.

Some of these queer faces amused Ben exceedingly; they
seemed to have just swallowed a dose of physic; but Van
Mounen declared he could not see anything funny about
them. A druggist showed his sense by putting a *Gaper*
before his door, so that his place could be known at once as
an "apotheek," and that was all there was about it.

Another thing attracted Ben—the milkmen's carts. These
were small affairs, filled with shiny brass kettles, or stone
jars, and drawn by dogs. The milkman walked meekly
beside his cart, keeping his dog in order, and delivering the
milk to customers. Certain fish dealers had dog-carts also,
and when a herring-dog chanced to meet a milk-dog, he
invariably put on airs and growled as he passed them. Sometimes a milk-dog would recognise an acquaintance before
another milk-cart across the street, and then how the kettles
would rattle, especially if they were empty! Each dog would
give a bound, and, never caring for his master's whistle, insist
upon meeting the other half-way. Sometimes they contented

themselves with an inquisitive sniff, but, generally, the smaller
dog made an affectionate snap at the larger one's ear, or a
friendly tussle was engaged in by way of exercise. Then wo
to the milk kettles, and wo to the dogs !

The whipping over, each dog, expressing his feelings as best
he could, would trot leisurely back to his work.

If some of these animals were eccentric in their ways, others
were remarkably well-behaved. In fact, there was a school for
dogs in the city, established expressly for training them. Ben
probably saw some of its graduates. Many a time he noticed a
span of barkers trotting along the street with all the dignity of
horses, obeying the slightest hint of the man walking briskly
beside them. Sometimes, when their load was delivered, the
dealer would jump in the cart, and have a fine drive to his
home beyond the gates of the city; and sometimes, I regret to
say, a patient vrouw would trudge beside the cart, with fish-
basket upon her head and a child in her arms, while her lord
enjoyed his drive, carrying no heavier burden than a stumpy
clay pipe, the smoke of which mounted lovingly into her face.

CHAPTER XXIX

A DAY OF REST AND HOMEWARD BOUND

THE sight-seeing came to an end at last, and so did our
boys' visit to the Hague. They had spent three happy days
and nights with the Van Gends, and, strange to say, had not
once, in all that time, put on skates. The third day had indeed
been one of rest. The noise and bustle of the city was hushed;
sweet Sunday bells sent blessed, tranquil thoughts into their
hearts. Ben felt, as he listened to their familiar music, that
the Christian world is one, after all, however divided by sects
and differences it may be. As the clock speaks every one's
native language in whatever land it may strike the hour, so
church bells are never foreign if our hearts but listen.

On Monday morning, bright and early, our boys bade farewell to their kind entertainers and started on their homeward journey.

They were so happy to be on skates once more, so impatient to dart at once into the very heart of Broek, that they spun and wheeled about like crazy fellows, relieving themselves, meantime, by muttering something about " Peter and donder " not worth translating.

Even Lambert and Ben, who had been waiting at the street corner began to grow impatient.

The captain joined them at last ; they were soon on the canal with the rest.

" Hurry up, Peter," growled Ludwig, " we're freezing by inches—there ! I knew you'd be the last after all to get on your skates.

" Did you ? " said his brother, looking up with an air of deep interest—" a clever boy ! "

Ludwig laughed, but tried to look cross, as he said, " I'm in earnest, anyhow. We must get home some time this year."

" Now, boys," cried Peter, springing up, as he fastened the last buckle. " There's a clear way before us ! We will imagine it's the grand race. Ready ! One—two—three—START ! "

I assure you very little was said for the first half hour. They were six Mercuries skimming the ice. In plain English they went like lightning—no, that is imaginary too. The fact is, one cannot decide what to say when half-a-dozen boys are whizzing past at such a rate. I can only tell you that each did his best, flying, with bent body, and eager eyes, in and out among the placid skaters on the canal, until the very guard shouted to them to " hold up ! " This only served to send them onward with a two-boy power that startled all beholders.

But the laws of inertia are stronger even than canal-guards.

After a while Jacob slackened his speed—then Ludwig—then Lambert—then Carl.

They soon halted to take a long breath, and finally found themselves standing in a group gazing after Peter and Ben, who were still racing in the distance as if their lives were at stake.

"It is very evident," said Lambert, as he and his three companions started on again, "that neither of them will give up until he can't help it."

"What foolishness!" growled Carl, "to tire themselves at the beginning of the journey; but they're racing in earnest, that's certain. Hollo! Peter's flagging!"

"Not so!" cried Ludwig, "catch him being beaten!"

"Ha! ha!" sneered Carl. "I tell you, boy, Benjamin is ahead."

Now if Ludwig disliked anything in this world, it was to be called a boy—probably because he was nothing else. He grew indignant at once.

"Humph, what are *you*, I wonder? There sir! *now* look and see if Peter isn't ahead!"

"*I* think he *is*," interposed Lambert, "but I can't quite tell at this distance."

"*I* think he isn't!" retorted Carl.

Jacob was growing anxious—he always abhorred an argument—so he said in a coaxing tone, "Don't quarrel; don't quarrel!"

"Don't quarrel!" mocked Carl, looking back at Jacob as he skated. "Who's quarrelling? Poot, you're a goose!"

"I can't help that," was Jacob's meek reply. "See! they are nearing the turn of the canal."

"*Now* we can see!" cried Ludwig, in great excitement. "Peter will make it first, I know."

"He can't, for Ben is ahead!" insisted Carl. "Gunst! That ice-boat will run over him. No! he is clear! They're a couple of geese anyhow. Hurrah! they're at the turn. Who's ahead?"

"PETER!" cried Ludwig, joyfully.

"Good for the captain!" shouted Lambert and Jacob.

And Carl condescended to mutter—

"It *is* Peter, after all. I thought, all the time, that head fellow was Ben."

This turn in the canal had evidently been their goal, for the two racers came to a sudden halt after passing it.

Carl said something about being "glad that they had sense enough to stop and rest," and the four boys skated on in silence to overtake their companions.

All the while Carl was secretly wishing that he had kept on with Peter and Ben, as he felt sure he could easily have come out winner. He was a very rapid, though by no means a graceful skater.

Ben was looking at Peter with mingled vexation, admiration, and surprise as the boys drew near.

They heard him saying in English—

"You're a perfect bird on the ice, Peter Van Holp. The first fellow that ever beat me in a fair race, I can tell you!"

Peter, who understood the language better than he could speak it, returned a laughing bow at Ben's compliment, but made no further reply. Possibly he was scant of breath at the time.

"Now, Penchamin, vat you do mit yourself? get so hot as a fire-brick—dat ish no goot," was Jacob's plaintive comment.

"Nonsense!" answered Ben. "This frosty air will cool me soon enough. I am not tired."

"You are beaten, though, my boy," said Lambert in English, "and fairly, too. How will it be, I wonder, on the day of the grand race?"

Ben flushed, and gave a proud, defiant laugh, as if to say—

"This was mere pastime. I'm *determined* to beat then— come what will!"

CHAPTER XXX

BOYS AND GIRLS

BY the time the boys reached the village of Voorhout, which stands near the grand canal, about half-way between the Hague and Haarlem, they were forced to hold a council. The wind, though moderate at first, had grown stronger and stronger, until at last they could hardly skate against it. The weather-vanes through the country had evidently entered into a conspiracy.

"No use trying to face such a blow as this," said Ludwig. "It cuts its way down a man's throat like a knife."

"Keep your mouth shut, then," grunted the affable Carl, who was strong-chested as a young ox; "I'm for keeping on."

"In this case," interposed Peter, "we must consult the weakest of the party rather than the strongest."

The captain's principle was all right, but its application was not flattering to Master Ludwig; shrugging his shoulders, he retorted—

"Who's weak? Not I, for one—but the wind's stronger than any of us. I hope you'll condescend to admit that!"

"Ha! ha!" laughed Van Mounen, who could barely keep his feet; "so it is."

Just then the weather-vanes telegraphed to each other by a peculiar twich—and, in an instant, the gust came. It nearly threw the strong-chested Carl; it almost strangled Jacob, and quite upset Ludwig.

"This settles the question," shouted Peter; "off with your skates. We'll go into Voorhout."

At Voorhout they found a little inn with a big yard. The yard was well bricked, and, better than all, was provided with a complete set of skittles, so our boys soon turned the detention into a frolic. The wind was troublesome even in that sheltered quarter, but they were on good standing ground, and did not mind it.

First a hearty dinner; then the game. With pins as long as their arms, and balls as big as their heads, plenty of strength left for rolling, and a clean sweep of sixty yards for the strokes, no wonder they were happy.

That night Captain Peter and his men slept soundly. No prowling robber came to disturb them; and, as they were distributed in separate rooms, they did not even have a bolster-battle in the morning.

Such a breakfast as they ate! The landlord looked frightened. When he had asked them where they "belonged," he made up his mind that the Broek people starved their children. It was a shame. "Such fine young gentlemen, too!"

Fortunately the wind had tired itself out, and fallen asleep in the great sea-cradle beyond the Dunes. There were signs of snow; otherwise the weather was fine.

It was mere child's-play for the well-rested boys to skate to Leyden. Here they halted a while, for Peter had an errand at the "Golden Eagle." He left the city with a lightened heart. Dr. Boekman had been at the hotel, read the note containing Hans' message, and departed for Broek.

"I cannot say it was your letter sent him off so soon," explained the landlord. "Some rich lady in Broek was taken bad very sudden, and he was sent for in haste."

Peter turned pale.

"What was the name?" he asked.

"Indeed, it went in one ear, and out of the other, for all I hindered it. Plague to people who can't see a traveller in comfortable lodgings, but they must whisk him off before one can breathe."

"A lady in Broek, did you say?"

"Yes," very gruffly; "any other business young master?"

"No, mine host, except that I and my comrades here would like a bite of something, and a drink of hot coffee."

"Ah," said the landlord, sweetly, "a bite you shall have, and coffee too, the finest in Leyden. Walk up to the stove, my masters. Now I think again—that was a widow lady—from Rotterdam, I think they said—visiting at one Van Stoepel's, if I mistake not."

"Ah!" said Peter, greatly relieved. "They live in the white house by the Schlossen Mill. Now, Mynheer, the coffee please."

"What a goose I was," thought he, as the party left the Golden Eagle, "to feel so sure it was my mother—but she may be somebody's mother, poor woman, for all that. Who can she be, I wonder?"

There were not many upon the canal that day, between Leyden and Haarlem. However, as the boys neared Amster dam, they found themselves once more in the midst of a moving throng. The big *Ysbreker*[1] had been at work for the first time that season, but there was any amount of skating ground left yet.

"Three cheers for home!" cried Van Mounen, as they came in sight of the great western dock (Westelijk Dok). "Hurrah! hurrah!" shouted one and all, "Hurrah! hurrah!"

This trick of cheering was an importation among our party. Lambert Van Mounen had brought it from England. As they always gave it in English, it was considered quite an exploit, and, when circumstances permitted, always enthusiastically performed, to the sore dismay of their quiet-loving countrymen.

Therefore their arrival at Amsterdam created a great sensation, especially among the small boys on the wharfs.

The Y was crossed. They were on the Broek canal.

Lambert's home was reached first.

"Good-bye, boys!" he cried, as he left them; "we've had the greatest frolic ever known in Holland!"

"So we have. Good-bye, Van Mounen," answered the boys.

"Good-bye!"

Peter hailed him. "I say, Van Mounen, the classes begin to-morrow."

"I know it. Our holiday is over. Good-bye again."

"Good-bye!"

Broek came in sight. Such meetings! Katrinka was on the canal. Carl was delighted. Hilda was there. Peter felt rested in an instant. Rychie was there. Ludwig and Jacob nearly knocked each other over in their eagerness to shake hands with her.

Dutch girls are modest and generally quiet; but they have very glad eyes. For a few moments it was hard to decide whether Hilda, Rychie, or Katrinka felt the most happy.

---

[1] Ice-breaker—a heavy machine armed with iron spikes for breaking the ice as it is dragged along. Some of the small ones are worked by men, but the large ones are drawn by horses, sixty or seventy of which are sometimes attached to one Ysbreker.

Annie Bouman was also on the canal, looking even prettier than the other maidens in her graceful peasant's costume. But she did not mingle with Rychie's party. Neither did she look unusually happy.

The one she liked most to see was not among the new comers. Indeed, he was not upon the canal at all. She had not been near Broek before since the Eve of St. Nicholas, for she was staying with her sick grandmother in Amsterdam, and had been granted a brief resting-spell, as the grandmother called it, because she had been such a faithful little nurse night and day.

Annie had devoted her resting-spell to skating with all her might toward Broek, and back again, in the hope of meeting her mother, or some of her family, on the canal; or, it might be, Gretel Brinker—not one of them had she seen—and she must hurry back, without even catching a glimpse of her mother's cottage—for the poor helpless grandmother, she knew, was by this time moaning for some one to turn her upon her cot.

"Where can Gretel be?" thought Annie, as she flew over the ice, "she can almost always steal a few moments from her work at this time of day—poor Gretel—what a dreadful thing it must be to have a dull father—I should be woefully afraid of him, I know. So strong, and yet so strange!"

Annie had not heard of his illness. Dame Brinker and her affairs received but little notice from the people of the place.

If Gretel had not been known as a goose-girl, she might have had more friends among the peasantry of the neighbourhood. As it was, Annie Bouman was the only one who did not feel ashamed to avow herself by word and deed the companion of Gretel and Hans.

When the neighbours' children laughed at her for keeping such poor company, she would simply flush when Hans was ridiculed, or laugh in a careless, disdainful way; but to hear little Gretel abused always awakened her wrath.

"Goose girl! indeed!" she would say; "I can tell you any

of you are fitter for the work than she. My father often said last summer that it troubled him to see such a bright-eyed, patient little maiden tending geese. Humph! She would not harm them, as you would, Janzoon Kolp; and she would not tread upon them, as you might, Kate Wouters."

This would be pretty sure to start a laugh at the clumsy, ill-natured Kate's expense; and Annie would walk loftily away from the group of young gossips. Perhaps some memory of Gretel's assailants crossed her mind as she skated rapidly toward Amsterdam, for her eyes sparkled ominously, and she more than once gave her pretty head a defiant toss. When that mood passed, such a bright, rosy, affectionate look illumined her face, that more than one weary working-man turned to gaze after her, and to wish that he had a glad, contented lass like that for a daughter.

There were five joyous households in Broek that night.

The boys were back safe and sound; and they found all well at home. Even the sick lady at neighbour Van Stoepel's was out of danger.

But the next morning! Ah, how stupidly school-bells will ding-dong! ding-dong! when one is tired.

Ludwig was sure he had never listened to anything so odious. Even Peter felt pathetic on the occasion. Carl said it was a shame for a fellow to have to turn out when his bones were splitting—and Jacob soberly bade Ben "Goot Pye!" and walked off with his satchel as if it weighed a hundred pounds.

CHAPTER XXXI

THE CRISIS

WHILE the boys are nursing their fatigue, we will take a peep into the Brinker cottage.

Can it be that Gretel and her mother have not stirred since we saw them last? That the sick man upon the bed has not

even turned over? It was four days ago, and there is the sad
group just as it was before. No, not precisely the same, for
Raff Brinker is paler; his fever is gone, though he knows
nothing of what is passing. Then, they were alone in the bare,
clear room. Now there is another group in an opposite corner.

Dr. Boekman is there, talking in a low tone with a stout
young man who listens intently. The stout young man is
his student and assistant. Hans is there also. He stands
near the window, respectfully waiting until he shall be accosted.

"You see, Vollenhoven," said Dr. Boekman, "it is a clear
case of "——and here the doctor went off into a queer jumble of
Latin and Dutch that I cannot conveniently translate.

After a while, as Vollenhoven looked at him rather blankly,
the learned man condescended to speak to him in simpler
phrase.

"It is probably like Rip Donderdunck's case," he exclaimed,
in a low mumbling tone. "He fell from the top of Voppelploot's
windmill. After the accident the man was stupid, and finally
became idiotic. In time he lay helpless like yon fellow on the
bed, moaned, too, like him, and kept constantly lifting his hand
to his head. My learned friend, Von Choppem, performed an
operation upon this Dunderdunck, and discovered under the
skull a small dark sac, which pressed upon the brain. This had
been the cause of the trouble. My friend Von Choppem
removed it — a splendid operation! You see, according to
Celsus "——and here the doctor again went off into Latin.

"Did the man live?" asked the assistant, respectfully.

Dr. Boekman scowled. "That is of no consequence. I
believe he died, but why not fix your mind on the grand features
of the case. Consider a moment how "——and he plunged
into Latin mysteries more deeply than ever.

"But, Mynheer," gently persisted the student, who knew
that the doctor would not rise to the surface for hours unless
pulled at once from his favourite depths. "Mynheer, you have
other engagements to-day, three legs in Amsterdam, you
remember, and an eye in Broek, and that tumour up the canal."

"The tumour can wait," said the doctor, reflectively. "That

is another beautiful case—a beautiful case! The woman has not lifted her head from her shoulder for two months—magnificent tumour, sir!"

The doctor by this time was speaking aloud. He had quite forgotten where he was.

Vollenhoven made another attempt.

"This poor fellow on the bed, Mynheer. Do you think you can save him?"

"Ah, indeed, certainly," stammered the doctor, suddenly perceiving that he had been talking rather off the point—"certainly, that is—I hope so"——

"If any one in Holland can, Mynheer," murmured the assistant, with honest bluntness—"it is yourself."

The doctor looked displeased — growled out a tender request for the student to talk less, and beckoned Hans to draw near.

This strange man had a great horror of speaking to women, especially on surgical matters. "One can never tell," he said, "what moment the creatures will scream or faint." Therefore he explained Raff Brinker's case to Hans, and told him what he believed should be done to save the patient.

Hans listened attentively, growing red and pale by turns, and throwing quick, anxious glances toward the bed.

"It may *kill* the father—did you say, Mynheer?" he exclaimed at last, in a trembling whisper.

"It may, my boy. But I have a strong belief that it will cure and not kill. Ah! if boys were not such dunces, I could lay the whole matter before you, but it would be of no use."

Hans looked blank at this compliment.

"It would be of no use," repeated Doctor Boekman, indignantly; "a great operation is proposed—but one might as well do it with a hatchet. The only question asked is—'Will it kill?'"

"The question is *everything* to us, Mynheer," said Hans, with tearful dignity.

Doctor Boekman looked at him in sudden dismay.

"Ah! exactly so. You are right, boy, I am a fool. Good

boy.   One does not wish one's father killed—of course not.
I am a fool."

"Will he die, Mynheer, if this sickness goes on?"

"Humph! this is no new illness.   The same thing growing
worse every instant—pressure on the brain—will take him off
soon like *that*," said the doctor, snapping his fingers.

"And the operation *may* save him," pursued Hans.   "How
soon, Mynheer, can we know?"

Doctor Boekman grew impatient.

"In a day—perhaps, an hour.   Talk with your mother, boy,
and let her decide.   My time is short."

Hans approached his mother; at first, when she looked up
at him, he could not utter a syllable; then turning his eyes
away he said in a firm voice:

"I must speak with the mother alone."

Quick little Gretel, who could not quite understand what
was passing, threw rather an indignant look at Hans, and
walked away.

"Come back, Gretel, and sit down," said Hans, sorrowfully.
She obeyed.

Dame Brinker and her boy stood by the window while the
doctor and his assistant, bending over the bedside, conversed
together in a low tone.   There was no danger of disturbing the
patient.   He appeared like one blind and deaf.   Only his faint,
piteous moans showed him to be a living man.   Hans was
talking earnestly, and in a low voice, for he did not wish his
sister to hear.

With dry, parted lips, Dame Brinker leaned toward him
searching his face, as if suspecting a meaning beyond his words.
Once she gave a quick, frightened sob that made Gretel start,
but, after that, listened calmly.

When Hans ceased to speak, his mother turned, gave one
long, agonised look at her husband, lying there so pale and
unconscious, and threw herself on her knees, beside the bed.

Poor little Gretel! what did all this mean?   She looked
with questioning eyes at Hans; he was standing, but his head
was bent as if in prayer;—at the doctor, he was gently feeling

her father's head, and looked like one examining some curious stone ;—at the assistant ; the man coughed and turned away ;— at her mother ; Ah ! little Gretel, that was the best you could do—to kneel beside her and twine your warm, young arms about her neck—to weep and implore God to listen.

When the mother arose, Doctor Boekman, with a show of trouble in his eyes, asked gruffly, "Well, jufvrouw, shall it be done?"

"Will it pain him, Mynheer?" she asked in a trembling voice.

"I cannot say. Probably not. Shall it be done?"

"It may *cure* him, you said, and—Mynheer, did you tell my boy that?—perhaps—perhaps" she could not finish.

"Yes, jufvrouw, I said the patient might sink under the operation—but we will hope it may prove otherwise"—(he looked at his watch. The assistant moved impatiently toward the window.) "Come, jufvrouw, time presses. Yes or no?"

Hans wound his arm about his mother. It was not his usual way. He even leaned his head against her shoulder.

"The meester awaits an answer," he whispered.

Dame Brinker had long been the head of her house in every sense. Many a time she had been very stern with Hans, ruling him with a strong hand, and rejoicing in her motherly discipline—*now* she felt so weak, so helpless. It was something to feel that firm embrace. There was strength even in the touch of that yellow hair.

She turned to her boy imploringly.

"Oh Hans ! What shall I say?"

"Say what God tells thee, mother," answered Hans, bowing his head.

One quick, questioning prayer to Heaven rose from the mother's heart. The answer came.

She turned toward Doctor Boekman.

"It is right, Mynheer. I consent."

"Humph !" grunted the doctor, as if to say, "You've been long enough about it." Then he conferred a moment with his assistant, who listened with great outward deference, but was inwardly rejoicing at the grand joke he would have to tell his fellow-students. He had actually seen a tear in "old Boekman's" eye.

Meanwhile Gretel looked on in trembling silence—but when she saw the doctor open a leathern case, and take out one sharp, gleaming instrument after another, she sprang forward.

"Oh mother—the poor father meant no wrong. Are they going to *murder* him?"

"I do not know, child," screamed Dame Brinker, looking fiercely at Gretel. "I DO NOT KNOW."

"This will not do, jufvrouw," said Dr. Boekman sternly, and at the same time he cast a quick, penetrating look at Hans; "you and the girl must leave the room. The boy may stay."

Dame Brinker drew herself up in a instant. Her eyes flashed. Her whole countenance was changed. She looked like one who had never wept, never felt a moment's weakness. Her voice was low, but decided. "I stay with my husband, Mynheer."

Doctor Boekman looked astonished. His orders were seldom disregarded in this style. For an instant his eye met hers.

"You may remain, jufvrouw," he said, in an altered voice.

Gretel had already disappeared.

In one corner of the cottage was a small closet where her rough box-like bed was fastened against the wall. None would think of the trembling little creature crouching there in the dark.

Dr. Boekman took off his heavy coat; he filled an earthen basin with water, and placed it near the bed. Then turning to Hans, he asked—

"Can I depend upon you, boy?"

"You can, Mynheer."

"I believe you. Stand at the head, here—your mother may sit at your right—so," and he placed a chair near the cot.

"Remember, jufvrouw, there must be no cries, no fainting."

Dame Brinker answered him with a look.

He was satisfied.

"Now, Vollenhoven."

Oh, that case with the terrible instruments! The assistant

lifted them. Gretel, who had been peering, with brimming eyes, through the crack of the closet door, could remain silent no longer.

She rushed frantically across the apartment, seized her hood, and ran from the cottage.

CHAPTER XXXII

GRETEL AND HILDA

IT was recess hour. At the first stroke of the school-house bell the canal seemed to give a tremendous shout, and grow suddenly alive with boys and girls. The sly thing, shining so quietly under the noonday sun, was a kaleidoscope at heart, and only needed a shake from that great clapper to start it into dazzling changes.

Dozens of gaily-clad children were skating in and out among each other, and all their pent-up merriment of the morning was relieving itself in song and shout and laughter. There was nothing to check the flow of frolic. Not a thought of school-books came out with them into the sunshine. Latin, arithmetic, grammar, all were locked up for an hour in the dingy school-room. The teacher might be a noun if he wished, and a proper one at that, but *they* meant to enjoy themselves. As long as the skating was as perfect as this, it made no difference whether Holland were on the North Pole or the Equator; and as for philosophy, how could they bother themselves about inertia, and gravitation, and such things, when it was as much as they could do to keep from getting knocked over in the commotion.

In the height of the fun, one of the children called out—

"What is that?"

"What? Where?" cried a dozen voices.

"Why, don't you see? That dark thing over there by the idiot's cottage."

"I don't see anything," said one.

"I do!" shouted another; "it's a dog!"

"Where's any dog?" put in a squeaky voice that we have heard before! "it's no such thing—it's a heap of rags."

"Pooh! Voost," retorted another gruffly, "that's about as near the fact as you ever get; it's the goose girl, Gretel, looking for rats."

"Well, what of it?" squeaked Voost; "isn't *she* a bundle of rags, I'd like to know?"

"Ha! ha! Pretty good for you, Voost! You'll get a medal for wit yet, if you keep on."

"You'd get something else, if her brother Hans were here, I'll warrant you would!" said a muffled-up little fellow, with a cold in his head.

As Hans was *not* there, Voost could afford to scout the insinuation.

"Who cares for *him*, little sneezer? I'd fight a dozen like him any day, and you in the bargain."

"You would! would you? I'd like to catch you at it," and, by way of proving his words, the sneezer skated off at the top of his speed.

Just then a general chase after three of the biggest boys of the school was proposed, and friend and foe, frolicsome as ever, were soon united in a common cause.

Only one of all that happy throng remembered the dark little form by the idiot's cottage. Poor, frightened Gretel! She was not thinking of them, though their merry laughter floated lightly toward her, making her feel like one in a dream.

How loud the moans were behind the darkened window; what if those strange men were really killing her father!

The thought made her spring to her feet with a cry of horror.

"Ah, no!" she sobbed, sinking upon the frozen mound of earth where she had been sitting; "mother is there, and Hans. They will care for him. But how pale they were! And even Hans was crying!"

"Why did the cross old meester keep *him*, and send me away?" she thought. "I could have clung to the mother and kissed her. That always makes her stroke my hair and speak gentle, even after she has scolded me. How quiet it is now! Oh, if the father should die! and Hans, and the mother! what *would* I do?" and Gretel, shivering with cold, buried her face in her arms, and cried as if her heart would break.

The poor child had been tasked beyond her strength during the past four days. Through all, she had been her mother's willing little handmaiden, soothing, helping, and cheering the half-widowed woman by day, and watching and praying beside her all the long night. She knew that something terrible and mysterious was taking place at this moment, something that had been too terrible and mysterious for even kind, good Hans to tell.

Then new thoughts came. Why had not Hans told her? It was a shame. It was *her* father as well as his. She was no baby. She had once taken a sharp knife from the father's hand. She had even drawn him away from the mother on that awful night when Hans, big as he was, could not help her. Why then must she be treated like one who could do nothing? Oh, how very still it was!—how bitter, bitter cold! If Annie Bouman had only stayed home instead of going to Amsterdam, it wouldn't be so lonely. How cold her feet were growing; was it the moaning that made her feel as if she were floating in the air?

This would not do; the mother might need her help at any moment.

Rousing herself with an effort, Gretel sat upright, rubbing her eyes and wondering—wondering that the sky was so bright and blue—wondering at the stillness in the cottage—more than all, at the laughter rising and falling in the distance.

Soon she sank down again, the strange medley of thought growing more and more confused in her bewildered brain.

What a strange lip the meester had. How the stork's nest upon the roof seemed to rustle and whisper down to her! How bright those knives were in the leathern case—brighter perhaps than the silver skates. If she had but worn her new jacket she would not shiver so. The new jacket was pretty, the only pretty thing she had ever worn. God had taken care of her father so long, He would do it still, if those two men would but go away. Ah, now the meesters were on the roof, they were clambering to the top—no—it was her mother and Hans—or the storks. It was so dark, who could tell? and the mound rocking, swinging in that strange way. How sweetly the birds were singing. They must be winter birds, for the air was thick with icicles—not one bird, but twenty. Oh! hear them, mother —wake me, mother, for the race. I am so tired with crying, and crying.

A firm hand was laid upon her shoulder.

"Get up, little girl!" cried a kind voice. "This will not do, for you to lie here and freeze."

Gretel slowly raised her head. She was so sleepy that it seemed nothing strange to her that Hilda van Gleck should be leaning over her, looking with kind beautiful eyes into her face. She had often dreamed it before.

But she had never dreamed that Hilda was shaking her roughly, almost dragging her by main force—never dreamed that she heard her saying, "Gretel! Gretel Brinker! you *must* wake!"

This was real. Gretel looked up. Still the lovely delicate young lady was shaking, rubbing, fairly pounding her. It must be a dream. No; there was the cottage, and the stork's nest, and the meester's coach by the canal. She could see them now quite plainly. Her hands were tingling, her feet throbbing. Hilda was forcing her to walk.

At last Gretel began to feel like herself again.

"I have been asleep," she faltered, rubbing her eyes with both hands, and looking very much ashamed.

"Yes, indeed; entirely too much asleep," laughed Hilda, whose lips were very pale; "but. you are well enough now. Lean upon me, Gretel; there, keep moving; you will soon be warm enough to go by the fire. Now let me take you into the cottage."

"Oh! no, no, no, jufvrouw! not in there! The meester is there. He sent me away."

Hilda was puzzled, but she wisely forbore to ask at present for an explanation. "Very well, Gretel; try to walk faster. I saw

you upon the mound some time ago, but I thought you were
playing. That is right—keep moving."

All this time the kind-hearted girl had been forcing Gretel to
walk up and down, supporting her with one arm, and, with the
other, striving as well as she could to take off her own warm
sacque.

Suddenly Gretel suspected her intention.

"Oh, jufvrouw ! jufrvouw !" she cried, imploringly. "*Please*
never think of such a thing as *that*. Oh ! please keep it on.
I am burning all over, jufvrouw ! I really am burning—not
burning exactly, but pins and needles pricking all over me—oh,
jufvrouw ! don't."

The poor child's dismay was so genuine that Hilda hastened
to reasure her.

"Very well, Gretel ; move your arms then—so. Why, your
cheeks are as pink as roses already. I think the meester would
let you in now. He certainly would. Is your father so very
ill ?"

"Ah, jufvrouw !" cried Gretel, weeping afresh, "he is dying,
I think. There are two meesters in with him at this moment,
and the mother has scarce spoken to-day. Can you hear him
moan, jufvrouw ?" she added, with sudden terror ; "the air
buzzes so I cannot hear. He may be dead ! Oh, I do wish I
could hear him ! "

Hilda listened. The cottage was very near, but not a sound
could be heard

Something told her that Gretel was right. She ran to the
window.

"You cannot see there, my lady," sobbed Gretel, eagerly ;
"the mother has oiled paper hanging inside. But at the other
one, in the south end of the cottage, you can look in where the
paper is torn."

Hilda in her anxiety ran round, past the corner where the
low roof was fringed with its loosened thatch.

A sudden thought checked her.

"It is not right for me to peep into another's house in this
way," she said to herself ; then softly calling to Gretel, she

added, in a whisper, "You may look—perhaps he is only sleeping."

Gretel tried to walk briskly toward the spot, but her limbs were trembling. Hilda hastened to her support.

"You are sick yourself, I fear," she said, kindly.

"No, not sick, jufvrouw; but my heart cries all the time now, even when my eyes are as dry as yours. Why, jufvrouw, your eyes are not dry! Are you crying for *us*? Oh, jufvrouw, if God sees you! Oh, I know father will get better now!" And the little creature, even while reaching to look through the tiny window, kissed Hilda's hand again and again.

The sash was sadly patched and broken, a torn piece of paper hung half-way down across it. Gretel's face was pressed to the window.

"Can you see anything?" whispered Hilda, at last.

"Yes; the father lies very still, his head is bandaged, and all their eyes are fastened upon him. Oh, jufvrouw!" almost screamed Gretel, as she started back, and by a quick, dexterous movement shook off her heavy wooden shoes, "I *must* go in to my mother! Will you come with me?"

"Not now, the bell is ringing; I shall come again soon. Good-bye!"

Gretel scarce heard the words. She remembered for many a day afterward the bright, pitying smile on Hilda's face, as she turned away.

CHAPTER XXXIII

THE AWAKENING

AN angel could not have entered the cottage more noiselessly. Gretel, not daring to look at any one, slid softly to her mother's side.

The room was very still. She could hear the old doctor breathe. She could almost hear the sparks as they fell into the ashes on the hearth. The mother's hand was very cold, but a burning spot glowed on her cheek, and her eyes were like a deer's—so bright, so sad, so eager.

At last there was a movement upon the bed, very slight, but enough to cause them all to start. Dr. Boekman leaned eagerly forward.

Another movement. The large hand, so white and soft for a poor man's hand, twitched—then raised itself steadily toward the forehead.

It felt the bandage, not in a restless, crazy way, but with a questioning movement that caused even Dr. Boekman to hold his breath. Then the eyes opened slowly.

"Steady! steady!" said a voice that sounded very strangely to Gretel. "Shift that mat higher, boys! now throw on the clay. The waters are rising fast—no time to——"

Dame Brinker sprang forward like a young panther.

She seized his hands, and leaning over him, cried "Raff, Raff, boy! speak to me!"

"Is it you, Meitje?" he asked, faintly; "I have been asleep—hurt, I think; where is little Hans?"

"Here I am, father!" shouted Hans, half mad with joy.

But the doctor held him back.

"He knows us!" screamed Dame Brinker. "Great God! he knows us. Gretel! Gretel! come, see your father!"

In vain Dr. Boekman commanded "silence!" and tried to force them from the bedside. He could not keep them off.

Hans and his mother laughed and cried together, as they hung over the newly-awakened man. Gretel made no sound, but gazed at them all with glad, startled eyes. Her father was speaking in a faint voice.

"Is the baby asleep, Meitje?"

"The baby!" echoed Dame Brinker. "Oh, Gretel, that is *you*! And he calls Hans 'little Hans.' Ten years asleep! Oh, Mynheer, you have saved us all! He has known nothing for ten years! Children, why don't you thank the meester?"

The good woman was beside herself with joy. Dr. Boekman said nothing; but as his eye met hers, he pointed upward. She understood. So did Hans and Gretel.

With one accord they knelt by the cot, side by side. Dame Brinker felt for her husband's hand even while she was praying. Dr. Boekman's head was bowed; the assistant stood by the hearth with his back toward them.

"Why do you pray?" murmured the father, looking feebly from the bed, as they rose. "Is it God's day?"

It was not Sunday; but his vrouw bowed her head—she could not speak.

"Then we should have a chapter," said Raff Brinker, speaking slowly, and with difficulty. "I do not know how it is. I am very, very weak. Mayhap the minister will read to us."

Gretel lifted the big Dutch Bible from its carved shelf. Dr. Boekman, rather dismayed at being called a minister, coughed and handed the volume to his assistant.

"Read," he muttered; "these people must be kept quiet, or the man will die yet."

When the chapter was finished, Dame Brinker motioned mysteriously to the rest, by way of telling them that her husband was asleep.

"Now, jufvrouw," said the doctor, in a subdued tone, as he drew on his thick woollen mittens, "there must be perfect quiet. You understand. This is truly a most remarkable case. I shall come again to-morrow. Give the patient no food to-day," and bowing hastily, he left the cottage, followed by his assistant.

His grand coach was not far away; the driver had kept the horses moving slowly up and down by the canal nearly all the time the doctor had been in the cottage.

Hans went out also.

"May God bless you, Mynheer!" he said, blushing and trembling; "I can never repay you, but if ——"

"Yes, you can," interrupted the doctor, crossly. "You can use your wits when the patient wakes again. This clacking and snivelling is enough to kill a well man, let alone one lying on the edge of his grave. If you want your father to get well, keep 'em quiet."

So saying, Doctor Boekman, without another word, stalked

off to meet his coach, leaving Hans standing there with eyes and mouth wide open.

Hilda was reprimanded severely that day for returning late to school after recess, and for imperfect recitations.

She had remained near the cottage until she heard Dame Brinker laugh, until she had heard Hans say, "Here I am, father!" and then she had gone back to her lessons. What wonder that she missed them! How could she get a long string of Latin verbs by heart, when her heart did not care a fig for them, but would keep saying to itself, "Oh, I am so glad! I am so glad!"

CHAPTER XXXIV

BONES AND TONGUES

BONES are strange things. One would suppose that they knew nothing at all about school affairs, but they do. Even Jacob Poot's bones, buried as they were in flesh, were sharp in the matter of study hours.

Early on the morning of his return they ached through and through, giving Jacob a twinge at every stroke of the school-bell —as if to say, "Stop that clapper! There's trouble in it." After school, on the contrary, they were quiet and comfortable; in fact, seemed to be taking a nap among their cushions.

The other boys' bones behaved in a similar manner—but that is not so remarkable. Being nearer the daylight than Jacob's, they might be expected to be more learned in the ways of the world. Master Ludwig's, especially, were like beauty, only skin deep; they were the most knowing bones you ever heard of. Just put before him, ever so quietly, a grammar-book with a long lesson marked in it, and immediately the sly bone over his eyes would set up such an aching! Request him to go to the garret for your footstove—instantly the bones would remind him that he was "too tired." Ask him to go to the confectioner's, a mile way, and *presto*! not a bone would remember that it ever had been used before.

Bearing all this in mind, you will not wonder when I tell you that our five boys were among the happiest of the happy throng pouring forth from the school-house that day.

Peter was in excellent spirits. He had heard through Hilda of Dame Brinker's laugh and of Hans' joyous words, and he needed no further proof that Raff Brinker was a cured man. In fact the news had gone forth in every direction, for miles around. Persons who had never before cared for the Brinkers, or even mentioned them, except with a contemptuous sneer or a shrug of pretended pity, now became singularly familiar with every point of their history. There was no end to the number of ridiculous stories that were flying about.

Hilda, in the excitement of the moment, had stopped to exchange a word with the doctor's coachman, as he stood by the horses, pommelling his chest and clapping his hands. Her kind heart was overflowing. She could not help pausing to tell the cold, tired-looking man, that she thought the doctor would be out soon; she even hinted to him that she suspected—only suspected—that a wonderful cure had been performed—an idiot brought to his senses. Nay, she was *sure* of it—for she had heard his widow laugh—no, not his widow, of course, but his wife—for the man was as much alive as anybody, and, for all she knew, sitting up and talking like a lawyer.

All this was very indiscreet. Hilda, in an impenitent sort of way, felt it to be so.

But it is always so delightful to impart pleasant or surprising news!

She went tripping along by the canal, quite resolved to repeat the sin *ad infinitum*, and tell nearly every girl and boy in the school.

Meantime Janzoon Kolp came skating by. Of course in two seconds he was striking slippery attitudes, and shouting saucy things to the coachman, who stared at him in indolent disdain.

This, to Janzoon, was equivalent to an invitation to draw nearer. The coachman was now upon his box, gathering up the reins and grumbling at his horses.

Janzoon accosted him.

"I say! what's going on at the idiot's cottage? Is your boss in there?"

Coachman nodded mysteriously.

"Whew!" whistled Janzoon, drawing closer. "Old Brinker dead?"

The driver grew big with importance, and silent in proportion.

"See here, old pincushion! I'd run home yonder and get you a chunk of gingerbread, if I thought you could open your mouth."

Old pincushion was human—long hours of waiting had made him ravenously hungry. At Janzoon's hint, his countenance showed signs of a collapse.

"That's right, old fellow," pursued his tempter; "hurry up —what news—old Brinker dead?"

"No—CURED! got his wits," said the coachman, shooting forth his words, one at a time, like so many bullets.

Like bullets (figuratively speaking) they hit Janzoon Kolp. He jumped as if he had been shot.

"Goede Gunst! you don't say so!"

The man pressed his lips together, and looked significantly toward Master Kolp's shabby residence.

Just then Janzoon saw a group of boys in the distance. Hailing them in a rowdy style, common to boys of his stamp all over the world, whether in Africa, Japan, Amsterdam, or Paris, he scampered toward them, forgetting coachman, gingerbread, everything but the wonderful news.

Therefore by sundown it was well known throughout the neighbouring country that Dr. Boekman, chancing to stop at the cottage, had given the idiot Brinker a tremendous dose of medicine, as brown as gingerbread. It had taken six men to hold him while it was poured down. The idiot had immediately sprung to his feet, in full possession of all his faculties—

knocked over the doctor, or thrashed him (there was admitted to be a slight uncertainty as to which of these penalties was inflicted), then sat down and addressed him for all the world like a lawyer. After that he had turned and spoken beautifully to his wife and children. Dame Brinker had laughed herself into violent hysterics. Hans had said, "Here I am, father! your own dear son"; and Gretel had said, "Here I am, father! your own dear Gretel!" and the doctor had afterward been seen leaning back in his carriage looking just as white as a corpse.

CHAPTER XXXV

A NEW ALARM

WHEN Dr. Boekman called the next day at the Brinker cottage, he could not help noticing the cheerful, comfortable aspect of the place. An atmosphere of happiness breathed upon him as he opened the door. Dame Brinker sat complacently knitting beside the bed, her husband was enjoying a tranquil slumber, and Gretel was noiselessly kneading rye-bread on the table in the corner.

The doctor did not remain long. He asked a few simple questions, appeared satisfied with the answers, and after feeling his patient's pulse, said, "Ah, very weak yet, jufvrouw; very weak, indeed. He must have nourishment. You may begin to feed the patient—ahem!—not too much, but what you do give him let it be strong and of the best."

"Black bread we have, Mynheer, and porridge," replied Dame Brinker, cheerily; "they have always agreed with him well."

"Tut! tut!" said the doctor, frowning; "nothing of the kind. He must have the juice of fresh meat, white bread, dried and toasted, good Malaga wine, and—ahem!—the man looks cold—give him more covering, something light and warm. Where is the boy?"

"Hans, Mynheer, has gone into Broek to look for work. He will be back soon. Will the meester please be seated?"

Whether the hard, polished stool offered by Dame Brinker did not look particularly tempting, or whether the dame herself frightened him, partly because she was a woman, and partly because an anxious, distressed look had suddenly appeared in her face, I cannot say. Certain it is that our eccentric doctor looked hurriedly about him, muttered something about "extraordinary case," bowed, and disappeared, before Dame Brinker had time to say another word.

Strange that the visit of their good benefactor should have left a cloud, yet so it was. Gretel frowned, an anxious childish frown, and kneaded the bread-dough violently, without looking up. Dame Brinker hurried to her husband's bedside, leaned over him, and fell into silent but passionate weeping.

In a moment Hans entered.

"Why, mother," he whispered, in alarm, "what ails thee? Is the father worse?"

She turned her quivering face toward him, making no attempt to conceal her distress.

"Yes. He is starving—perishing. The meester said it."

Hans turned pale.

"What does this mean, mother? We must feed him at once. Here, Gretel, give me the porridge."

"Nay!" cried his mother, distractedly, yet without raising her voice, "it may kill him. Our poor fare is too heavy for him. Oh, Hans, he will die—the father will *die* if we use him this way. He must have meat, and sweet wine, and a dek-bed. Oh, what shall I do? what shall I do?" she sobbed, wringing her hands. "There is not a stiver in the house."

Gretel pouted. It was the only way she could express sympathy just then. Her tears fell one by one into the dough.

"Did the meester say he *must* have these things, mother?" asked Hans.

"Yes, he did."

"Well, mother, don't cry, *he shall have them.* I shall bring meat and wine before night. Take the cover from my bed. I can sleep in the straw."

"Yes, Hans, but it is heavy, scant as it is. The meester said he must have something light and warm. He will perish! Out peat is giving out, Hans. The father has wasted it sorely, throwing it on when I was not looking, dear man!"

"Never mind, mother," whispered Hans, cheerfully. "We can cut down the willow-tree and burn it, if need be. But I'll bring home something to-night. There *must* be work in Amsterdam, though there's none in Broek. Never fear, mother; the worst trouble of all is past. We can brave anything now that the father is himself again."

"Ay," sobbed Dame Brinker, hastily drying her eyes, "that is true indeed."

"Of course it is. Look at him, mother, how softly he sleeps. Do you think God would let him starve, just after giving him back to us. Why, mother, I'm as *sure* of getting all the father needs, as if my pocket was bursting with gold. There now, don't fret." And hurriedly kissing her, Hans caught up his skates, and slipped from the cottage.

Poor Hans! Disappointed in his morning's errand, half sickened with this new trouble, he wore a brave look, and tried to whistle as he tramped resolutely off with the firm intention of mending matters.

Want had never before pressed as sorely upon the Brinker family. Their stock of peat was nearly exhausted, and all the flour in the cottage was in Gretel's dough. They had scarcely cared to eat during the past few days—scarcely realised their condition. Dame Brinker had felt so sure that she and the children could earn money before the worst came, that she had given herself up to the joy of her husband's recovery. She had not even told Hans that the few pieces of silver in the old mitten were quite gone.

Hans reproached himself now that he had not hailed the doctor when he saw him enter his coach and drive rapidly away in the direction of Amsterdam.

"Perhaps there is some mistake," he thought. "The meester

surely would have known that meat and sweet wine were not at our command ; and yet the father looks very weak, he certainly does. I *must* get work. If Mynheer van Holp were back from Rotterdam I could get plenty to do. But Master Peter told me to let him know if he could do aught to serve us. I shall go to him at once. Oh, if it were but summer ! "

All this time Hans was hastening towards the canal. Soon his skates were on, and he was skimming rapidly toward the residence of Mynheer van Holp.

"The father must have meat and wine at once," he muttered, "but how can I earn the money in time to buy them to-day. There is no other way but to go, as I *promised*, to Master Peter. What would a gift of meat and wine be to him ? When the father is once fed, I can rush down to Amsterdam and earn the morrow's supply."

Then came other thoughts—thoughts that made his heart thump heavily and his cheeks burn with a new shame—"It is *begging*, to say the least. Not one of the Brinkers has ever been a beggar. Shall I be the first ? Shall my poor father, just coming back into life, learn that his family have asked for charity—he, always so wise and thrifty ? No !" cried Hans aloud, "better a thousand times to part with the watch."

"I can at least borrow money on it in Amsterdam," he thought, turning around. "That will be no disgrace. I can find work at once, and get it back again. Nay, perhaps I can even *speak to the father about it.*"

This last thought almost made the lad dance for joy. Why not, indeed, speak to the father ? He was a rational being now. "He may wake," thought Hans, "quite bright and rested— may tell us the watch is of no consequence, to sell it of course ! Hoezza !" and Hans almost flew over the ice.

A few moments more and the skates were again swinging from his arm. He was running towards the cottage.

His mother met him at the door.

"Oh Hans !" she cried, her face radiant with joy, "the young lady has been here with her maid. She brought everything— meat, jelly, wine, and bread—a whole basketful ! Then the meester sent a man from town with more wine, and a fine bed and blankets for the father. Oh! he will get well now. God bless them!"

"God bless them!" echoed Hans, and for the first time that day his eyes filled with tears.

CHAPTER XXXVI

THE FATHER'S RETURN

THAT evening Raff Brinker felt so much better that he insisted upon sitting up a while on the rough, high-backed chair by the fire. For a few moments there was quite a commotion in the little cottage. Hans was all-important on the occasion, for his father was a heavy man, and needed something firm to lean upon. The dame, though none of your fragile ladies, was in such a state of alarm and excitement at the bold step they were taking in lifting him without the meester's orders, that she came near pulling her husband over, even while she believed herself to be his main prop and support.

"Steady, vrouw, steady," panted Raff, "have I grown old and feeble, or is it the fever makes me thus helpless?"

"Hear the man!" laughed Dame Brinker, "talking like any other Christian. Why you're only weak from the fever, Raff. Here's the chair, sit thee down—there we are!"

With these words, Dame Brinker let her half of the burden settle slowly into the chair. Hans prudently did the same.

Meanwhile Gretel flew about generally, bringing every possible thing to her mother to tuck behind the father's back and spread over his knees. Then she twitched the carved bench under his feet, and Hans kicked the fire to make it brighter.

The father was "sitting up" at last. What wonder that he looked about him like one bewildered. "Little Hans" had just been almost carrying him. "The baby" was over four feet long, and was demurely brushing up the hearth with a bundle of

willow wisps.   Meitje, the vrouw, winsome and fair as ever, had
gained at least fifty pounds in what seemed to him a few hours.
She also had some new lines in her face that puzzled him.   The
only familiar things in the room were the pine table that he had
made before he was married, the Bible upon the shelf, and the
cupboard in the corner.

Ah ! Raff Brinker, it was only natural that your eyes should
fill with hot tears, even while looking at the joyful faces of your
loved ones.   Ten years dropped from a man's life are no small
loss ; ten years of manhood, of household happiness and care ;
ten years of honest labour, of conscious enjoyment of sunshine
and out-door beauty, ten years of grateful life.   One day looking
forward to all this ; the next, waking to find them passed, and a
blank.   What wonder the scalding tears dropped one by one
upon your cheek !

Tender little Gretel ! The prayer of her life was answered
through those tears.   She *loved* her father from that moment.
Hans and his mother glanced silently at each other when they
saw her spring towards him, and throw her arms about his neck.

" Father, *dear* father," she whispered, pressing her cheek close
to his, " don't cry.   We are all here."

" God bless thee," sobbed Raff, kissing her again and again ;
" I had forgotten that."

Soon he looked up again, and spoke in a cheerful voice : " I
should know her, vrouw," he said, holding the sweet young face
between his hands, and gazing at it as though he were watching
it grow.   " I should know her.   The same blue eyes, and the
lips, and, ah me ! the little song she could sing almost before
she could stand.   But that was long ago," he added, with a sigh,
still looking at her dreamily, " long ago ; it's all gone now."

" Not so, indeed," cried Dame Brinker, eagerly.   " Do you
think I would let her forget it ?   Gretel, child, sing the old song
thou hast known so long."

Raff Brinker's hands fell wearily, and his eyes closed ; but it
was something to see the smile playing about his mouth as
Gretel's voice floated about him like an incense.

It was a simple air.   She had never known the words.

With loving instinct she softened every note, until Raff almost fancied that his two - year - old baby was once more beside him.

As soon as the song was finished, Hans mounted a wooden stool and began to rummage in the cupboard.

"Have a care, Hans," said Dame Brinker, who, through all her poverty, was ever a tidy housewife. "Have a care, the wine is there at your right, and the white bread beyond it."

"Never fear, mother," answered Hans, reaching far back on an upper shelf, "I shall do no mischief."

Jumping down, he walked toward his father, and placed an oblong block of pine-wood in his hands. One of its ends was rounded off, and some deep cuts had been made on the top.

"Do you know what it is, father?" asked Hans.

Raff Brinker's face brightened. "Indeed I do, boy; it is the boat I was making you yest——alack, not yesterday, but years ago."

"I have kept it ever since, father; it can be finished when your hand grows strong again."

"Yes, but not for you, my lad. I must wait for the grand-children. Why, you are nearly a man. Have you helped your mother, boy, through all these years?"

"Ay, and bravely," put in Dame Brinker.

"Let me see," muttered the father, looking in a puzzled way at them all; "how long is it since the night when the waters were coming in? 'Tis the last I remember."

"We have told thee true, Raff. It was ten years last Pinxter-week."

"Ten years—and I fell then, you say. Has the fever been on me ever since?"

Dame Brinker scarce knew how to reply. Should she tell him all? Tell him that he had been an idiot, almost a lunatic? The doctor had charged her on no account to worry or excite his patient.

Hans and Gretel looked astonished when the answer came.

"Like enough, Raff," she said, nodding her head, and raising her eyebrows. "When a heavy man like thee falls on his head, it's hard to say what will come; but thou'rt well *now*, Raff. Thank the good Lord!"

The newly-awakened man bowed his head.

"Ay, well enough, mine vrouw," he said, after a moment's silence; "but my brain turns somehow like a spinning-wheel. It will not be right till I get on the dykes again. When shall I be at work, think you!"

"Hear the man!" cried Dame Brinker, delighted, yet frightened, too, for that matter; "we must get him on the bed, Hans. Work, indeed!"

They tried to raise him from the chair, but he was not ready yet.

"Be off with ye!" he said, with something like his old smile (Gretel had never seen it before); "does a man want to be lifted about like a log? I tell you before three suns I shall be on the dykes again. Ah! there 'll be some stout fellows to greet me. Jan Kamphuisen and young Hoogsvliet. They have been good friends to thee, Hans, I'll warrant."

Hans looked at his mother. Young Hoogsvliet had been dead five years. Jan Kamphuisen was in the jail at Amsterdam.

"Ay, they'd have done their share, no doubt," said Dame Brinker, parrying the inquiry, "had we asked them. But what with working and studying, Hans has been busy enough without seeking comrades."

"Working and studying," echoed Raff, in a musing tone; "can the youngsters read and cipher, Meitje?"

"You should hear them!" she answered, proudly. "They can run through a book while I mop the floor. Hans there is as happy over a page of big words as a rabbit in a cabbage-patch. As for ciphering"——

"Here, lad, help a bit," interrupted Raff Brinker; "I must get me on the bed again."

CHAPTER XXXVII

THE THOUSAND GUILDERS

NONE seeing the humble supper eaten in the Brinker cottage that night would have dreamed of the dainty fare hidden away near by. Hans and Gretel looked rather wistfully toward the cupboard as they drank their cupful of water and ate their scanty share of black bread; but even in thought they did not rob their father.

"He relished his supper well," said Dame Brinker, nodding sideways toward the bed, "and fell asleep the next moment. Ah! the dear man will be feeble for many a day. He wanted sore to sit up again, but while I made show of humouring him and getting ready, he dropped off. Remember that, my girl, when you have a man of your own (and many a day may it be before that comes to pass), remember you can never rule by differing : 'Humble wife is husband's boss—' Tut ! tut ! never swallow such a mouthful as that again, child ; why, I could make a meal off two such pieces. What's in thee, Hans? One would think there were cobwebs on the wall ! "

"Oh, no, mother, I was only thinking——"

"Thinking, about what? Ah, no use asking," she added, in a changed tone, "I was thinking of the same a while ago. Well, well, it's no blame if we *did* look to hear something by this time about the thousand guilders ; but not a word—no, it's plain enough he knows naught about them."

Hans looked up anxiously, dreading lest his mother should grow agitated, as usual, when speaking of the lost money ; but she was silently nibbling her bread and looking with a doleful stare toward the window.

"Thousand guilders," echoed a faint voice from the bed. "Ah, I am sure they have been of good use to you, vrouw, through the long years while your man was idle."

The poor woman started up. These words quite destroyed the hope that of late had been glowing within her.

"Are you awake, Raff?" she faltered

"Yes, Meitje, and I feel much better. Our money was well saved, vrouw, I was saying. Did it last through all these ten years?"

"I—I—have not got it Raff, I"—she was going to tell him the whole truth, when Hans lifted his finger warningly and whispered—

"Remember what the meester told us; the father must not be worried."

"Speak to him, child," she answered, trembling.

Hans hurried to the bedside.

"I am glad you are feeling better," he said, leaning over his father; "another day will see you quite strong again."

"Ay, like enough. How long did the money last, Hans? I could not hear your mother. What did she say?"

"I said, Raff," stammered Dame Brinker in great distress, "that it was all gone."

"Well, well, wife, do not fret at that; one thousand guilders is not so very much for ten years, and with children to bring up; but it has helped to make you all comfortable. Have you had much sickness to bear?"

"N—no," sobbed Dame Brinker, lifting her apron to her eyes.

"Tut—tut, woman, why do you cry?" said Raff, kindly; "we will soon fill another pouch, when I am on my feet again. Lucky I told you all about it before I fell."

"Told me what, man?"

"Why, that I buried the money. In my dream just now, it seemed I had never said aught about it."

Dame Brinker started forward. Hans caught her arm.

"Hist! mother," he whispered, hastily leading her away, "we must be very careful." Then while she stood with clasped hands waiting in breathless anxiety, he once more approached the cot. Trembling with eagerness he said—

"That was a troublesome dream. Do you remember *when* you buried the money, father?"

"Yes, my boy. It was before daylight on the same day I was hurt. Jan Kamphuisen said something, the sundown before, that made me distrust his honesty. He was the only one living besides mother who knew we had saved a thousand guilders—so I rose up that night and buried the money—blockhead that I was ever to suspect an old friend!"

"I'll be bound, father," pursued Hans, in a laughing voice, motioning to his mother and Gretel to remain quiet—"that you've forgotten where you buried it."

"Ha! ha! not I, indeed—but good-night, my son, I can sleep again."

Hans would have walked away, but his mother's gestures were not to be disobeyed; so he said gently—

"Good-night, father. Where did you say you buried the money? I was only a little one then."

"Close by the willow sapling behind the cottage," said Raff Brinker, drowsily.

"Ah, yes. North side of the tree, wasn't it, father?"

"No, the south side. Ah, you know the spot well enough, you rogue—like enough you were there when your mother lifted it. Now, son—easy—shift this pillow—so. Good-night."

"Good-night, father!" said Hans, ready to dance for joy.

The moon rose very late that night, shining in, full and clear, at the little window; but its beams did not disturb Raff Brinker. He slept soundly, so did Gretel. As for Hans and his mother, they had something else to do.

After making a few hurried preparations, they stole forth with bright expectant faces, bearing a broken spade and a rusty implement that had done many a day's service when Raff was a hale worker on the dykes.

It was so light out of doors they could see the willow-tree distinctly. The frozen ground was hard as stone, but Hans and his mother were resolute. Their only dread was that they might disturb the sleepers in the cottage.

"This ysbreker is just the thing, mother," said Hans, striking many a vigorous blow; "but the ground has set so firm, it'll be a fair match for it."

"Never fear, Hans," she answered, watching him eagerly; "here, let me try a while."

They soon succeeded in making an impression; one opening, and the rest was not so difficult.

Still they worked on, taking turns and whispering cheerily to one another. Now and then Dame Brinker stepped noiselessly over the threshold and listened, to be certain that her husband slept.

"What grand news it will be for him," she said, laughing, "when he is strong enough to bear it. How I should like to put the pouch and the stocking, just as we find them, all full of money, near him this blessed night, for the dear man to see when he wakens."

"We must get them, first, mother," panted Hans, still tugging away at his work.

"There's no doubt of that. They can't slip away from us, now," she answered, shivering with cold and excitement, as she crouched beside the opening. "Like enough we'll find them stowed in the old earthen pot I lost long ago."

By this time Hans, too, began to tremble, but not with cold. He had penetrated a foot deep for quite a space on the south side of the tree. At any moment they might come upon the treasure.

Meantime the stars winked and blinked at each other as if to say, "Queer country, this Holland! How much we do see to be sure!"

"Strange that the dear father should have put it down so woeful deep," said Dame Brinker, in rather a provoked tone. "Ah, the ground was soft enough then, I warrant. How wise of him to mistrust Jan Kamphuisen, and Jan in full credit at the time. Little I thought that handsome fellow with his gay ways would ever go to jail! Now, Hans, let me take a turn— it's lighter work, d'ye see? the deeper we go. I'd be loath to kill the tree, Hans—will we harm it, think you?"

"I cannot say," he answered, gravely.

Hour after hour, mother and son worked on. The hole grew larger and deeper. Clouds began to gather in the sky, throwing elfish shadows as they passed. Not until moon and stars faded away and streaks of daylight began to appear, did Meitje Brinker and Hans looked hopelessly into each other's face.

They had searched thoroughly, desperately, all round the tree; South, North, East, West. *The hidden money was not there!*

CHAPTER XXXVIII

GLIMPSES

A NNIE BOUMAN had a healthy distaste for Janzoon Kolp. Janzoon Kolp, in his own rough way, adored Annie. Annie declared she could not "to save her life" say one civil word to that odious boy. Janzoon believed her to be the sweetest, sauciest creature in the world. Annie laughed among her playmates at the comical flapping of Janzoon's tattered and dingy jacket; he sighed in solitude over the floating grace of her jaunty blue petticoat. She thanked her stars that her brothers were not like the Klops; and he growled at his sister because she was not like the Boumans. They seemed to exchange natures whenever they met. His presence made her harsh and unfeeling; and the very sight of *her* made him gentle as a lamb. Of course they were thrown together very often. It is thus that in some mysterious way we are convinced of error and cured of prejudice. In this case, however, the scheme failed. Annie detested Janzoon more and more at each encounter; and Janzoon liked her better and better every day.

"He killed a stork, the wicked old wretch!" she would say to herself.

"She knows I am strong and fearless," thought Janzoon.

"How red and freckled and ugly he is!" was Annie's secret comment when she looked at him.

"How she stares, and stares!" thought Janzoon. "Well, I am a fine, weather-beaten fellow, anyway."

"Janzoon Kolp, you impudent boy, go right away from me!" Annie often said; "I don't want any of your company."

"Ha! ha!" laughed Janzoon to himself, "girls never say what they mean. I'll skate with her every chance I can get."

And so it came to pass that the pretty maid would not look up that morning when, skating homeward from Amsterdam, she became convinced that a great burly boy was coming down the canal toward her.

"Humph! if I look at him," thought Annie, "I'll——"

"Good-morrow, Annie Bouman," said a pleasant voice.

[How a smile brightens a girl's face!]

"Good-morrow, Master Hans; I am right glad to meet you."

[How a smile brightens a boy's face!]

"Good-morrow again, Annie. There has been a great change at our house since you left."

"How so?" she exclaimed, opening her eyes very wide.

Hans who had been in a great hurry, and rather moody, grew talkative and quite at leisure in Annie's sunshine. Turning about, and skating slowly with her towards Broek, he told the good news of his father. Annie was so true a friend that he told her even of their present distress, of how money was needed, and how everything depended upon his obtaining work, and he could find nothing to do in the neighbourhood.

All this was not said as a complaint, but just because she was looking at him, and really wished to know. He could not speak of last night's bitter disappointment, for that secret was not wholly his own.

"Good-bye, Annie!" he said at last. "The morning is going fast, and I must haste to Amsterdam and sell these skates. Mother must have money at once. Before nightfall I shall certainly find a job somewhere."

"Sell your new skates, Hans!" cried Annie, "you, the best skater around Broek! Why, the race is coming off in five days!"

"I know it," he answered, resolutely. "Good-bye! I shall skate home again on the old wooden ones."

Such a bright glance! So different from Janzoon's ugly grin—and Hans was off like an arrow.

"Hans! come back," she called.

Her voice changed the arrow into a top. Spinning around, he darted, in one long, leaning sweep, toward her.

"Then you really are going to sell your new skates if you can find a customer?"

"Of course I am," he replied, looking up with a surprised smile.

"Well, Hans, if you *are* going to sell your skates," said Annie, somewhat confused, "I mean if you——well I know somebody who would like to buy them—that's all."

"Not Janzoon Kolp?" asked Hans, flushing.

"Oh no," she pouted; "he is not one of my friends."

"But you *know* him," persisted Hans.

Annie laughed. "Yes, I know him, and it's all the worse for him that I do. Now please, Hans, don't ever talk any more to me about Janzoon. I hate him!"

"Hate him! *you* hate any one, Annie?"

She shook her head saucily. "Yes; and I'll hate you too, if you persist in calling him one of my friends. You boys may like him because he caught the greased goose at the Kermis last summer, and climbed the pole with his great, ugly body tied up in a sack, but I don't care for such things. I've disliked him ever since I saw him try to push his little sister out of the merry-go-round at Amsterdam; and it's no secret up *our* way who killed the stork on your mother's roof. But we mustn't talk about such a bad, wicked fellow. Really, Hans, I know somebody who would be glad to buy your skates. You won't get half a price for them in Amsterdam. *Please* give them to me. I'll take you the money this very afternoon."

If Annie was charming even when she said "hate," there was no withstanding her when she said "please;" at least Hans found it to be so.

"Annie," he said, taking off the skates, and rubbing them

carefully with a skein of twine before handing them to her, "I am sorry to be so particular; but if your friend should not want them, will you bring them back to me to-day? I must buy peat and meal for the mother early to-morrow morning."

"My friend *will* want them," laughed Annie, nodding gaily, and skating off at the top of her speed.

As Hans drew forth the wooden "runners" from his capacious pockets and fastened them on as best he could, he did not hear Annie murmur, "I wish I had not been so rude; poor, brave Hans; what a noble boy he is!" And as Annie skated homeward filled with pleasant thoughts, she did not hear Hans say, "I grumbled like a bear—but bless her! some girls are like angels!"

Perhaps it was all for the best. One cannot be expected to know everything that is going on in the world.

CHAPTER XXXIX

LOOKING FOR WORK

LUXURIES unfit us for returning to hardships easily endured before. The wooden runners squeaked more than ever. It was as much as Hans could do to get on with the clumsy old things; still he did not regret that he had parted with his beautiful skates—but resolutely pushed back the boyish trouble that he had not been able to keep them just a little longer, at least until after the race.

"Mother surely will not be angry with me," he thought, "for selling them without her leave. She has had care enough already. It will be full time to speak of it when I take home the money."

Hans went up and down the streets of Amsterdam that day, looking for work. He succeeded in earning a few stivers by assisting a man who was driving a train of loaded mules into the city, but he could not secure steady employment anywhere.

He would have been glad to obtain a situation as porter or errand-boy, but though he passed, on his way, many a loitering, shuffling urchin, laden with bundles, there was no place for him. Some shopkeepers had just supplied themselves; others needed a trimmer, more lightly-built fellow (they meant better dressed, but did not choose to say so); others told him to call again in a month or two, when the canals would probably be broken up; and many shook their heads at him without saying a word.

At the factories he met with no better luck. It seemed to him that in those great buildings, turning out respectively such tremendous quantities of woollen, cotton, and linen stuffs, such world-renowned dyes and paints, such precious diamonds cut from the rough, such supplies of meal, of bricks, of glass and china— that in at least one of these, a strong-armed boy, able and eager to work, could find something to do. But no—nearly the same answer met him everywhere,—"no need of more hands just now. If he had called before Nicholas' Day they might have given him a job, as they were hurried then; but at present they had more boys than they needed." Hans wished they could see, just for a moment, his mother and Gretel. He did not know how the anxiety of both looked out from his eyes, and how more than once, the gruffest denials were uttered with an uncomfortable consciousness that the lad ought not to be turned away. Certain fathers when they went home that night, spoke more kindly than usual to their own youngsters, from memory of a frank, young face saddened at their words; and before morning one man actually resolved that if the Broek boy came in again he would instruct his head man Blankert to set him at something.

But Hans knew nothing of all this. Toward sundown he started on his return to Broek, uncertain whether the strange, choking sensation in his throat arose from discouragement or resolution. There was certainly one more chance. Mynheer van Holp might have returned by this time. Master Peter, it was reported, had gone to Haarlem the night before, to attend to something connected with the great Skating Race. Still Hans would go and try.

Fortunately, Peter had returned early that morning. He was

at home when Hans reached there, and was just about starting for the Brinker cottage.

"Ah, Hans!" he cried, as the weary boy approached the door; "you are the very one I wished to see. Come in and warm yourself."

After tugging at his well-worn hat, which always *would* stick to his head when he was embarrassed, Hans knelt down—not by way of making a new style of oriental salute, nor to worship the goddess of cleanliness who presided there, but because his heavy shoes would have filled the soul of a Broek housewife with horror. When their owner stepped softly into the house, they were left outside to act as sentinels until his return.

Hans left the Van Holp mansion with a lightened heart. Peter had brought word from Haarlem that young Brinker was to commence working upon the summer-house doors immediately. There was a comfortable workshop on the place, and it was to be at his service until the carving was done.

Peter did not tell Hans that he had skated all the way to Haarlem for the purpose of arranging this plan with Mynheer van Holp. It was enough for him to see the glad eager look rise on young Brinker's face.

"I *think* I can do it," said Hans, "though I have never learned the trade."

"I am *sure* you can," responded Peter, heartily. "You will find every tool you require in the workshop. It is nearly hidden yonder by that wall of twigs. In summer when the hedge is green, one cannot see the shop from here at all. How is your father to-day?"

"Better, Mynheer; he improves every hour."

"It is the most astonishing thing I ever heard of. That gruff old doctor is a great fellow after all."

"Ah, Mynheer!" said Hans, warmly, "he is more than great. He is good. But for the meester's kind heart and great skill, my poor father would yet be in the dark. I think, Mynheer," he added, with kindling eyes, "surgery is the very noblest science in the world!"

Peter shrugged his shoulders. "Very noble it may be, but not quite to my taste. This Doctor Boekman certainly has skill. As for his heart, defend me from such hearts as his!"

"Why do you say so, Mynheer?" asked Hans.

Just then a lady slowly entered from an adjoining apartment. It was Mevrouw van Holp arrayed in the grandest of caps, and the longest of satin aprons ruffled with lace. She nodded placidly as Hans stepped back from the fire, bowing as well as he knew how.

Peter at once drew a high-backed oaken chair toward the fire, and the lady seated herself. There was a block of cork on each side of the chimney-place. One of these he placed under his mother's feet.

Hans turned to go.

"Wait a moment, if you please, young man," said the lady. "I accidentally overheard you and my son speaking, I think, of my friend, Dr. Boekman. You are right, young man. Doctor Boekman has a very kind heart. You perceive, Peter, we may be quite mistaken in judging of a person solely by their manners, though a courteous deportment is by no means to be despised."

"I intended no disrespect, mother," said Peter, "but surely one has no right to go growling and snarling through the world, as they say he does."

"They say. Ah, Peter, 'they' means everybody or nobody. Surgeon Boekman has had a great sorrow. Many years ago he lost his only child, under very painful circumstances—a fine lad, except that he was a thought too hasty and high-spirited. Before then Gerard Boekman was one of the most agreeable gentlemen I ever knew."

So saying, Mevrouw van Holp, looking kindly upon the two boys, arose and left the room with the same dignity with which she had entered.

Peter, only half convinced, muttered something about "the sin of allowing sorrow to turn all one's honey into gall," as he conducted his visitor to the narrow side-door. Before they parted, he advised Hans to keep himself in good skating order, "for," he added, "now that your father is all right, you will be in fine spirits for the race. That will be the prettiest skating show ever seen in this part of the world. Everybody is talking of it. You are to try for the prize, remember."

"I shall not be in the race, Mynheer," said Hans, looking down.

"Not be in the race! Why not, indeed?" and immediately Peter's thoughts swept on a full tide of suspicion towards Carl Schummel.

"Because I cannot, Mynheer," answered Hans, as he bent to slip his feet into his big shoes.

Something in the boy's manner warned Peter that it would be no kindness to press the matter further. He bade Hans "good-bye," and stood thoughtfully watching him as he walked away.

In a minute Peter called out—

"Hans Brinker!"

"Yes, Mynheer."

"I'll take back all I said about Dr. Boekman."

"Yes, Mynheer."

Both were laughing. But Peter's smile changed to a look of puzzled surprise when he saw Hans kneel down by the canal and put on the wooden skates.

"Very queer," muttered Peter, shaking his head as he turned to go into the house; "why in the world don't the boy wear his new ones?"

CHAPTER XL

THE FAIRY GODMOTHER

THE sun had gone down quite out of sight when our hero— with a happy heart, but with something like a sneer on his countenance, as he jerked off the wooden "runners"—trudged hopefully toward the tiny hut-like building, known of old as the Idiot's Cottage.

Duller eyes than his would have discerned two slight figures moving near the doorway.

That gray, well-patched jacket and the dull blue skirt, covered with an apron of still duller blue; that faded, close-fitting cap; and those quick little feet in their great boat-like shoes: they were Gretel's, of course. He would have known them anywhere.

That bright, coquettish, red jacket, with its pretty skirt, bordered with black; that graceful cap, bobbing over the gold ear-rings; that dainty apron, and those snug leather shoes that seemed to have grown with the feet: why, if the Pope of Rome had sent them to him by express, Hans could have sworn they were Annie's.

The two girls were slowly pacing up and down in front of the cottage. Their arms were entwined, of course, and their heads were nodding and shaking as emphatically as if all the affairs of the kingdom were under discussion.

With a joyous shout Hans hastened toward them.

"Huzza, girls, I've found work!"

This brought his mother to the cottage door.

She, too, had pleasant tidings. The father was still improving. He had been sitting up nearly all day, and was now sleeping, as Dame Brinker declared, "just as quiet as a lamb."

"It is my turn now, Hans," said Annie, drawing him aside after he had told his mother the good word from Mynheer van Holp. "Your skates are sold, and here's the money."

"Seven guilders!" cried Hans, counting the pieces in astonishment; "why that is three times as much as I paid for them."

"I cannot help that," said Annie. "If the buyer knew no better, it is not our fault."

Hans looked up quickly.

"Oh, Annie!"

"Oh, Hans!" she mimicked, pursing her lips and trying to look desperately wicked and unprincipled.

"Now, Annie, I know you would never mean that! You must return some of this money."

"But I'll not do any such thing," insisted Annie; "they're sold, and that's an end of it." Then seeing that he looked really pained, she added in a lower tone—

"Will you believe me, Hans, when I say that there has been no mistake—that the person who bought your skates *insisted* upon paying seven guilders for them."

"I will," he answered, and the light from his clear blue eyes seemed to settle and sparkle under Annie's lashes.

Dame Brinker was delighted at the sight of so much silver, but when she learned that Hans had parted with his treasures to obtain it, she sighed, as she exclaimed—

"Bless thee, child! That will be a sore loss for thee!"

"Here, mother," said the boy, plunging his hands far into his pocket, "here is more; we shall be rich if we keep on!"

"Ay, indeed," she answered, eagerly reaching forth her hand. Then, lowering her voice, added, "We *would* be rich but for that Jan Kamphuisen. He was at the willow-tree years ago, Hans. Depend upon it."

"Indeed, it seems likely," sighed Hans. "Well, mother, we must give up the money bravely. It is certainly gone, the father has told us all he knows. Let us think no more about it."

"That's easy saying, Hans. I shall try, but it's hard, and my poor man wanting so many comforts. Bless me! How girls fly about. They were here but this instant. Where did they run to?"

"They slipped behind the cottage," said Hans; "like enough to hide from us. Hist! I'll catch them for you. They both can move quicker and softer than yonder rabbit, but I'll give them a good start first."

"Why, there *is* a rabbit, sure enough. Hold, Hans, the poor thing must have been in sore need to venture from its burrow this bitter weather. I'll get a few crumbs for it within."

So saying, the good woman bustled into the cottage. She soon came out again, but Hans had forgotten to wait, and the rabbit, after taking a cool survey of the premises, had scampered off to unknown quarters. Turning the corner of the cottage,

Dame Brinker came upon the children. Hans and Gretel were standing before Annie, who was seated carelessly upon a stump.

"That is as good as a picture!" cried Dame Brinker, halting in admiration of the group. "Many a painting have I seen at the grand house at Heidelberg not a whit prettier. My two are rough chubs, Annie, but *you* look like a fairy!"

"Do I?" laughed Annie, sparkling with animation. "Well then, Gretel and Hans, imagine I'm your godmother just paying you a visit. Now, I'll grant you each a wish. What will you have, Master Hans?"

A shade of earnestness passed over Annie's face as she looked up at him. Perhaps it was because she wished from the depths of her heart that for once she could have a fairy's power.

Something whispered to Hans that, for the moment, she was more than mortal.

"I wish," said he solemnly, "I could find something I was searching for last night?"

Gretel laughed merrily. Dame Brinker moaned, "Shame on you, Hans!" and passed wearily into the cottage.

The fairy godmother sprang up and stamped her foot three times.

"Thou shalt have thy wish," said she, "let them say what they will." Then, with playful solemnity, she put her hand in her apron pocket, and drew forth a large glass bead. "Bury this," said she, giving it to Hans, "where I have stamped, and, ere moonrise, thy wish shall be granted."

Gretel laughed more merrily than ever.

The godmother pretended great displeasure.

"Naughty child," said she, scowling terribly. "In punishment for laughing at a fairy, *thy* wish shall not be granted."

"Ha!" cried Gretel, in high glee, "better wait till you're asked, godmother. I haven't made any wish!"

Annie acted her part well. Never smiling, through all their merry laughter, she stalked away, the embodiment of offended dignity.

"Good-night, fairy!" they cried again and again.

"Good-night, mortals!" she called out at last, as she sprang over a frozen ditch, and ran quickly homeward.

"Oh isn't she—just like flowers—so sweet and lovely!" cried Gretel, looking after her in great admiration, "and to think how many days she stays in that dark room with her grandmother. Why, brother Hans! what is the matter? What are you going to do?"

"Wait and see!" answered Hans, as he plunged into the cottage and came out again, all in an instant, bearing the spade and ysbreker in his hands. "I'm going to bury my magic bead!"

Raff Brinker still slept soundly; his wife took a small block of peat from her nearly exhausted store, and put it upon the embers. Then opening the door, she called gently—

"Come in, children."

"Mother! mother! See here!" shouted Hans.

"Holy St. Bavon!" exclaimed the dame, springing over the doorstep. "What ails the boy?"

"Come quick, mother," he cried, in great excitement, working with all his might, and driving in the ysbreker at each word. "Don't you see? *This* is the spot—right here on the south side of the stump. Why didn't we think of it last night? *The stump* is the old willow-tree—the one you cut down last spring because it shaded the potatoes. That little tree wasn't here when father—huzzah!"

Dame Brinker could not speak. She dropped on her knees beside Hans, just in time to see him drag forth—*the old stone pot!*

He thrust in his hand and took out a piece of brick,—then another—then another—then, the stocking and the pouch, black and mouldy, but filled with the long-lost treasure!

Such a time! Such laughing! Such crying! Such counting, after they went into the cottage! It was a wonder that Raff did not waken. His dreams were pleasant, however, for he smiled in his sleep.

Dame Brinker and her children had a fine supper, I can assure you. No need of saving the delicacies now.

"We'll get father some nice fresh things, to-morrow," said the dame, as she brought forth cold meat, wine, bread, and jelly, and placed them on the clean pine-table. "Sit by, children, sit by."

That night, Annie fell asleep wondering whether it was a knife Hans had lost, and thinking how funny it would be if he should find it, after all.

Hans had scarce closed his eyes, before he found himself trudging through a thicket ; pots of gold were lying all around, and watches, and skates, and glittering beads were swinging from every branch.

Strange to say, each tree, as he approached it, changed into a stump, and on the stump sat the prettiest fairy imaginable, clad in a scarlet jacket and blue petticoat.

CHAPTER XLI

THE MYSTERIOUS WATCH

SOMETHING else than the missing guilders was brought to light on the day of the fairy godmother's visit. This was the story of the watch that for ten long years had been so jealously guarded by Raff's faithful vrouw. Through many an hour of sore temptation she had dreaded almost to look upon it, lest she might be tempted to disobey her husband's request. It had been hard to see her children hungry and to know that the watch, if sold, would enable the roses to bloom in their cheeks again—"But nay," she would exclaim, "Meitje Brinker is not one to forget her man's last bidding, come what may."

"Take good care of this, mine vrouw," he had said, as he handed it to her—that was all. No explanation followed, for the words were scarcely spoken, when one of his fellow-workmen rushed into the cottage, crying, "Come, man! the waters are rising! you're wanted on the dykes."

Raff had started at once, and that, as Dame Brinker has already told you, was the last she saw of him in his right mind.

On the day when Hans was in Amsterdam looking for work, and Gretel, after performing her household labours, was wandering about in search of chips, twigs—anything that could be burned, Dame Brinker with suppressed excitement had laid the watch in her husband's hand.

"It wasn't in reason," as she afterwards said to Hans, "to wait any longer, when a word from the father would settle all; no woman living but would want to know how he came by that watch." Raff Brinker turned the bright, polished thing over and over in his hand—then he examined the bit of smoothly-ironed black ribbon fastened to it; he seemed hardly to recognise it. At last he said, "Ah, I remember this! Why you've been rubbing it, vrouw, till it shines like a new guilder."

"Ay," said Dame Brinker, nodding her head complacently.

Raff looked at it again. "Poor boy!" he murmured, then fell into a brown study.

This was too much for the dame. "Poor boy!" she echoed, somewhat tartly. "What do you think I'm standing here for, Raff Brinker, and my spinning awaiting, if not to hear more than that?"

"I told ye all, long since," said Raff, positively, as he looked up in surprise.

"Indeed, and you never did!" retorted the vrouw.

"Well, if not—since it's no affair of ours—we'll say no more about it," said Raff, shaking his head sadly; "like enough while I've been dead on the earth, all this time, the poor boy's died and been in Heaven. He looked near enough to it, poor lad!"

"Raff Brinker! If you're going to treat me this way, and I nursing you and bearing with you since I was twenty-two years old, it's a shame! ay, and a disgrace," cried the vrouw, growing quite red and scant of breath.

Raff's voice was feeble yet, "Treat you *what* way, Meitje?"

"What way," said Dame Brinker, mimicking his voice and

manner, "what way? why just as every woman in the world is treated after she's stood by a man through the worst, like a——"

"Meitje!"

Raff was leaning forward, with outstretched arms. His eyes were full of tears.

In an instant Dame Brinker was at his feet, clasping his hands in hers.

"Oh! what have I done? Made my good man cry, and he not back with me four days! Look up, Raff! nay, Raff, my own boy, I'm sorry I hurt thee. It's hard not to be told about the watch after waiting ten years to know—but I'll ask thee no more, Raff. Here, we'll put the thing away that's made the first trouble between us, after God just giving thee back to me."

"I was a fool to cry, Meitje," he said, kissing her, "and it's no more than right ye should know the truth. But it seemed like it might be telling the secrets of the dead to talk about the matter."

"Is the man—the lad—thou wert talking of dead, think thee?" asked the vrouw, hiding the watch in her hand, but seating herself expectantly on the end of his long foot-bench.

"It's hard telling," he answered.

"Was he so sick, Raff?"

"No, not sick, I may say; but troubled, vrouw, very troubled."

"Had he done any wrong, think ye?" she asked, lowering her voice.

Raff nodded.

"*Murder?*" whispered the wife, not daring to look up.

"He said it was like to that, indeed."

"Oh! Raff, you frighten me! Tell me more. You speak so strange, and you tremble. I must know all."

"If I tremble, mine vrouw, it must be from the fever. There is no guilt on my soul, thank God!"

"Take a sip of this wine, Raff. There, now you are better. It was like to a crime you were saying?"

"Ay, Meitje, like to murder. *That* he told me himself.

But I'll never believe it. A likely lad, fresh and honest-looking as our own youngster, but with something not so bold and straight about him."

"Ay, I know," said the dame, gently, fearing to interrupt the story.

"He came upon me quite sudden," continued Raff. "I had never seen his face before, the palest, frightenedst face that ever was. He caught me by the arm, 'You look like an honest man,' says he."

"Ay, he was right in that," interrupted the dame, emphatically.

Raff looked somewhat bewildered.

"Where was I, mine vrouw?"

"The lad took hold of your arm, Raff," she said, gazing at him anxiously.

"Ay, so. The words come awkward to me, and everything is half like a dream, ye see."

"S-stut! What wonder, poor man," sighed the dame, stroking his hand. "If ye had not head enough for a dozen, the wit would never have come to ye again. Well, the lad caught ye by the arm, and said ye looked honest (well he might!) What then? Was it noontime?"

"Nay, before daylight. Long before early chimes."

"It was the same day you were hurt," said the dame. "I know it seemed you went to your work in the middle of the night. You left off, where he caught your arm, Raff."

"Yes," resumed her husband; "and I can see his face this minute, so white and wild-looking. 'Take me down the river a way,' says he. I was working then, you'll remember, far down on the line, across from Amsterdam. I told him I was no boatman. 'It's an affair of life and death,' says he, 'take me on a few miles. Yonder skiff is not locked, but it may be a poor man's boat, and I'd be loath to rob him!' The words might differ some, vrouw, for it's all like a dream. Well, I took him down, it might be six or eight miles, and then he said he could run the rest of the way on shore. I was in haste to get the boat back. Before he jumped out, he says, sobbing-like, 'I can trust you. I've done a thing—God knows I never intended it—but the man is dead! I must fly from Holland.'"

"What was it, did he say, Raff? Had he been shooting at a comrade, like they do down at the University at Gottingen?"

"I can't recall that. Mayhap he told me. But it's all like a dream. I said it wasn't for me, a good Hollander, to cheat the laws of my country by helping him off that way; but he kept saying, 'God knows I am innocent!' and looked at me in the starlight as fair, now, and clear-eyed as our little Hans might, and I just pulled away faster."

"It must have been Jan Kamphuisen's boat," remarked Dame Brinker, dryly; "none other would have left his oars out that careless."

"Ay, it was Jan's boat, sure enough. The man will be coming in to see me, Sunday, likely, if he's heard; and young Hoogsvliet too. Where was I?"

[It was lucky the dame restrained herself. To have spoken at all of Jan, after the last night's cruel disappointment, would have been to have let out more sorrow and suspicion than Raff could bear.]

"Where were you? Why, not very far, forsooth—the lad hadn't yet given ye the watch; alack, I misgive whether he came by it honestly!"

"Why, vrouw," exclaimed Raff, in an injured tone, "he was dressed soft and fine as the prince himself. The watch was his own, clear enough."

"How came he to give it up?" asked the dame, looking uneasily at the fire, for it needed another block of peat.

"I told ye just now," he answered, with a puzzled air.

"Tell me again," said Dame Brinker, wisely warding off another digression.

"Well, just before jumping from the boat, he says, handing me the watch, 'I'm flying from my country as I never thought I could. I'll trust you, because you look honest. Will you take this to my father—not to-day, but in a week—and tell him his unhappy boy sent it; and tell him if ever the time comes that he wants me to come back to him, I'll brave everything and

come. Tell him to send a letter to—to—' there the rest is all
gone from me. I *can't* remember where the letter was to go.
Poor lad! poor lad!" resumed Raff, sorrowfully, taking the
watch from his vrouw's lap as he spoke—"and it's never been
sent to his father to this day."

"I'll take it, Raff, never fear, the moment Gretel gets back.
She will be in soon. What was the father's name did you say?
Where were you to find him?"

"Alack!" answered Raff, speaking very slowly, "it's all
slipped me. I can see the lad's face, and his great eyes, just as
plain—and I remember his opening the watch, and snatching
something from it and kissing it, but no more. All the rest
whirls past me; there's a kind of sound like rushing waters
comes over me when I try to think."

"Ay, that's plain to see, Raff; but I've had the same feeling
after a fever. You're tired now; I must get ye straight on the
bed again. Where *is* the child, I wonder?"

Dame Brinker opened the door, and called, "Gretel! Gretel!"

"Stand aside, vrouw," said Raff, feebly, as he leaned forward
and endeavoured to look out upon the bare landscape, "I've
half a mind to stand beyond the door just once."

"Nay, nay," she laughed; "I'll tell the meester how ye tease
and fidget and bother to be let out in the air; and, if he says it,
I'll bundle ye warm to-morrow, and give ye a turn on your feet.
But I'm freezing you with this door open. I declare if there
isn't Gretel with her apron full, skating on the canal like wild.
Why man," she continued almost in a scream as she slammed
the door, "thou'rt walking to the bed without my touching
thee! Thou'lt fall!"

The dame's "thee" proved her mingled fear and delight, even
more than the rush which she made toward her husband. Soon
he was comfortably settled under the new cover, declaring as his
vrouw tucked him in snug and warm, that it was the last daylight that should see him abed.

"Ay! I can hope it myself," laughed Dame Brinker, "now
you have been frisking about at that rate." As Raff closed his
eyes, the dame hastened to revive her fire, or rather to dull it,

for Dutch peat is like a Dutchman, slow to kindle, but very good at a blaze when once started. Then putting her neglected spinning-wheel away, she drew forth her knitting from some invisible pocket and seated herself by the bedside.

"If you could remember that man's name, Raff," she began cautiously, "I might take the watch to him, while you're sleeping; Gretel can't but be in soon."

Raff tried to think; but in vain.

"Could it be Boomphoffen?" suggested the dame. "I've heard how they've had two sons turn out bad—Gerard and Lambert?"

"It might be," said Raff; "look if there's letters on the watch, that'll guide us some."

"Bless thee, man," cried the happy dame, eagerly lifting the watch, "why, thou'rt sharper than ever! Sure enough. Well I know the letters! They're L. J. B. That's Lambert Boomphoffen, you may depend—what the J. is for I can't say; but they used to be grand kind o' people, high-feathered as fancy fowl. Just the kind to give their children all double names, which isn't Scripture anyway."

"I don't know about that, vrouw. Seems to me there's long, mixed names in the Holy Book, hard enough to make out. But you've got the right guess at a jump. It was your way always," said Raff, closing his eyes; "take the watch to Boompkinks and try."

"Not Boompkinks, I know no such name; it's Boomphoffen."

"Ay, take it there."

"Take it there, man! why, the whole brood of 'em's been gone to America these four years. But go to sleep, Raff; you look pale and out of strength. It'll all come to you, what's best to do, in the morning.

"So, Mistress Gretel! Here you are at last!"

Before Raff awoke that evening, the fairy godmother, as we know, had been at the cottage, the guilders were once more safely locked in the big chest, and Dame Brinker and the children were faring sumptuously on meat and white bread and wine.

So the mother, in the joy of her heart, told them the story of the watch as far as she deemed it prudent to divulge it. It was no more than fair, she thought, that the poor things should know, after keeping the secret so safe, ever since they had been old enough to know anything.

CHAPTER XLII

A DISCOVERY

THE next sun brought a busy day to the Brinkers. In the first place, the news of the thousand guilders had of course to be told to the father. Such tidings as that surely could not harm him. Then while Gretel was diligently obeying her mother's injunction to "clean the place fresh as a new brewing," Hans and the dame sallied forth to revel in the purchasing of peat and provisions.

Hans was careless and contented; the dame was filled with delightful anxieties caused by the unreasonable demands of ten thousand guilders' worth of new wants that had sprung up like mushrooms in a single night. The happy woman talked so largely to Hans on their way to Amsterdam, and brought back such little bundles after all, that he scratched his bewildered head, as he leaned against the chimney-piece, wondering whether "Bigger the pouch tighter the string" was in "Jacob Cats," and therefore true, or whether he had dreamed it when he lay in a fever.

"What thinking on, Big-eyes?" chirruped his mother, half reading his thoughts, as she bustled about preparing the dinner, "what thinking on? Why, Raff, would ye believe it, the child thought to carry half Amsterdam back on his head. Bless us! he would have bought as much coffee as would have filled this fire-pot. 'No, no, my lad,' says I, 'no time for leaks when the ship is rich laden;' and then how he stared—ay, just as he stares this minute. Hoot, lad! fly around a mite. Ye'll grow to the chimney-place with your staring and wondering. Now, Raff, here's your chair at the head of the table, where it should be, for there's A MAN to the house now—I'd say it to the king's face. Ay, that's the way, lean on Hans: there's a strong staff for you!—growing like a weed too, and it seems only yesterday since he was toddling. Sit by, my man, sit by."

"Can you call to mind, vrouw," said Raff, settling himself cautiously in the big chair, "the wonderful music-box that cheered your working in the big house at Heidelberg?"

"Ay, that I can," answered the dame; "three turns of a brass key, and the witchy thing would send the music fairly running up and down one's back; I remember it well. But, Raff" (growing solemn in an instant), "you would never throw our guilders away for a thing like that?"

"No, no, not I, vrouw—for the good Lord has already given me a music-box without pay."

All three cast quick, frightened glances at one another and at Raff. Were his wits on the wing again?

"Ay, and a music-box that fifty pouchful would not buy from me," insisted Raff; "and it's set going by the turn of a mop-handle, and it slips and glides around the room, everywhere in a flash, carrying the music about till you'd swear the birds were back again."

"What's in the man?" cried the dame, "what's in the man?"

"Comfort and joy, vrouw, that's what's in him! Ask Gretel, ask my little music-box Gretel, if your man has lacked comfort and joy this day."

"Not he, mother," laughed Gretel. "He's been *my* music-box, too. We sang together half the time you were gone."

"Ay, so," said the dame, greatly relieved. "Now, Hans, you'll never get through with a piece like that; but never mind, chick, thou'st had a long fasting; here, Gretel, take another slice of the sausage, it'll put blood in your cheeks."

"Oh! oh! mother," laughed Gretel, eagerly holding forth her platter, "blood don't grow in girls' cheeks—you mean roses —isn't it roses, Hans?"

While Hans was hastily swallowing a mammoth mouthful in order to give a suitable reply to this poetic appeal, Dame Brinker settled the matter with a quick—

"Well, roses or blood, it's all one to me, so the red finds its way on your sunny face. It's enough for mother to get pale and weary-looking, without——"

"Hoot, vrouw," spoke up Raff hastily, "thou'rt fresher and rosier this minute than both our chicks put together."

This remark, though not bearing very strong testimony to the clearness of Raff's newly-awakened intellect, nevertheless afforded the dame intense satisfaction; the meal accordingly passed off in the most delightful manner.

After dinner, the affair of the watch was talked over, and the mysterious initials duly discussed.

Hans had just pushed back his stool, intending to start at once for Mynheer van Holp's, and his mother had risen to put the watch away in its old hiding-place, when they heard the sound of wheels upon the frozen ground.

Some one knocked at the door, opening it at the same time.

"Come in," stammered Dame Brinker, hastily trying to hide the watch in her bosom. "Oh! is it you, Mynheer? Good day; the father is nearly well, as you see. It's a poor place to greet you in, Mynheer, and the dinner not cleared away."

Dr. Boekman scarcely noticed the dame's apology. He was evidently in haste.

"Ahem!" he exclaimed, "not needed here, I perceive. The patient is mending fast."

"Well he may, Mynheer," cried the dame, "for only last night we found a thousand guilders that's been lost to us these ten years."

Dr. Boekman opened his eyes.

"Yes, Mynheer," said Raff. "I bid the vrouw tell you, though it's to be held a secret among us, for I see you can keep your lips closed as well as any man."

The doctor scowled. He never liked personal remarks.

"Now, Mynheer," continued Raff, "you can take your rightful pay. God knows you have earned it, if bringing such a poor tool back to the world and his family can be called a service. Tell the vrouw what's to pay, Mynheer; she will hand out the sum right willingly."

"Tut! tut!" said the doctor, kindly, "say nothing about money. I can find plenty of such pay any time, but gratitude comes seldom. That boy's 'thank you,'" he added, nodding sidewise towards Hans, "was pay enough for me."

"Like enough ye have a boy of your own," said Dame Brinker, quite delighted to see the great man becoming so sociable.

Doctor Boekman's good-nature vanished at once. He gave a growl (at least, it seemed so to Gretel) but made no actual reply.

"Do not think the vrouw meddlesome, Mynheer," said Raff; "she has been sore touched of late about a lad whose folks have gone away, none know where; and I had a message for them from the young gentleman."

"The name was Boomphoffen," said the dame, eagerly. "Do you know aught of the family, Mynheer?"

The doctor's reply was brief and gruff.

"Yes. A troublesome set. They went long since to America."

"It might be, Raff," persisted Dame Brinker, timidly, "that the meester knows somebody in that country, though I'm told they are mostly savages over there. If he could get the watch to the Boomphoffens with the poor lad's message, it would be a most blessed thing."

"Tut! vrouw, why pester the good meester, and dying men and women wanting him everywhere. How do ye know ye have the true name?"

"I'm sure of it," she replied. "They had a son Lambert, and there's an L for Lambert and a B for Boomphoffen, on the back; though to be sure there's an odd J too, but the meester can look for himself."

So saying, she drew forth the watch.

"L. J. B.!" cried Doctor Boekman springing toward her.

Why attempt to describe the scene that followed! I need

only say that the lad's message was delivered to his father at last—delivered while the great surgeon was sobbing like a little child.

"Laurens! my Laurens!" he cried, gazing with yearning eyes at the watch as he held it tenderly in his palm. "Ah, if I had but known sooner! Laurens a homeless wanderer—Great Heaven! he may be suffering, dying at this moment! Think, man, where is he? Where did my boy say the letter must be sent?"

Raff shook his head sadly.

"Think!" implored the doctor. Surely the memory so lately awakened through his aid could not refuse to serve him in a moment like this.

"It is all gone, Mynheer," sighed Raff.

Hans, forgetting distinctions of rank and station, forgetting everything but that his good friend was in trouble, threw his arms around the doctor's neck.

"I can find your son, Mynheer. If alive, he is *somewhere*. The earth is not so very large; I will devote every day of my life to the search. Mother can spare me, now. You are rich Mynheer; send me where you will."

Gretel began to cry. It was right for Hans to go; but how could they ever live without him?

Doctor Boekman made no reply, neither did he push Hans away. His eyes were fixed anxiously upon Raff Brinker. Suddenly he lifted the watch, and with trembling eagerness attempted to open it. Its stiffened spring yielded at last; the case flew open, disclosing a watch-paper in the back bearing a group of blue forget-me-nots. Raff, seeing a shade of intense disappointment pass over the doctor's face, hastened to say—

"There was something else in it, Mynheer, but the young gentleman tore it out before he handed it to me. I saw him kiss it as he put it away."

"It was his mother's picture," moaned the doctor; "she died when he was ten years old. Thank God! the boy had not forgotten. Both dead! It is impossible," he cried, starting up. "My boy is alive. You shall hear his story. Laurens acted as my assistant. By mistake he portioned out the wrong medicine for one of my patients,—a deadly poison,—but it was never administered, for I discovered the error in time. The man died that day. I was detained with other bad cases until the next evening. When I reached home, my boy was gone. Poor Laurens!" sobbed the doctor, breaking down completely; "never to hear from me through all these years. His message disregarded. Oh, what must he have suffered!"

Dame Brinker ventured to speak. Anything was better than to see the meester cry.

"It is a mercy to know the young gentleman was innocent. Ah, how he fretted! Telling you, Raff, that his crime was like unto murder. It was sending the wrong physic he meant. Crime indeed! why, our own Gretel might have done that. Like enough the poor young gentleman heard that the man was dead; that's why he ran, Mynheer. He said, you know, Raff, that he never could come back to Holland again unless"—she hesitated —"Ah, your honour, ten years is a dreary time to be waiting to hear from——"

"Hist, vrouw!" said Raff, sharply.

"Waiting to hear," groaned the doctor; "and I, like a fool, sitting stubbornly at home, thinking he had abandoned me. I never dreamed, Brinker, that the boy had discovered the mistake. I believed it was youthful folly, ingratitude, love of adventure, that sent him away. My poor, poor Laurens!"

"But you know all, now, Mynheer," whispered Hans. "You know he was innocent of wrong, that he loved you and his dead mother. We will find him. You shall see him again, dear meester."

"God bless you!" said Doctor Boekman, seizing the boy's hand. "It may be as you say. I shall try—I shall try. And, Brinker, if ever the faintest gleam of recollection concerning him should come to you, you will send me word at once?"

"Indeed we will!" cried all but Hans, whose silent promise would have satisfied the doctor, even had the others not spoken.

"Your boy's eyes," he said, turning to Dame Brinker, "are

strangely like my son's. The first time I met him, it seemed that Laurens himself was looking at me."

"Ay, Mynheer," replied the mother, proudly. "I have marked that you were much drawn to the child."

For a few moments the meester seemed lost in thought; then, arousing himself, he spoke in a new voice.

"Forgive me, Raff Brinker, for this tumult. Do not feel distressed on my account. I leave your house to-day a happier man than I have been for many a long year. Shall I take the watch?"

"Certain you must, Mynheer. It was your son's wish."

"Even so," responded the doctor—regarding his treasure with a queer frown, for his face could not throw off its bad habits in an hour—"even so. And now, I must be gone. No medicine is needed by my patient; only peace and cheerfulness, and both are here in plenty. Heaven bless you, my good friends! I shall ever be grateful to you."

"May Heaven bless you, too, Mynheer, and may you soon find the dear young gentleman," said Dame Brinker, earnestly, after hurriedly wiping her eyes upon the corner of her apron.

Raff uttered a hearty "Amen!" and Gretel threw such a wistful, eager glance at the doctor, that he patted her head as he turned to leave the cottage.

Hans went out also.

"When I can serve you, Mynheer, I am ready."

"Very well, boy," replied Doctor Boekman with peculiar mildness. "Tell them within to say nothing of what has just passed. Meantime, Hans, when you are with your father watch his mood. You have tact. At any moment he may suddenly be able to tell us more."

"Trust me for that, Mynheer."

"Good-day, my boy!" cried the doctor, as he sprang into his stately coach.

"Aha!' thought Hans, as it rolled away, "the meester has more life in him than I thought."

CHAPTER XLIII

THE RACE

THE Twentieth of December came at last, bringing with it the perfection of winter weather. All over the level landscape lay the warm sunlight. It tried its power on lake, canal, and river; but the ice flashed defiance and showed no sign of melting. The very weathercocks stood still to enjoy the sight. This gave the windmills a holiday. Nearly all the past week they had been whirling briskly; now, being rather out of breath, they rocked lazily in the clear, still air. Catch a windmill working when the weathercocks have nothing to do!

There was an end to grinding, crushing, and sawing for that day. It was a good thing for the millers near Broek. Long before noon they concluded to take in their sails, and go to the race. Everybody would be there—already the north side of the frozen Y was bordered with eager spectators; the news of the great skating match had travelled far and wide. Men, women, and children in holiday attire were flocking toward the spot. Some wore furs, and wintry cloaks or shawls; but many, consulting their feelings rather than the almanac, were dressed as for an October day.

The site selected for the race was a faultless plain of ice near Amsterdam, on that great *arm* of the Zuider Zee which Dutchmen of course must call—the Eye. The townspeople turned out in large numbers. Strangers in the city deemed it a fine chance to see what was to be seen. Many a peasant from the northward had wisely chosen the Twentieth as the day for the next city-trading. It seemed that everybody, young and old, who had wheels, skates, or feet at command, had hastened to the scene.

There were the gentry in their coaches, dressed like Parisians fresh from the Boulevards; Amsterdam children in charity

uniforms; girls from the Roman Catholic Orphan House, in
sable gowns and white head-bands; boys from the Burgher
Asylum, with their black tights and short-skirted, harlequin
coats.[1] There were old-fashioned gentlemen in cocked hats and
velvet knee-breeches; old-fashioned ladies, too, in stiff, quilted
skirts and bodies of dazzling brocade. These were accompanied
by servants bearing foot-stoves and cloaks. There were the
peasant folk arrayed in every possible Dutch costume. Shy
young rustics in brazen buckles; simple village maidens con-
cealing their flaxen hair under fillets of gold; women whose
long, narrow aprons were stiff with embroidery; women with
short, corkscrew curls hanging over their foreheads; women
with shaved heads and close-fitting caps; and women in striped
skirts and windmill bonnets. Men in leather, in homespun,
in velvet, and broadcloth; burghers in model European attire;
and burghers in short jackets, wide trousers, and steeple-
crowned hats.

There were beautiful Friesland girls in wooden shoes and
coarse petticoats, with solid gold crescents encircling their heads,
finished at each temple with a golden rosette, and hung with
lace a century old. Some wore necklaces, pendants, and ear-
rings, of the purest gold. Many were content with gilt or even
with brass, but it is not an uncommon thing for a Friesland
woman to have all the family treasure in her head-gear. More
than one rustic lass displayed the value of two thousand
guilders upon her head that day.

Scattered throughout the crowd were peasants from the
Island of Marken, with sabots, black stockings, and the widest
of breeches; also women from Marken with short, blue petticoats, and black jackets, gaily figured in front. They wore red
sleeves, white aprons, and a cap like a bishop's mitre over their
golden hair.

---

[1] This is not said in derision. Both the girls and boys of this Institution
wear garments quartered in red and black alternately. By making the dress
thus conspicuous, the children are, in a measure, deterred from wrong-doing
while going about the city. The Burgher Orphan Asylum affords a comfortable home to several hundred boys and girls. Holland is famous for its
charitable institutions.

The children often were as quaint and odd-looking as their elders. In short, one-third of the crowd seemed to have stepped bodily from a collection of Dutch paintings.

Everywhere could be seen tall women and stumpy men, lively-faced girls, and youths whose expression never changed from sunrise to sunset.

There seemed to be at least one specimen from every known town in Holland. There were Utrecht water-bearers, Gouda cheese-makers, Delft pottery-men, Schiedam distillers, Amsterdam diamond-cutters, Rotterdam merchants, dried-up herring-packers, and two sleepy-eyed shepherds from Texel. Every man of them had his pipe and tobacco-pouch. Some carried what might be called the smoker's complete outfit—a pipe, tobacco, a pricker, with which to clean the tube, a silver net for protecting the bowl, and a box of the strongest of brimstone matches.

A true Dutchman, you must remember, is rarely without his pipe on any possible occasion. He may for a moment neglect to breathe, but when the pipe is forgotten, he must be dying indeed. There were no such sad cases here. Wreaths of smoke were rising from every possible quarter. The more fantastic the smoke wreath, the more placid and solemn the smoker.

Look at those boys and girls on stilts! That is a good idea. They can see over the heads of the tallest. It is strange to see those little bodies high in the air carried about on mysterious legs. They have such a resolute look on their round faces, what wonder that nervous old gentlemen, with tender feet, wince and tremble while the long-legged little monsters stride past them.

You will read in certain books that the Dutch are a quiet people—so they are generally—but listen: did ever you hear such a din? All made up of human voices—no, the horses are helping somewhat, and the fiddles are squeaking pitifully (how it must pain fiddles to be tuned!), but the mass of the sound comes from the great *vox humana* that belongs to a crowd.

That queer little dwarf going about with a heavy basket,

winding in and out among the people, helps not a little. You
can hear his shrill cry above all the other sounds, "Pypen en
tabac ! Pypen en tabac !"

Another, his big brother, though evidently some years
younger, is selling doughnuts and bon-bons. He is calling on
all pretty children far and near to come quickly or the cakes
will be gone.

You know quite a number among the spectators. High up
in yonder pavilion, erected upon the border of the ice, are some
persons whom you have seen very lately. In the centre is
Madame van Gleck. It is her birthday, you remember; she
has the post of honour. There is Mynheer van Gleck, whose
meerschaum has not really grown fast to his lips—it only appears
so. There are grandfather and grandmother, whom you met
at the St. Nicholas *fête*. All the children are with them. It
is so mild they have brought even the baby. The poor little
creature is swaddled very much after the manner of an Egyptian
mummy, but it can crow with delight, and, when the band is
playing, open and shut its animated mittens in perfect time to
the music.

Grandfather, with his pipe and spectacles and fur-cap, makes
quite a picture as he holds baby upon his knee. Perched high
upon their canopied platforms, the party can see all that is
going on. No wonder the ladies look complacently at the
glassy ice; with a stove for a footstool one might sit cosily
beside the North Pole.

There is a gentleman with them who somewhat resembles St.
Nicholas as he appeared to the young Van Glecks on the fifth
of December. But the saint had a flowing white beard; and
this face is as smooth as a pippin. His saintship was larger
around the body, too, and (between ourselves) he had a pair of
thimbles in his mouth, which this gentleman certainly has not.
It cannot be Saint Nicholas after all.

Near by, in the next pavilion, sit the Van Holps with their
son and daughter (the Van Gends) from the Hague. Peter's
sister is not one to forget her promises. She has brought
bouquets of exquisite hothouse flowers for the winners.

These pavilions, and there are others beside, have all been erected since daylight. That semicircular one, containing Mynheer Korbes' family, is very pretty, and proves that the Hollanders are quite skilled at tent-making; but I like the Van Glecks' best—the centre one—striped red and white and hung with evergreens.

The one with the blue flags contains the musicians. Those pagoda-like affairs, decked with sea-shells and streamers of every possible hue, are the judges' stands, and those columns and flag-staffs upon the ice mark the limit of the race-course. The two white columns twined with green, connected at the top by that long, floating strip of drapery, form the starting-point. Those flag-staffs, half a mile off, stand at each end of the boundary line, cut sufficiently deep to be distinct to the skaters, though not enough so to trip them when they turn to come back to the starting-point.

The air is so clear it seems scarcely possible that the columns and flag-staffs are so far apart. Of course the judges' stands are but little nearer together.

Half a mile on the ice, when the atmosphere is like this, is but a short distance after all, especially when fenced with a living chain of spectators.

The music has commenced. How melody seems to enjoy itself in the open air! The fiddles have forgotten their agony, and everything is harmonious. Until you look at the blue tent it seems that the music springs from the sunshine, it is so boundless, so joyous. Only when you see the staid-faced musicians you realise the truth.

Where are the racers? All assembled together near the white columns. It is a beautiful sight. Forty boys and girls in picturesque attire darting with electric swiftness in and out among each other, or sailing in pairs and triplets, beckoning, chatting, whispering in the fulness of youthful glee.

A few careful ones are soberly tightening their straps; others halting on one leg, with flushed, eager faces, suddenly cross the suspected skate over their knee, give it an examining shake, and dart off again. One and all are possessed with the

spirit of motion. They cannot stand still. Their skates are a
part of them, and every runner seems bewitched.

Holland is the place for skaters after all. Where else can
nearly every boy and girl perform feats on the ice that would
attract a crowd if seen on any of our parks? Look at Ben! I
did not see him before. He is really astonishing the natives;
no easy thing to do in the Netherlands. Save your strength,
Ben; you will need it soon. Now other boys are trying! Ben
is surpassed already. Such jumping, such poising, such
spinning, such india-rubber exploits generally! That boy with
a red cap is the lion now; his back is a watch-spring, his body
is cork—no, it is iron, or it would snap at that! He is a bird,
a top, a rabbit, a corkscrew, a sprite, a flesh-ball, all in an
instant. When you think he's erect he is down, and when you
think he is down he is up. He drops his glove on the ice and
turns a somersault as he picks it up. Without stopping, he
snatches the cap from Jacob Poot's astonished head and claps it
back again "hind side before." Lookers-on hurrah and laugh.
Foolish boy! it is Arctic weather under your feet, but more
than temperate overhead. Big drops already are rolling down
your forehead. Superb skater as you are, you may lose the race.

A French traveller, standing with a note-book in his hand,
sees our English friend, Ben, buy a doughnut off the dwarf's
brother, and eat it. Thereupon he writes in his note-book that
the Dutch take enormous mouthfuls, and universally are fond of
potatoes boiled in molasses.

There are some familiar faces near the white columns.
Lambert, Ludwig, Peter, and Carl, are all there, cool, and in
good skating order. Hans is not far off. Evidently he is going
to join in the race, for his skates are on, the very pair that he
sold for seven guilders! He had soon suspected that his fairy
godmother was the mysterious "friend" who bought them.
This settled, he had boldly charged her with the deed, and she,
knowing well that all her little savings had been spent in the
purchase, had not had the face to deny it. Through the fairy
godmother, too, he had been rendered amply able to buy them
back again. Therefore Hans is to be in the race. Carl is more

indignant than ever about it, but as three other peasant boys have entered, Hans is not alone.

Twenty boys and twenty girls. The latter by this time are standing in front, braced for the start, for they are to have the first "run." Hilda, Rychie, and Katrinka are among them. Two or three bend hastily to give a last pull at their skate straps. It is pretty to see them stamp, to be sure that all is firm. Hilda is speaking pleasantly to a graceful little creature in a red jacket, and a new brown petticoat. Why, it is Gretel! What a difference those pretty shoes make, and the skirt, and the new cap. Annie Bouman is there too. Even Janzoon Kolp's sister has been admitted, but Janzoon himself has been voted out by the directors, because he killed the stork, and only last summer was caught in the act of robbing a bird's nest, a legal offence in Holland.

This Janzoon Kolp, you see, was—— There, I cannot tell the story just now. The race is about to commence.

Twenty girls are formed in a line. The music has ceased.

A man, whom we shall call the Crier, stands between the columns and the first judges' stand. He reads the rules in a loud voice.

"THE GIRLS AND BOYS ARE TO RACE IN TURN, UNTIL ONE GIRL AND ONE BOY HAS BEATEN TWICE. THEY ARE TO START IN A LINE FROM THE UNITED COLUMNS, SKATE TO THE FLAG-STAFF LINE, TURN, AND THEN COME BACK TO THE STARTING-POINT, THUS MAKING A MILE AT EACH RUN."

A flag is waved from the judges' stand. Madame van Gleck rises in her pavilion. She leans forward with a white handkerchief in her hand. When she drops it, a bugler is to give the signal for them to start.

The handkerchief is fluttering to the ground. Hark!

They are off.

No. Back again. Their line was not true in passing the judges' stand.

The signal is repeated.

Off again. No mistake this time. Whew! how fast they go!

The multitude is quiet for an instant, absorbed in eager, breathless watching.

Cheers spring up along the line of spectators. Huzza! five girls are ahead. Who comes flying back from the boundary-mark? We cannot tell. Something red, that is all. There is a blue spot flitting near it, and a dash of yellow nearer still. Spectators at this end of the line strain their eyes and wish they had taken their post nearer the flag-staff.

The wave of cheers is coming back again. Now we can see! Katrinka is ahead!

She passes the Van Holp pavilion. The next is Madam van Gleck's. That leaning figure gazing from it is a magnet. Hilda shoots past Katrinka, waving her hand to her mother as she passes. Two others are close now, whizzing on like arrows. What is that flash of red and gray? Hurrah, it is Gretel! She too waves her hand, but toward no gay pavilion. The crowd is cheering, but she hears only her father's voice, "Well done, little Gretel!" Soon Katrinka, with a quick merry laugh, shoots past Hilda. The girl in yellow is gaining now. She passes them all, all except Gretel. The judges lean forward without seeming to lift their eyes from their watches. Cheer after cheer fills the air; the very columns seem rocking. Gretel has passed them. She has won.

"GRETEL BRINKER, ONE MILE!" shouts the crier.

The judges nod. They write something upon a table which each holds in his hand.

While the girls are resting—some crowding eagerly around our frightened little Gretel, some standing aside in high disdain —the boys form in a line.

Mynheer van Gleck drops the handkerchief this time. The buglers give a vigorous blast!

The boys have started.

Half-way already! Did ever you see the like!

Three hundred legs flashing by in an instant. But there are only twenty boys. No matter, there were hundreds of legs I am sure! Where are they now? There is such a noise one gets bewildered. What are the people laughing at? Oh, at that fat boy in the rear. See him go! See him! He'll be down in an instant; no, he won't. I wonder if he knows he is all alone; the other boys are nearly at the boundary-line. Yes, he knows it. He stops! He wipes his hot face. He takes off his cap and looks about him. Better to give up with a good grace. He has made a hundred friends by that hearty, astonished laugh. Good Jacob Poot!

The fine fellow is already among the spectators, gazing as eagerly as the rest.

A cloud of feathery ice flies from the heels of the skaters as they "bring to" and turn at the flag-staffs.

Something black is coming now, one of the boys—it is all we know. He has touched the *vox humana* stop of the crowd, it fairly roars. Now they come nearer—we can see the red cap. There's Ben—there's Peter—there's Hans!

Hans is ahead! Young Madame van Gend almost crushes the flowers in her hand; she had been quite sure that Peter would be first. Carl Schummel is next, then Ben, and the youth with the red cap. The others are pressing close. A tall figure darts from among them. He passes the red cap, he passes Ben, then Carl. Now it is an even race between him and Hans. Madame van Gend catches her breath.

It is Peter! He is ahead! Hans shoots past him. Hilda's eyes fill with tears; Peter *must* beat. Annie's eyes flash proudly. Gretel gazes with clasped hands—four strokes more will take her brother to the columns.

He is there! Yes, but so was young Schummel just a second before. At the last instant, Carl, gathering his powers, had whizzed between them and passed the goal.

"CARL SCHUMMEL, ONE MILE!" shouts the crier.

Soon Madame Van Gleck rises again. The falling hand-kerchief starts the bugle; and the bugle, using its voice as a bow string, shoots off twenty girls like so many arrows.

It is a beautiful sight, but one has not long to look; before we can fairly distinguish them they are far in the distance. This time they are close upon one another; it is hard to say as they come speeding back from the flag-staff which will reach

the columns first. There are new faces among the foremost—
eager, glowing faces, unnoticed before. Katrinka is there, and
Hilda, but Gretel and Rychie are in the rear. Gretel is
wavering, but when Rychie passes her, she starts forward
afresh Now they are nearly beside Katrinka. Hilda is still
in advance, she is almost "home." She has not faltered since
that bugle note sent her flying; like an arrow still she is
speeding toward the goal. Cheer after cheer rises in the air.
Peter is silent, but his eyes shine like stars. "Huzza! Huzza!"

The crier's voice is heard again.

"HILDA VAN GLECK, ONE MILE!"

A loud murmur of approval runs through the crowd, catching
the music in its course, till all seems one sound, with a glad
rhythmic throbbing in its depths. When the flag waves all is
still.

Once more the bugle blows a terrific blast. It sends off the
boys like chaff before the wind—dark chaff I admit, and in big
pieces.

It is whisked round at the flag-staff, driven faster yet by the
cheers and shouts along the line. We begin to see what is
coming. There are three boys in advance this time, and all
abreast. Hans, Peter, and Lambert. Carl soon breaks the ranks,
rushing through with a whiff! Fly, Hans; fly, Peter; don't let
Carl beat again. Carl the bitter, Carl the insolent. Van
Mounen is flagging, but you are strong as ever. Hans and
Peter, Peter and Hans; which is foremost? We love them
both. We scarcely care which is the fleeter.

Hilda, Annie, and Gretel seated upon the long crimson
bench, can remain quiet no longer. They spring to their feet
—so different, and yet one in eagerness. Hilda instantly reseats
herself; none shall know how interested she is, none shall know
how anxious, how filled with one hope. Shut your eyes then,
Hilda—hide your face rippling with joy. Peter has beaten.

"PETER VAN HOLP, ONE MILE!" calls the crier

The same buzz of excitement as before, while the judges
take notes, the same throbbing of music through the din—but
something is different. A little crowd presses close about some

object, near the column. Carl has fallen. He is not hurt, though somewhat stunned.   If he were less sullen he would find more sympathy in these warm young hearts. As it is they forget him as soon as he is fairly on his feet again.

The girls are to skate their third mile.

How resolute the little maidens look as they stand in a line ! Some are solemn with a sense of responsibility, some wear a smile half bashful, half provoked, but one air of determination pervades them all.

This third mile may decide the race. Still, if neither Gretel nor Hilda win, there is a yet chance among the rest for the Silver Skates.

Each girl feels sure that this time she will accomplish the distance in one half the time. How they stamp to try their runners, how nervously they examine each strap, how erect they stand at last, every eye upon Madame van Gleck.

The bugle thrills through them again. With quivering eagerness they spring forward, bending, but in perfect balance. Each flashing stroke seems longer than the last.

Now they are skimming off in the distance.

Again the eager straining of eyes ; again the shouts and cheering, again the thrill of excitement, as, after a few moments, four or five, in advance of the rest, come speeding back, nearer, nearer to the white columns.

Who is first ? Not Rychie, Katrinka, Annie, nor Hilda, nor the girl in yellow ; but Gretel—Gretel, the fleetest sprite of a girl that ever skated. She was but playing in the earlier race, *now* she is in earnest, or rather something within her has determined to win. That lithe little form makes no effort, but it cannot stop, not until the goal is passed.

In fain the crier lifts his voice. He cannot be heard. He has no news to tell. It is already ringing through the crowd. *Gretel has won the Silver Skates !*

Like a bird she has flown over the ice, like a bird she looks about her in a timid, startled way. She longs to dart to the sheltered nook where her father and mother stand. But Hans is beside her. The girls are crowding round. Hilda's kind, joyous voice breathes in her ear. From that hour none will depise her. Goose-girl or not, Gretel stands acknowledged Queen of the Skaters!

With natural pride Hans turns to see if Peter Van Holp is witnessing his sister's triumph. Peter is not looking toward them at all. He is kneeling, bending his troubled face low, and working hastily at his skate-strap. Hans is beside him at once.

"Are you in trouble, Mynheer?"

"Ah, Hans! that you? Yes, my fun is over. I tried to tighten my strap—to make a new hole—and this botheration of a knife has cut it nearly in two."

"Mynheer," said Hans, at the same time pulling off a skate, "you must use my strap!"

"Not I, indeed, Hans Brinker," cried Peter, looking up, "though I thank you warmly. Go to your post, my friend, the bugle will sounded in a minute."

"Mynheer," pleaded Hans, in a husky voice. "You have called me your friend. Take this strap—quick! There is not an instant to lose. I shall not skate this time. Indeed, I am out of practice. Mynheer, you *must* take it," and Hans, blind and deaf to any remonstrance, slipped his strap into Peter's skate, and implored him to put it on.

"Come Peter," cried Lambert, from the line, "we are waiting for you."

"For Madame's sake," pleaded Hans, "be quick. She is motioning to you to join the racers. There, the skate is almost on. Quick, Mynheer, fasten it. I could not possibly win. The race lies between Master Schummel and yourself."

"You are a noble fellow, Hans!" cried Peter, yielding at last. He sprang to his post just as the white handkerchief fell to the ground. The bugle sends forth its blast, loud, clear, and ringing.

Off go the boys!

"See them!" cries a tough old fellow from Delft. "They beat everything, these Amsterdam youngsters."

See them, indeed! They are winged Mercuries every one of them. What mad errand are they on? Ah, I know; they are hunting Peter Van Holp. He is some fleet-footed runaway from Olympus. Mercury and his troop of winged cousins are in full chase. They will catch him ! Now Carl is the runaway—the pursuit grows furious—Ben is foremost !

The chase turns in a cloud of mist. It is coming this way. Who is hunted now ? Mercury himself. It is Peter—Peter Van Holp ; fly, Peter—Hans is watching you. He is sending all his fleetness, all his strength into your feet. Your mother and sister are pale with eagerness. Hilda is trembling, and dare not look up. Fly, Peter ! the crowd has not gone deranged—it is only cheering. The pursuers are close upon you ! Touch the white column ! It beckons—it is reeling before you—it——

Huzza ! huzza ! Peter has won the Silver Skates !

"PETER VAN HOLP !" shouted the crier. But who heard him ? "Peter Van Holp !" shouted a hundred voices, for he was the favourite boy of the place. Huzza ! huzza !

Now the music was resolved to be heard. It struck up a lively air, then a tremendous march. The spectators, thinking something new was about to happen, deigned to listen and to look.

The racers formed in single file. Peter, being tallest, stood first. Gretel, the smallest of all, took her place at the end. Hans, who had borrowed a strap from the cake-boy, was near the head.

Three gaily-twined arches were placed at intervals upon the river, facing the Van Gleck pavilion.

Skating slowly, and in perfect time to the music, the boys and girls moved forward, led on by Peter. It was beautiful to see the bright procession glide along like a living creature. It curved and doubled, and drew its graceful length in and out among the arches—whichever way Peter the head went, the body was sure to follow. Sometimes it steered direct for the centre arch, then, as if seized with a new impulse, turned away and curled itself about the first one ; then unwound slowly and bending low, with quick, snake-like curvings, crossed the river, passing at length through the furthest arch.

When the music was slow, the procession seemed to crawl

like a thing afraid, it grew livelier, and the creature darted forward with a spring, gliding rapidly among the arches, in and out, curling, twisting, turning, never losing form until, at the shrill call of the bugle rising above the music, it suddenly resolved itself into boys and girls standing in double semicircle before Madame van Gleck's pavilion.

Peter and Gretel stand in the centre in advance of the others. Madame van Gleck rises majestically. Gretel trembles, but feels that she must look at the beautiful lady. She cannot hear what is said, there is such a buzzing all around her. She is thinking that she ought to try and make a curtsey, such as her mother makes to the meester, when suddenly something so dazzling is placed in her hand that she gives a cry of joy.

Then she ventures to look about her. Peter, too, has something in his hands—"Oh! oh! how splendid!" she cries; and "Oh! how splendid!" is echoed as far as people can see.

Meantime the silver skates flash in the sunshine, throwing dashes of light upon those two happy faces.

Mevrouw van Gend sends a little messenger with her bouquets. One for Hilda, one for Carl, and others for Peter and Gretel.

At sight of the flowers the Queen of the Skaters becomes uncontrollable. With a bright stare of gratitude she gathers skates and bouquet in her apron—hugs them to her bosom, and darts off to search for her father and mother in the scattering crowd.

CHAPTER XLIV

JOY IN THE COTTAGE

PERHAPS you were surprised to learn that Raff and his vrouw were at the skating-race; you would have been more so had you been with them on the evening of that merry twentieth of December. To see the Brinker cottage standing sulkily alone on the frozen marsh, with its bulgy, rheumatic-looking walls, and its slouched hat of a roof pulled far over its eyes, one would never suspect that a lively scene was passing within. Without, nothing was left of the day but a low line of blaze at the horizon. A few venturesome clouds had already taken fire, and others, with their edges burning, were lost in the gathering smoke.

A stray gleam of sunshine, slipping down from the willow stump, crept stealthily under the cottage. It seemed to feel that the inmates would give it welcome if it could only get near them. The room under which it hid was as clean as clean could be. The very cracks in the rafters were polished. Delicious odours filled the air. A huge peat fire upon the hearth sent flashes of harmless lightning at the sombre walls. It played in turn upon the great leathern Bible, upon Gretel's closet-bed, the household things on their pegs, and the beautiful Silver Skates and the flowers upon the table. Dame Brinker's honest face shone and twinkled in the changing light. Gretel and Hans, with arms entwined, were leaning against the fireplace, laughing merrily, and Raff Brinker was dancing!

I do not mean that he was pirouetting or cutting a pigeon-wing, either of which would have been entirely too undignified for the father of a family : I simply affirm that while they were chatting pleasantly together Raff suddenly sprang from his seat, snapped his fingers, and performed two or three flourishes very much like the climax of a Highland Fling. Next he caught his vrouw in his arms, and fairly lifted her from the ground in his delight.

"Huzza!" he cried, "I have it! I have it! It's THOMAS HIGGS. That's the name! It came upon me like a flash; write it down, lad, write it down!"

Some one knocked at the door.

"It's the meester," cried the delighted dame ; "Goede Gunst! how things come to pass!"

Mother and children came in merry collision as they rushed to open the door.

It was not the doctor, after all, but three boys—Peter van Holp, Lambert, and Ben.

"Good evening, young gentlemen," said Dame Brinker, so

happy and proud that she would scarce have been surprised at a visit from the king himself.

"Good evening, jufvrouw," said the trio, making magnificent bows.

"Dear me," thought Dame Brinker, as she bobbed up and down like a churn-dasher, "it's lucky I learned to curtsey at Heidelberg!"

Raff was content to return the boys' salutations with a respectful nod.

"Pray be seated, young masters," said the dame, as Gretel bashfully thrust a stool toward them. "There's a lack of chairs, as you see, but this one by the fire is at your service, and if you don't mind the hardness, that oak-chest is as good a seat as the best. That's right, Hans; pull it out!"

By the time the boys were seated to the dame's satisfaction, Peter, acting as spokesman, had explained that they were going to attend a lecture at Amsterdam, and had stopped on the way to return Hans' strap.

"Oh, Mynheer," cried Hans, earnestly, "it is too much trouble. I am very sorry."

"No trouble at all, Hans; I could have waited for you to come to your work to-morrow had I not wished to call. And, Hans, talking of your work, my father is much pleased with it —a carver by trade could not have done it better. He would like to have the south arbour ornamented also, but I told him you were going to school again."

"Ay!" put in Raff Brinker, emphatically. "Hans must go to school at once—and Gretel as well—that is true."

"I am glad to hear you say so," responded Peter, turning towards the father, "and very glad to know that you are again a well man."

"Yes, young master, a well man, and able to work as steady as ever—thank God!"

Here Hans hastily wrote something on the edge of a time-worn almanac that hung by the chimney-place.

"Ay, that's right, lad; set it down. Figgs! Wiggs! Alack! alack!" added Raff, in great dismay, "it's gone again!"

"All right, father," said Hans, "the name's down now in black and white. Here, look at it, father; mayhap the rest will come to you. If we had the place as well, it would be complete;" then turning to Peter, he said in a low tone, "I have an important errand in town, Mynheer, and if——"

"Wist!" exclaimed the dame, lifting her hands, "not to Amsterdam to-night, and you've owned your legs were aching under you. Nay, nay—it'll be soon enough to go at early day-light."

"Daylight indeed!" echoed Raff, "that would never do. Nay, Meitje, he must go this hour."

"Very well, Raff," she said, smilingly; "it is thy boy as well as mine. Ah! I've a troublesome house, young masters."

Just then Peter drew a long strap from his pocket.

Handing it to Hans he said in an undertone, "I need not thank you for lending me this, Hans Brinker. Such boys as you do not ask for thanks—but I must say you did me a great kind-ness, and I am proud to acknowledge it. I did not know," he added, laughingly, "until fairly in the race how anxious I was to win."

Hans was glad to join in Peter's laugh—it covered his embarrassment and gave his face a chance to cool off a little. Honest, generous boys like Hans have such a stupid way of blushing when you least expect it.

"It was nothing, Mynheer," said the dame, hastening to her son's relief; "the lad's whole soul was in having you win the race, I know it was!"

This helped matters beautifully.

"Ah, Mynheer," Hans hurried to say, "from the first start I felt stiff and strange on my feet; I was well out of it so long as I had no chance of winning."

Peter looked rather distressed.

"We may hold different opinions there. That part of the business troubles me. It is too late to mend it now, but it would be really a kindness to me if——"

The rest of Peter's speech was uttered so confidentially that I cannot record it. Enough to say, Hans soon started back in dismay, and Peter, looking very much ashamed, stammered out something to the effect that he would keep them, since he won the race, but it was "all wrong."

Here Van Mounen coughed, as if to remind Peter that lecture hour was approaching fast. At the same moment Ben laid something upon the table.

"Ah," exclaimed Peter, "I forgot my other errand. Your sister ran off so quickly to-day, that Madame van Gleck had no opportunity to give her the case for her skates."

"S-s-t!" said Dame Brinker, shaking her head reproachfully at Gretel, "she was a very rude girl, I'm sure." Secretly she was thinking that very few women had such a fine little daughter.

"No, indeed," laughed Peter; "she did exactly the right thing—ran home with her richly won treasures—who would not? Don't let us detain you, Hans," he continued, turning around as he spoke; but Hans, who was eagerly watching the father, seemed to have forgotten their presence.

Meantime Raff, lost in thought, was repeating under his breath, "Thomas Higgs—Thomas Higgs; ay, that's the name. Alack! if I could but tell the place as well."

The skate-case was elegantly made of crimson morocco, ornamented with silver. If a fairy had breathed upon its tiny key, or Jack Frost himself designed its delicate tracery, they could not have been more daintily beautiful. FOR THE FLEETEST was written upon the cover in sparkling letters. It was lined with velvet, and in one corner was stamped the name and address of the maker.

Gretel thanked Peter in her own simple way. Then, being quite delighted and confused, and not knowing what else to do, lifted the case, carefully examining it in every part. "It's made by Mynheer Birmingham," she said after a while, still blushing, and holding it before her eyes.

"Birmingham!" replied Lambert van Mounen; "that's the name of a place in England. Let me see it."

"Ha! ha!" he laughed, holding the open case toward the firelight; "no wonder you thought so, but it's a slight mistake.

The case was made at Birmingham, but the maker's name is in smaller letters.   Humph! they're so small, I can't read them."

"Let me try," said Peter, leaning over his shoulder; "why, man, it's perfectly distinct.   It's T—H—it's T——"

"Well!" exclaimed Lambert, triumphantly, "if you can read it so easily, let's hear it, T—H, what?"

"T. H—T. H.   Oh! why, Thomas Higgs, to be sure," replied Peter, pleased to be able to decipher it at last.   Then, feeling they had been behaving rather unceremoniously, he turned toward Hans.

Peter turned pale.   What was the matter with the people? Raff and Hans had started up, and were staring at him in glad amazement.   Gretel looked wild.   Dame Brinker, with an unlighted candle in her hand, was rushing about the room, crying, "Hans! Hans! where's your hat?   Oh, the meester! Oh, the meester!"

"Birmingham! Higgs!" exclaimed Hans.   "Did you say Higgs?   We've found him!   I must be off."

"You see, young masters," panted the dame, at the same time snatching Hans' hat from the bed.   "You see—we know him.   He's our—no, he isn't.   I mean—oh, Hans, you must go to Amsterdam this minute!"

"Good-night, Mynheers," panted Hans, radiant with sudden joy.   "Good-night.   You will excuse me.   I must go.   Birmingham—Higgs! Higgs—Birmingham!" and seizing his hat from his mother, and his skates from Gretel, he rushed from the cottage.

What could the boys think, but that the entire Brinker family had suddenly gone crazy.

They bade an embarrassed "good-evening," and turned to go. But Raff stopped them.

"This Thomas Higgs, young masters, is a—a person."

"Ah!" exclaimed Peter, quite sure that Raff was the most crazy of all.

"Yes—a person—a—ahem!—a friend.   We thought him dead.   I hope it is the same man.   In England, did you say?"

"Yes, Birmingham," answered Peter, "it must be Birmingham in England."

"I know the man," said Ben, addressing Lambert. "His factory is not four miles from our place—a queer fellow—still as an oyster—don't seem at all like an Englishman. I've often seen him—a solemn-looking chap, with magnificent eyes. He made a beautiful writing-case once for me to give Jenny on her birthday—makes pocket-books, telescope-cases, and all kinds of leather work."

As this was said in English, Van Mounen of course translated it for the benefit of all concerned, noticing meanwhile that neither Raff nor his vrouw looked very miserable, though Raff was trembling, and the dame's eyes were swimming with tears.

You may believe the doctor heard every word of the story, when later in the evening he came driving back with Hans. "The three young gentlemen had been gone some time," Dame Brinker said, "but like enough, by hurrying, it would be easy to find them coming out from the lecture, wherever that was."

"True," said Raff, nodding his head, "the vrouw always hits upon the right thing. It would be well to see the young English gentleman, Mynheer, before he forgets all about Thomas Higgs—it's a slippery name, d'ye see?—one can't hold it safe a minute. It came upon me sudden and strong as a pile-driver, and my boy writ it down. Ay, Mynheer, I'd haste to talk with the English lad; he's seen your son many a time—only to think on't!"

Dame Brinker took up the thread of the discourse.

"You'll pick out the lad quick enough, Mynheer, because he's in company with Master Peter van Holp; and his hair curls all up over his forehead like foreign folks, and, if you hear him speak, he talks kind of big and fast, only it's English; but that wouldn't be any hindrance to your honour."

The doctor had already lifted his hat to go. With a beaming face, he muttered something about its being just like the young scamp to give himself a rascally English name; called Hans

" my son "—thereby making that young gentleman happy as a lord—and left the cottage with very little ceremony, considering what a great meester he was.

The grumbling coachman comforted himself by speaking his mind, as he drove back to Amsterdam. Since the doctor was safely stowed away in the coach, and could not hear a word, it was a fine time to say terrible things of folks who hadn't no manner of feeling for nobody, and who were always wanting the horses a dozen times of a night.

CHAPTER XLV

BROAD SUNSHINE

ONE snowy day in January, Thomas Higgs, restored to all the honours of Laurens Boekman, went with his father to pay his respects to the Brinker family.

Raff was resting after the labours of the day; Gretel, having filled and lighted his pipe, was brushing every speck of ash from the hearth; the dame was spinning; and Hans, perched upon a stool by the window, was diligently studying his lessons—a peaceful, happy household, whose main excitement during the past week had been the looking forward to this possible visit from Thomas Higgs.

As soon as the grand presentation was over, Dame Brinker insisted upon giving her guests some hot tea; it was enough to freeze any one, she said, to be out in such crazy, blustering weather. While they were talking with her husband, she whispered to Gretel that the young gentleman's eyes and her boy's were certainly as much alike as four beans, to say nothing of a way they both had of looking as if they were stupid and yet knew as much as a body's grandfather.

Gretel was disappointed. She had looked forward to a tragic scene, such as Annie Bouman had often described to her from story books; and here was the gentleman who came so near being a murderer, who for ten years had been wandering over the face of the earth, who had believed himself deserted and scorned by his father—the very young gentleman who had fled from his country in such magnificent trouble, sitting by the fire just as pleasant and natural as could be !

To be sure his voice had trembled when he talked with her parents, and he had met his father's look with a bright kind of smile that would have suited a dragon-killer bringing the waters of perpetual youth to his king—but after all he wasn't at all like the conquered hero in Annie's book. He did not say, lifting his hand toward Heaven, "I hereby swear to be for ever faithful to my home, my king, and my country !" which would have been only right and proper under the circumstances.

All things considered, Gretel was disappointed. Raff, however, was perfectly satisfied. The message was delivered ; Doctor Boekman had his son safe and sound ; and the poor lad had done nothing sinful after all, except in thinking his father would have abandoned him for an accident. To be sure, the graceful stripling had become rather a heavy man—Raff had unconsciously hoped to clasp that same boyish hand again—but all things were changed to Raff, for that matter. So he pushed back every feeling but joy, as he saw father and son sitting side by side at his hearth-stone. Meantime, Hans was wholly occupied in the thought of Thomas Higgs' happiness in being able to be the meester's assistant again ; and Dame Brinker was sighing softly to herself, wishing that the lad's mother were alive to see him— such a fine young gentleman as he was ; and wondering how Doctor Boekman could bear to see the silver watch getting so dull. He had worn it ever since Raff handed it over, that was evident. What had he done with the gold one he used to wear ?

The light was shining full upon Doctor Boekman's face. How contented he looked ; how much younger and brighter than formerly. The hard lines were quite melting away. He was laughing, as he said to the father—

"Am I not a happy man, Raff Brinker ? My son will sell out his factory this month, and open a warehouse in Amsterdam. I shall have all my spectacle-cases for nothing."

Hans started from his reverie. "A warehouse, Mynheer! and will Thomas Higgs—I mean—is your son not to be your assistant again?"

A shade passed over the meester's face, but he brightened with an effort, as he replied—

"Oh no, Laurens has had quite enough of that. He wishes to be a merchant."

Hans appeared so surprised and disappointed that his friend asked good-naturedly—

"Why so silent, boy? Is it any disgrace to be a merchant?"

"N—not a disgrace, Mynheer," stammered Hans, "but——"

"But what?"

"Why, the other calling is so much better," answered Hans, "so much nobler. I think, Mynheer," he added, kindling with enthusiasm, "that to be a surgeon—to cure the sick and crippled, to save human life, to be able to do what you have done for my father—is the grandest thing on earth."

The doctor was regarding him sternly. Hans felt rebuked. His cheeks were flushed; hot tears were gathering under his lashes.

"It is an ugly business, boy, this surgery," said the doctor, still frowning at Hans; "it requires great patience, self-denial and perseverance."

"I am sure it does," cried Hans, kindling again. "It calls for wisdom too, and a reverence for God's work. Ah, Mynheer, it may have its trials and drawbacks—but you do not mean what you say—it is great and noble, not ugly! Pardon me, Mynheer. It is not for me to speak so boldly."

Doctor Boekman was evidently displeased. He turned his back on the boy, and conferred aside with Laurens. Meanwhile the dame scowled a terrible warning at Hans. These great people, she knew well enough, never like to hear poor folk speak up so pert.

The meester turned around.

"How old are you, Hans Brinker?"

"Fifteen, Mynheer," was the startled reply.

"Would you like to become a physician?"

"Yes, Mynheer," answered Hans, quivering with excitement.

"Would you be willing, with your parents' consent, to devote yourself to study, to go to the University—and, in time, be a student in my office?"

"YES, Mynheer."

"You would not grow restless, think you, and change your mind just as I had set my heart upon preparing you to be my successor?"

Hans' eyes flashed.

"No, Mynheer; I would not change."

"You may believe him there," cried the dame, who could remain quiet no longer; "Hans is like a rock, when once he decides; and as for study, Mynheer, the child has almost grown fast to his books of late. He can jumble off Latin already, like any priest!"

The doctor smiled. "Well, Hans, I see nothing to prevent us from carrying out this plan, if your father agrees."

"Ahem," said Raff, too proud of his boy to be very meek, "the fact is, Mynheer, I prefer an active, out-of-door life myself. But if the lad's inclined to study for a meester, and he'd have the benefit of your good word to push him on in the world, it's all one to me. The money's all that's a-wanting, but it mightn't be long, with two strong pair of arms to earn it, before we——"

"Tut! tut!" interrupted the doctor, "if I take your right-hand man away, I must pay the cost, and glad enough will I be to do it. It will be like having *two* sons—eh, Laurens? One a merchant and the other a surgeon—I shall be the happiest man in Holland! Come to me in the morning, Hans, and we will arrange matters at once."

Hans bowed assent. He dared not trust himself to speak.

"And, Brinker," continued the doctor, "my son Laurens will need a trusty, ready man like you, when he opens his warehouse in Amsterdam; some one to overlook matters, and see that the lazy clowns round about the place do their duty. Some one to—— Why don't you tell him yourself, you rascal!"

This last was addressed to the son, and did not sound half as fierce as it looks in print. The rascal and Raff soon understood each other perfectly.

"I'm loath to leave the dykes," said the latter, after they had talked together a while ; "but you have made me such a good offer, Mynheer, I'd be robbing my family if I let it go past me."

Take a long look at Hans, as he sits there staring gratefully at the meester, for you shall not see him again for many years.

And Gretel. Ah, what a vista of puzzling work suddenly opens before her ! Yes, for dear Hans' sake she will study now. If he really is to be a meester, his sister must not shame his greatness.

How faithfully those glancing eyes shall yet seek for the jewels that lie hidden in rocky school-books ! And how they shall yet brighten and droop at the coming of one whom she knows of now only as the boy who wore a red cap on that wonderful day when she found the Silver Skates in her apron !

But the doctor and Laurens are going. Dame Brinker is making her best curtsey. Raff stands beside her, looking every inch a man as he grasps the meester's hand. Through the open cottage door we can look out upon the level Dutch landscape all alive with the falling snow.

CONCLUSION

OUR story is nearly told. Time passes in Holland just as surely and steadily as here. In that respect no country is odd.

To the Brinker family it has brought great changes. Hans has spent the years faithfully and profitably, conquering obstacles as they arose, and pursuing one object with all the energy of his nature. If often the way has been rugged, his resolution has never failed. Sometimes he echoes, with his good old friend, the words said long ago in that little cottage near Broek: "Surgery is an ugly business;" but always in his heart of hearts lingers the echo of those truer words: "It is great and noble! it awakes a reverence for God's work!"

Were you in Amsterdam to-day you might see the famous Doctor Brinker riding in his grand coach to visit his patients; or, it might be, you would see him skating with his own boys and girls upon the frozen canal. For Annie Bouman, the beautiful, frank-hearted peasant girl, you would inquire in vain; but Annie Brinker, the vrouw of the great physician, is very like her—only, as Hans says, she is even lovelier, wiser, more like a fairy godmother than ever.

Peter van Holp also is a married man. I could have told you before, that he and Hilda would join hands and glide through life together, just as years ago they skimmed side by side over the frozen, sunlit river.

At one time, I came near hinting that Katrinka and Carl would unite their fortunes. It is well now that the report was not started, for Katrinka changed her mind, and is single to this day. The lady is not quite so merry as formerly, and, I grieve to add, some of the tinkling bells are out of tune. But she is the life of her social circle still. I wish she would be in earnest, just for a little while, but no; it is not her nature. Her cares and sorrows do nothing more than disturb the tinkling; they never waken any deeper music.

Rychie's soul has been stirred to its depths during these long years. Her history would tell how seed carelessly sown is sometimes reaped in anguish, and how a golden harvest may follow a painful planting. If I mistake not, you may be able to read the written record before long; that is, if you are familiar with the Dutch language. In the witty, but earnest author, whose words are welcomed at this day, in thousands of Holland homes, few could recognise the haughty, flippant Rychie who scoffed at little Gretel.

Lambert van Mounen, and Ludwig van Holp, are good Christian men, and, what is more easily to be seen at a glance, thriving citizens. Both are dwellers in Amsterdam, but one clings to the old city of that name, and the other is a pilgrim to the new. Van Mounen's present home is not far from the Central Park in the city of New York, and he says if the New Yorkers do their duty, the Park will, in time, equal his beautiful Bosch, near the Hague. He often thinks of the Katrinka, of his boyhood, but he is glad now that Katrinka, the woman, sent him away; though it seemed at the time his darkest hour. Ben's sister Jennie has made him very happy, happier than he could have been with any one else in the wide world.

Carl Schummel has had a hard life. His father met with reverses in business; and as Carl had not many warm friends, and, above all, was not sustained by noble principles, he has been tossed about by Fortune's battledore until his gayest feathers are nearly all knocked off. He is a book-keeper, in the thriving Amsterdam house of Boekman and Schimmelpenninck. Voostenwalbert, the junior partner, treats him kindly; and he, in turn, is very respectful to the "monkey with a long name for a tail."

Of all our group of Holland friends, Jacob Poot is the only one who has passed away. Good-natured, true-hearted, and unselfish to the last, he is mourned now, as heartily as he was loved and laughed at while on earth. He grew to be very thin before he died—thinner than Benjamin Dobbs, who is now portliest among the portly.

Raff Brinker and his vrouw have been living comfortably in Amsterdam for many years—a faithful, happy pair, as simple and straightforward in their good fortune as they were patient and trustful in darker days. They have a zommerhuis near the old cottage, and thither they often repair with their children and grandchildren on the pleasant summer afternoons when the pond-lilies rear their queenly heads above the water.

The story of Hans Brinker would be but half told, if we did not leave him with Gretel standing near. Dear, quick, patient little Gretel! What is she now? Ask old Doctor Boekman— he will declare she is the finest singer, the loveliest woman in Amsterdam; ask Hans and Annie—they will assure you she is the dearest sister ever known; ask her husband—he will tell you she is the brightest, sweetest little wife in Holland ; ask Dame Brinker and Raff—their eyes will glisten with joyous tears ; ask the poor—the air will be filled with blessings.

But, lest you forget a tiny form trembling and sobbing on the mound before the Brinker cottage, ask the Van Glecks ; they will never weary telling of the darling little girl who won The Silver Skates.